# MILLHOUSE

## D. KING

Under the oaks Publications,

www.undertheoaks.co.uk

For my wife Louise for understanding my overactive imagination!

# MILLHOUSE.

## Chapter One

Brambles tore through the linen of her skirt, lacerating the bareness of the pale skin that lay beneath. Eleanor desperately fought against the thicket surrounding the sanctuary of Somercarres wood. A dark foreboding place, unfrequented by any traveller, its contorted skeletal branches offering no shelter against the harshness of the biting wind as winter's icy fingers stretched out across the land. Reaching the centre Eleanor crouched down breathlessly, shielding herself from view as she hid between the rows of hazel trees. Her heart beat faster and faster as the voices drew ever nearer. Their voices, the voices of the men, who were sent to rid the land of any that they deemed to be impure. From her secluded position, Eleanor watched as the flaming torches of the chanting hoard flashed intermittently as they passed between the trees. In a short time, they would be upon her. Eleanor knew that she needed to escape or suffer at their hands, as those who had been too frail to run had suffered before her.

Eleanor stood, hitching up the remnants of her clothing she quickly turned and began yet again to run through the darkness of Somercarres wood.

"THERE SHE IS!" Eleanor heard from behind, she could smell their breath on the wind as again they gave chase. If only she could reach the village of Wallowmead then maybe, just maybe Eleanor could use the cover to throw them off her trail. Leaving Somercarres wood Eleanor struggled against the unevenness of the marshy ground. Where gorse bushes grew sporadically between the wetness of the earth, their needles waiting to stab anyone who veered too near. The sharpened points of the gorse were nothing in comparison to the tips of the pitchforks the men waved in the air as they emerged from the darkness of the trees. Ahead, Eleanor could just make out the silhouettes of houses as she battled against the driving rain.

"PLEASE, PLEASE OPEN UP!" Eleanor screamed as she reached the first house. From the window, she could just make out a face illuminated by a candle, The face watched as Eleanor was surrounded, she could run no more, her screams matching the ferocity of the howling wind. The jeering of the men continued as they grabbed Eleanor from behind, ripping out clumps of her hair as she tried to break free. And then she stopped struggling, turned and faced the angry crowd.

"I just find it hard to understand what is so hard about choosing floor tiles. We must have looked at a hundred different ones now!" Liam moaned as they walked around yet another flooring store.

"Really Liam, I would have thought that by now you, of all people would know how particular I can be!" Chloe retorted sharply, as she continued to study the many different slabs of stone.

It was true, Chloe could be indecisive, or *particular* as she had put it. Her inability to make decisions on the spot had begun to irritate Liam somewhat. The renovation of 'Millhouse' was supposed to take no longer than two years, but the constant changing of her mind meant that work had been halted until she committed herself to choosing between antique limestone or travertine.

From the moment Chloe first set eyes on Millhouse, she had fallen in love with the place. Much to Liam's displeasure who constantly stated that old buildings were nothing more than holes in the ground, places in which to just throw good money into. But Chloe saw more than that in the crumbling red bricks of its façade, she saw the potential of the building and the tranquility of the river as it flowed steadily through the old millrace. She watched as a willow tree bowed its leafy head down in the breeze to the water as if to offer her a silent welcome. That was nearly three years ago now, but still, it would greet her in the same noble fashion each time she visited.

In her mind, Millhouse deserved only the best, she never considered the place as an investment, a way in which to move higher up the property ladder. Chloe instead saw Millhouse as a home where she could see herself never wanting to leave.

"Ok, I have come to a decision, antique limestone it is! I think," Chloe said as she pointed at the whiteness of the stone in front of her. Liam sighed with relief as he gestured to the salesman to complete the order quickly before she changed her mind again.

It was fast approaching autumn and the leaves of the trees that stood on the banks flanking Millhouse and the river had started to fall, carpeting the earth below them in a hue of oranges and golden browns. In the small orchard, a solitary apple defied the calling of its brothers long since gone, as it desperately clung to the branch, like a baby to its mother.

White smoke rose steadily from the rooftop, encircling the chimney pot before being carried away by the gentleness of the wind. It had been two weeks since they had moved into Millhouse, and certain jobs still needed to be completed, but Chloe could wait no longer. Liam had been called away on business, something that, in his line of work, being an engineer for a large marine company happened quite a lot. Chloe understood the importance surrounding his work, and also the importance of his income, after all, freelance artists made nowhere near as much money. Especially in Chloe's case, where the blank canvases that lined the walls of her studio heavily outweighed the orders to use them. But the lack of interest in her artistic talents suited her for now. At least she could throw all of her attention to finalising Millhouse and being there full-time meant that Chloe could oversee the completion first-hand.

She breathed in the crisp autumnal air, and apart from the gentleness of the breeze and the motion of the river the whole place was silent. Chloe shivered, the quietness of her surroundings had an eeriness about it. From behind the trees, she felt as though eyes watched her every move, as though they were scrutinising this new addition to the valley. The telephone started to ring breaking Chloe's overactive imaginative thoughts. Shaking her head, she shrugged off the stupidity of it all and returned to the house.

"Hello, Chloe Stevenson," she said answering the call as she stood in the kitchen.

"Hey, sweetheart it's me, I just thought I would see how everything is going and tell you that, that Simpson guy called. He said it was about something that you had shown an interest in?" Liam said as he sat on his hotel bed.

"Oh hi, everything is good here, I managed to light the fire and the builder says he will be finished by Friday at the latest. Did he say anything else, the guy from the emporium I mean?" Chloe asked suspiciously. If she was honest she had shown interest in so many different things over at Simpsons Place that quite frankly it could be anything.

"No, he just said that something had arrived that he thought might be of interest to you and that he would be there all day tomorrow," Liam replied as he looked at his phone screen. "Listen, babe, work is calling me so I had better answer it, I will call you tomorrow evening, okay? Love you," he said quickly.

"Oh ok, bye love you," Chloe said quickly into the mouthpiece before the line went dead as Liam ended the call. "Well, guess it's just you and me kid," Chloe said as she looked at the old rag doll on the rocking chair in the corner of the kitchen. Annie had been with Chloe since childhood when she had rescued her from a jumble sale at the local village hall. From her worn-out eyes, the small woollen haired girl looked back at Chloe in her usual motionless way of approval.

The morning sun was shining through the gap in the curtains as Chloe sat up and climbed out of bed. From outside she could hear the builders discussing what needed to be done that day, wrapping her dressing gown tightly around her she made her way downstairs and unlocked the front door.

"Morning Frank, early as usual I see," Chloe said sarcastically as she headed toward the kitchen.

"Morning Mrs. Stevenson, you know me up with the lark," he called out, whistling his way along the hallway as he followed her to the kitchen.

"Coffee?" Chloe asked in the same sarcastic manner. *Only if you're making one,* Chloe thought to herself as she filled the kettle.

"Only if you're making one," Frank chirped, as he sat down on a stool next to the island.

*Only one sugar mind!* Chloe again replayed in her head as she filled two mugs.

"Only one sugar mind," Frank said bang on queue as though he was her very own ventriloquist dummy.

"I need to visit Simpsons today, apparently he has something interesting to show me," Chloe said innocently as Frank stifled a laugh.

"You want to watch him," Frank chuckled unable to control himself.

Chloe tutted, "He's in his seventies! I think I'm more than safe on that score."

She liked Frank, he always had a smile on his face and a twinkle in his eye, and nothing Chloe ever asked him to do was considered too much trouble. He had lived in Little Lawton all of his life and as a child had played and fished in the river next to Millhouse. Just like Chloe, she shared her love for the building, and over the past few years had painstakingly brought the house back to its former glory.

"Well, I will leave the place in your capable hands, Frank, I'm off to see what new arrivals Simpsons are eager to show me," Chloe called out as she collected her keys from the bowl in the centre of the kitchen island and headed for the door."

Frank quickly lifted his head to reply, "BLOODY HELL!" he shouted out loud.

Chloe smirked as she watched Frank crawl backwards from out of the cupboard as he rubbed the top of his head. "Oh, are you ok?" she asked, trying to compose herself.

"You made me jump then! But aye I'm ok," Frank replied as he readjusted his cap.

"Right, well I will see you later, I have left the biscuits in the usual place," Chloe replied as she headed for the door.

"You spoil me something rotten Mrs Stevenson!" Frank said as he began to whistle his rendition of 'memories you gave to me'.

"Don't I know it!" Chloe muttered to herself.

Closing the front door behind her she headed out into the garden, shielding her eyes from the morning sun as it tried its hardest to warm the damp valley air. On the lawn, a blackbird hopped about eagerly as it sourced its breakfast, noticing Chloe flew up quickly onto the garden wall to watch her with unblinking eyes from a safe distance. She bowed her head to the willow tree, which silently acknowledged the greeting as its thin branches moved back and forth on the surface of the water. Reaching the small wrought iron gate Chloe stopped and pinched herself on the arm. "Just so that I know I'm not dreaming," she sighed. Feeling contented with the fact that she was indeed very awake, Chloe closed the gate behind her with a clatter of the latch and began the walk to her car.

Millhouse had stood beside the river long before motor vehicles were invented. The narrow rutted track that wound its way down the steep side of the valley originally served a horse and cart. Chloe had attempted the precarious journey only once before and in her words 'that was one time too many!' Instead, she chose to leave her small but practical car at the top of the track, after all the exercise was good for her. Halfway Chloe stopped to catch her breath, she stood hand on hips as she looked at the climb ahead. *Maybe they should have the track sorted,* she thought as she started walking again.

Simpson's Emporium was just over ten miles away on the outskirts of Wellton, a small market town, overrun by tourists in summer and reputedly famous for cheeses. Chloe in all honesty only ever visited Wellton when she needed to, she had a nausea inducing dislike for cheese of any description and tourists too for that matter! Turning off the main road she drove into the entrance of Simpson's yard and parked next to the vast display of garden sculptures. Eclectic was a word that Chloe would often use to describe this place, a hideous collection of Tat, and expensive Tat at that, was how Liam generally would choose to reference it. But what did he know, his idea of home furnishing and décor would happily be supplied in the modern Nordic flat-packed way. Not handmade traditionally with the love and care of that of a true craftsman.

Chloe would happily spend the entirety of a king's ransom here. Unfortunately for her, Liam had insisted that this was not the case, and she was to keep her spending limit to the absolute minimum. "Ah, Mrs. Stevenson," Old Mr. Simpson called out from across the yard. Chloe waved happily as she made her way over to him. *He must have earned thousands over the years owning this place,* Chloe thought to herself. Yet here he stood in old corduroy trousers held up by a belt, and battered boots that had been in service long before she had even been born.

"Hello again, Liam tells me that you have something interesting to show me," Chloe said smiling, as she reached old Mr. Simpson.

"Ah I do indeed, I do indeed, follow me, young lady," the old man uttered with an air of mystery in his voice. Chloe followed in his footsteps as he led her through a barn filled with old bicycles and other motoring paraphernalia. Passing a row of old-fashioned telephone boxes, that stood like guards outside a palace they entered the second large shed. "Here we are!" Mr. Simpson declared eagerly, as he lifted away a sheet to reveal a complete Victorian bathroom. Chloe gasped as she laid her eyes upon the beauty of the rolltop bath still wearing its original cast iron feet.

"It's beautiful!" Chloe exclaimed as she stroked her hand along the edge of the enamel, "I'll take it!"

"But you don't know how much it is," Old Mr Simpson stated as he stood scratching the stubble on his chin.

"I am sure that whatever it is will be a fair price," Chloe replied adamantly, convincing Liam of its worthiness would be a different story, but that could wait for now. Mr. Simpson nodded his head as he wrote a small note reading 'sold, Mrs Stevenson' before placing it down onto the edge of the sink. "What other exciting treasures do you have?" she asked as her eyes scanned the contents of the building. Within twenty minutes, Chloe's purchases had now racked up to an unknown sum, as she selected items to enhance her soon-to-be antique bathing experience.

"Well, that's about all my new stock I have to show you, except for what's inside that storage container over there, but to be honest with you I haven't looked in there yet myself," he said as he pointed out the large blue metal exterior of the container that sat alone outside.

"Let's go then!" Chloe suggested eagerly, "No time like the present."

Old Mr Simpson sighed to himself, how did he always allow her to twist him around her finger? Deep down he knew exactly why, Chloe over the past couple of years had become one of his best customers. The hard-faced attitudes of the usual interior designers, who saw everything as a way of making money made his blood boil. But in Chloe, he saw the love she felt for every item she had ever bought, and over the years this had amounted to a lot! He had trouble remembering the majority, except for the items that stood out, like the old millstone she had purchased to turn into a fireplace and a whole crate full of antique books, which she never intended to read and were only for decorative purposes.

The doors to the storage container swung open with a low growl from their hinges. Chloe breathed in as the musty scent of the interior slowly filled her nostrils as she gazed inside.

"Well from what I know this all came from different places, it was someone's collection from what I understand. Take a look inside, and if anything takes your eye then I will be in the office, it's time for another of those horrible pills again," he said, smiling at Chloe before making his way slowly across the yard.

"Gross!" Chloe muttered as she looked at the many glass cabinets, taxidermy was never her thing. She never did understand the reason behind filling an animal with straw to make it look alive. The whole thing creeped her out somewhat, and being surrounded by the things made the experience a thing of nightmares. At the back of the container, something caught her eye, it was ideal, and surely Frank would be able to do something with it. Confident in her decision she closed the container doors and made her way back to Old Mr Simpson.

"I'm sure I could have it all delivered this week Mrs Stevenson, will there be someone to help with the unloading as a few of the items are quite heavy," the old man asked as he filled out the invoice.

"Yes, Mr. Willcott my builder, and of course, there will be me," Chloe replied smiling, as she checked out her bicep in a way to look big and strong. Much to the amusement of Mr Simpson who sat chuckling to himself, all the time thinking who she was trying to prove it to, him or her?

# Chapter Two

It was the weekend and Old Mr Simpson had stood by his word and delivered the items to Millhouse, much to the displeasure of Frank and Ted the labourer. Chloe had watched awkwardly as they carried each piece between them, huffing and puffing as they went along the path that ran down the side of the house and into the old outbuilding. She had listened to Frank, who just did not understand why a perfectly sized double bedroom would be converted into a bathroom. After all, he had recently completed the en-suite and saw no necessity for another place to wash. Chloe had gone on to tell the moaning builder that the Victorian bathroom from old Simpson's had been a steal and with his excellent skills would make the room the icing on the cake. Of course, Frank as always could not say no to Chloe even though he was due to finish work on Millhouse that week. She left him to his moaning and set about filling the floor to ceiling bookshelves that he had fitted in the lounge with the vast array of literature she had purchased some time ago, freeing up space in the now overcrowded out building.

Liam had returned to Millhouse late on Friday evening, the traffic had been a nightmare to contend with and all he wanted to do was just relax. Chloe on the other hand was buzzing with excitement and just wanted him to see all of the new additions Frank had completed in his absence. However, the revelation that the spare double bedroom would now become a haven of Victorian antiquity did not exactly fill him with the same amount of enthusiasm as it did for Chloe. And by Sunday it was still number one on the list of topics open for discussion by Liam.

"What I fail to understand is where my mother is supposed to sleep, I cannot expect her to sleep in the box room Chloe, there isn't enough room to swing a cat!" Liam grumbled as he sat on a stool next to the kitchen island reading the newspaper.

"Well, it's a good job that your mother doesn't have a cat then, isn't it!" she responded harshly as she flicked loudly through the pages of the Sunday supplement. Liam's mother was not what you would class as a fan of Chloe. Her sometimes rather brash outbursts and comments were not what she saw as how a lady should behave. Coupled with the fact that she had always seen her son marrying a barrister or the manager of a bank, not an artist, or more to the point an unemployed artist at that! Made their relationship somewhat strained to say the least. Of course, for Liam's sake, Chloe always tried her best to make Liam's mother feel welcome whenever she came to visit. Secretly though Chloe just wanted to place her hands around the old bag's neck and squeeze the life out of her, but she didn't, instead, she would smile sweetly and pretend to be interested in anything she had to say.

"Just come to the outbuilding and have a look at the bathroom suite, I promise it's amazing Liam," Chloe pleaded, "Look even Annie thinks it's a good idea!" She continued to say as she pointed to the rocking chair, where the ragdoll sat, still wearing the same expression as always.

"In case it has slipped your memory, I spend the majority of my time working to pay for all of this. I'm sorry if my enthusiasm somewhat lacks gusto, but washing in a bath over a hundred years old does not excite me in any way!" Liam replied sharply, "And that is a stuffed toy with as much common sense as you have understanding about saving money," he continued to rant as he pointed over to Annie.

By Monday morning Chloe was again alone. Liam had left early to avoid the traffic and more importantly to avoid another confrontation with Chloe. He loved her dearly and had only agreed to purchase Millhouse to keep her happy, but how she could spend money faster than he could earn it concerned him somewhat.

Frank had telephoned to say that he would be back again on Wednesday. This was because he had thought his work at Millhouse was completed for the time being and had promised his services to another customer. The weatherman on the radio had joyfully announced that a large band of rain was on its way by midday. It was nowhere near midday as Chloe sighed and watched the continuous drops of rain running down the window pane as she looked outside at the dark looming clouds above. The day's inclement weather had now spoilt her plans, she had decided to attempt the tidying of the garden. But the invite of a soaking had discouraged her somewhat from undertaking the task.

The dark clouds seemed to mask the arrival of nightfall as still, the rain fell heavily to the ground. Logs crackled in the fireplace as their glowing flames flickered along the walls of the lounge. As if their very movements were those of trance like golden-clad dancers moving to an unheard but mesmerising rhythm of the fire. She must have fallen asleep, for how long she did not know. The logs on the fire had now become embers of their former lives as they lay brightly in the hearth.

She sat bolt upright, listening intently as she scanned the dimly lit room from the sofa. There it was again, the same sound as if metal was being rubbed against a stone. Chloe held her breath and listened, the palms of her hands had become nervously clammy as she waited, but the noise had stopped. Slowly she stood and made her way over to the window. The moon was slowly becoming visible from behind the dark clouds and from its silver hue she could just make out the silhouettes of the trees as they appeared from out of the darkness. Scraping, scraping, the same sound again froze Chloe on the spot. Had the Grim Reaper himself arrived to sharpen his scythe on the millers stone? Chloe exhaled deeply and laughed to herself as she realised that no taker to the afterlife had arrived, but instead, the garden gate had been left open and was rubbing slowly back and forth against the hardness of the stone gatepost.

In the kitchen, Chloe sipped slowly from her glass of water. For the first time since moving into Millhouse, she felt fearful, unnerved by the isolation surrounding her. She looked over to where Annie still sat unemotionally detached, her silence deafening, but she was the only companion Chloe had. Scooping Annie up quickly in her arms, Chloe climbed the stairs and carried her to bed. Outside the rain had stopped, leaving puddles illuminated by the moon behind. As Chloe turned out the light and snuggled beneath the safety of the duvet with Annie, a hand slowly closed the gate and fastened the latch securely before walking away into the night, their path lit only by the moon and the lantern that they carried.

The next morning any fears from the night before had vanished. Chloe drew back the curtains and smiled as she looked out at the valley now bathed in the morning sunshine. "Good morning," Chloe said happily, as she picked Annie up by the arm and led her back down to her usual observant position on the rocking chair in the corner of the kitchen. As she sat at the kitchen island sipping her morning coffee the telephone rang breaking the sequestered harmony of Millhouse. It was Liam apologising for the way he had acted over the weekend and making sure that everything was as it should be with Chloe. It seemed to have completely slipped his mind that in fact, he was only a day late with his weak attempt at forgiveness. Chloe thought about telling him about the night before and how she had felt so alone, but in the light of day, she knew that Liam would just use her insecurity as a way to sell Millhouse.

The garden was more of a challenge than Chloe had first thought, as she struggled to clear the overgrown flowerbed next to the wall of brambles. Liam of course had suggested that the job be left to someone with more horticultural knowledge, Chloe being Chloe had insisted all along that she was more than capable of returning the garden to its former self, something that she now was beginning to regret.

Two hours had passed, and Chloe smiled as she looked at the results of her perseverance. In the centre of the small lawn, a mass of weeds and brambles now sat awaiting their journey to the bonfire. And in the corner of the garden, where the two walls met a rose bush stood patiently awaiting the tentative care of Chloe's hands. Slowly and carefully, she cut away at the dead stems, confident in her pruning, just like she had watched her Grandfather do when she was just a small girl. As she cleared the bottom of the bush something caught her eye, kneeling on the damp grass Chloe reached in to retrieve the item from its earthy resting place. "And what might you be?" she asked, rubbing the mud away with her fingers. "A key, and why would you be hidden away in the garden?" Chloe questioned the earth covered object in her hand. "I wonder what else is hiding in here?" she said quickly, returning her attention to the bottom of the rose bush. "SHIT!" she yelped, as thorns dug into the flesh of her arm, forcing her to pull back quickly. Blood had begun to slowly flow from the open wounds on her forearm and hand, as she stood at the kitchen sink carefully addressing the cuts with cotton wool and antiseptic lotion.

Content with her nursing skills, Chloe set about cleaning the key. As she washed the dirt away the key revealed its beauty, each piece of mud giving way to the finely engraved scrolls that had been carved around the entirety of the handle. It seemed strange that such a piece of craftsmanship would just be discarded, surely it would have been missed. And the lock that once would have been its companion, what of that? All the Millhouse doors had their locks and keys intact when they had purchased the place. Chloe allowed her mind to be filled with what-ifs and maybes as she thought about the origins of the key. Turning the key around in her fingers, the movement forced one of the cuts on the back of her hand to again start to bleed. Slowly unnoticed the trickle of blood flowed down the edge of her finger and onto the surface of the key.

A sudden gust of wind blew through the valley, and the trees seemed to be shaking with its very presence. Chloe jumped as the back door slammed shut aggressively causing her to drop the key down onto the limestone floor, where it lay spinning slowly in a circle. In the corner of the room, Annie sat completely still, her eyes transfixed as she stared blankly into thin air. Chloe stood holding her chest as she exhaled slowly, "It was just the wind!" she said, laughing nervously to herself. Slowly she knelt and stopped the key from spinning, before carefully picking it up. "How strange!" she said, noticing that the key felt oddly warm to the touch. "I think that we need to put you somewhere safe in case you get lost again," she said, winking at Annie and hanging the key on an old hook that had been found fastened to the wall when they had first started the renovations. Liam of course had wanted to just rip it out, but Chloe deemed it to be an important original feature and so it stayed.

By the afternoon the sun had again been smothered by the darkening of the clouds, as they gathered heavily over Millhouse. She decided to take the small path that ran alongside the river. It was a beautiful walk where the air was filled with the heavy scent of wild garlic and the sound of the river swollen by the rain as it gushed its way over rocks and made its way downstream. Standing on the small stone bridge that arched its ancient back low over the river, Chloe took out her phone and began to take photograph after photograph back along the river and the valley towards Millhouse. She needed to start painting again, it seemed like an age since she had last taken a brush to canvas, and she needed to occupy her mind while Liam was away. Happy that she had enough references to begin Chloe turned to make her way back along the path. All around her nature busied itself in preparation for nightfall as she returned to the millrace. She watched as a kingfisher sat tracing the silver lines of the small fish through the surface of the water, before diving down quickly to redeem his prize. As she neared the crossing to Millhouse she stopped and looked around at the willow tree, which bowed gracefully as its branches hung playfully upon the surface of the water.

That evening Chloe sat sipping slowly from her glass of wine as Vivaldi serenaded her from the CD player in the corner of the studio. Carefully she began to copy the image of the photograph onto the stark white canvas that stood in front of her on the easel. Architecture was not the usual form that Chloe would paint, far from it. She had perfected the ability to capture the true likeness of a person, whether the sitter agreed or not was another story entirely. Chloe had lost track of how many people had questioned if their nose was really that big and if she could at least remove some of the wrinkles from the portrait. Her love for Millhouse seemed to inspire her to paint, freely she applied stroke after stroke to the canvas, pausing briefly to admire her work or to take in another mouthful of wine. Before reaching for her brush and beginning once more.

The evening had slipped away quickly for Chloe, checking the time she realised that it was fast approaching midnight. The liberation of painting and the consumption of maybe too much wine made her stretch as she yawned. It was most definitely time for bed, her days of painting into the wee small hours as she had done at university were now well and truly behind her. Climbing into bed she turned out the bedside lamp and drifted off into a deep sleep.

All the time Annie kept a close watch over Millhouse, silently looking out across the kitchen, the ticking of the clock counting down the hours towards sunrise. Chloe remained fast asleep, safe in her bed as Annie sat motionless, watching as the key began to slowly sway from side to side, as it hung from the hook. She watched as the movement of the key became more and more apparent as the arc of the swaying increased. Until unannounced it flicked up into the air and landed with a clank onto the paleness of the limestone floor.

The following morning, early as usual Chloe woke to the sound of Frank unloading his van outside. Stretching, she climbed out of bed and made her way downstairs wrapped in the warmth of her dressing gown. "Morning Frank," she said sleepily as she opened the front door and made her way to the kitchen.

"Morning!" Frank replied cheerfully as he followed Chloe's yawning form into the kitchen, perching himself on the edge of a stool at the island.

"Coffee?" Chloe asked foolishly, she already knew the

answer to that question far too well.

"Only if you are having one," Frank replied in his usual jolly tone as he looked down at the floor. "Well, what's this then?" He asked, climbing off the stool, and bending down. Chloe clicked on the kettle and turned to find Frank picking something up and holding it in his rough hands.

"What? What is it?" Chloe asked as she took two mugs from the cupboard and placed them down on the worktop next to the kettle.

"It's a key and an old one at that! Look at the time that someone put into making it," Frank said, holding out the key for Chloe to see.

"I found it yesterday in the garden, underneath a rose bush. Vicious it was too, look!" Chloe said as she rolled up the arm of her dressing gown to reveal the cuts to Frank. Who winced at the sight of the rose's brutality it had shown towards her. "What I don't get is why it was on the floor, I hung it on that hook," Chloe continued to say as she looked with a puzzled expression first at the key and then at the hook that was still fastened securely to the wall.

All the time Annie sat silently screaming out as to what she had witnessed, as Frank carefully placed the key back securely onto the hook. "Well, it's an old house maybe it moved a little bit in the night," he stated reassuringly as he smiled at Chloe.

"Maybe," she replied as she passed a mug of steaming coffee to the welcoming hand of Frank.

"Mind the walls!" Frank moaned as Ted struggled to carry the Victorian wash basin up the stairs. "Honestly, I'd be better training a chimp to do the job," he tutted, as Chloe sat examining the painting of Millhouse.

"Sorry, what did you say?" Chloe asked breaking herself away from the canvas, for some reason, she felt compelled to stare at the image.

"I said.." Frank began to say as he entered the studio before pausing as he looked at what Chloe had created. "I must say your painting of Millhouse is incredible Mrs Stevenson, is that you in between the trees?" he asked as he studied the picture more closely.

"Where, what are you talking about?" Chloe asked as she looked to where Frank was pointing his thick finger.

As she looked closely at the painting she saw that Frank was indeed correct, in between the trees was the form of a dark figure stood as though they were looking directly at Millhouse.

# Chapter Three

Nothing seemed to add up, had she unknowingly painted in the figure by complete accident? After all the shadows and silhouettes of the trees could mistakenly be seen as a person, couldn't they? Chloe again returned her gaze to the painting, this was most definitely not a trick of the light, nor was it random brushstrokes giving off the illusion.

She quickly walked down to the kitchen, apart from the noise created by Frank and Ted the place was silent. Grabbing her coat from the peg by the door Chloe made her way out into the small back garden and down the path that led to the trees. "I was standing on the bridge when I took the photos, so the figure must have been standing somewhere here," She said curiously, as she looked back in the direction of the house. The path was soddened and muddy from the rain and Chloe could see the footprints that she had left behind, but that was it, only her footprints and none that would have belonged to the mysterious figure in the painting. "They must have used the path!" Chloe said to herself adamantly as she looked around at the ground between the trees. Everywhere was covered with thick vegetation, entwined by the tangles of brambles that wrapped themselves closely around the shrubs and trees.

Chloe stood completely still, she had an immense feeling that at that moment she wasn't alone. She felt as though she was being scrutinised by hidden eyes that watched her every move. "Hello, is there anybody there?" she called out nervously, but there was no reply. From the bridge, the figure of a person dressed in black stood listening as they watched Chloe, before turning and disappearing into the wood. Chloe turned around slowly as she called out again, "Hello, I know someone's there!" But again, there was no reply. As she looked around, all that she could see were the familiar trees and the old stone bridge at the bottom of the path. She shuddered as a feeling of uneasiness rushed through her, pulling the collar of her coat up Chloe quickly made her way back along the path to the welcoming sight of Millhouse.

Entering the kitchen, Chloe was met by Frank and Ted, who, after lugging the bathroom suite upstairs, decided they deserved a well-earned break. "Here she is," Frank said cheerfully as Chloe hurried into the kitchen, closing the backdoor quickly behind her. "My, Mrs Stevenson you look worried, what's the matter?" Frank asked as he looked at the nervous expression on Chloe's face.

"Oh, nothing, I just get a little jumpy sometimes, it's a childhood thing that I suppose I never grew out of," Chloe sighed as she looked at Frank who was sitting on his usual stool next to the island.

"Ah I see, like the fear of ghosts and ghouls and things that go bump in the night kind of thing," Frank replied as he dunked a biscuit into his coffee before placing it whole into his mouth.

"No, I never said anything about being afraid of ghosts! Besides I would say that the living are far scarier than the dead Frank!" Chloe responded defensively as she tutted at the very thought of Frank thinking that she was scared of the dark.

All the time Ted the labourer stood looking at the key that hung from the hook on the wall. "Is this what you found in the garden then Mrs Stevenson?" Ted asked without averting his gaze from the key.

"Yes, under the rose bush," Chloe replied as she stood at the kitchen sink refilling the kettle with water.

"That's old that is!" Ted stated confidently as he sipped loudly from his mug of tea.

*No shit Sherlock!* Chloe thought sarcastically to herself as she turned to where Ted was still standing admiring the key.

"I reckon that's from the 17th century," Ted again said in the same confident manner.

"And what makes you so sure?" Chloe asked as she placed her mug next to the now boiling kettle.

"He's a bit of a history buff is old Ted here and if he says it's the 17th century then I'd put money on him being right Mrs. Stevenson," Frank interrupted as he placed another biscuit into his mouth.

"Really? Well, I must say I'm impressed Ted," Chloe smiled as she looked back over at him, "And what else can you tell me about the key?"

"Late 17th century, possibly French-made, but I could be wrong on that score, everybody copied everyone else's work you see, I will say one thing though," Ted stated, before pausing as he placed his mug down.

"What? What is it?" Chloe asked, now fully intrigued by what Ted had been about to say.

"Well," he began, "It's just these scrolls," he said pointing at the handle of the key.

"What, what about the scrolls?" Chloe asked impatiently as she made her way over to where he was standing.

"It's just, well, I seem to have seen them before somewhere, not on a key of course but."

"But, but what Ted?" Chloe asked again, her impatience now growing by the second.

"At a house when I was labouring for another firm. I seem to recall the same scrollwork on maybe the hinges of a door or something. I can't remember it was a while ago now Mrs Stevenson."

"Well come on Ted, I'm sure Mrs Stevenson has got better things to do with her time than listen to us waffling on. Besides that, the bathroom won't fit itself," Frank said placing his empty mug on top of the equally empty plate which had been piled with biscuits.

Chloe knew that when they agreed to buy Millhouse, they had also agreed to become somewhat custodians of the place's history. Of course, they knew about its former life as a miller's home, where he would rest after a hard day of grinding the wheat into flour between the turning stones. A hard, yet tranquil life all the same.

"Local history," Chloe whispered to herself as she studied the titles of the books in the library in the centre of Wellton. "The History of Little Lawton," she said sliding the book from the shelf carefully. Sitting at a table, Chloe flicked through the pages, as she looked at the images of the village from times gone by. Lawton Mill 1836, photograph by Mr. B. Chambers, Chloe read as she studied the image of Millhouse. From what she could see nothing much had changed, apart from the fact that the small porch on the front of the house, where they now stored their firewood, had a door fitted. Liam had often suggested that having the porch open to the elements would cause problems in the winter months but like other parts of the house, Chloe and Liam could not agree or compromise over what they thought would look best. Turning the page Chloe's eyes were met by the image of the miller, who stood proudly at the front door, his thick forearms folded in front of him. Alfred Barnet, miller, Lawton Mill 1836, photograph by Mr B Chambers. As

Chloe studied the photograph closely, she not only saw the image of a former resident of Millhouse but also a close-up of the door. Taking out her mobile phone Chloe took copies of the two images before returning the book to its position on the shelf.

By the time Chloe returned home Frank and Ted were packing their tools away in boxes on the back of the van. "Well, that's us done for the day, we'll see you at the same time tomorrow," Frank called out as the last box was filled and the lid slammed shut.

"Ok, thank you both, see you tomorrow," Chloe replied waving goodbye as she made her way indoors.

"Hi Babe, it's me. Give me a call when you can, miss you," Chloe said as she spoke to Liam's answerphone. "What riveting subject of conversation shall we have this evening then Annie?" she sighed as she looked over to her silent companion. As Chloe suspected her reply was the same as usual, nothing.

That evening Chloe decided to eat her dinner in the comfort of the living room, something that Liam would have surely complained about. But he wasn't there, so she decided to just do as she damn well pleased. She sat beside the roaring fire studying the photographs that she had taken earlier that day at the library and had the foresight to print them out when she returned home. The door as she had presumed was nothing more than just that, a door. It was plain in its appearance, with no

decorative scrolls or fancy carvings to signal its
importance, apart from the fact that it made Millhouse
appear somewhat more secure. *Maybe Liam was right after
all?* She thought to herself as she looked at the clock on
the mantlepiece. *It was nearly 9 p.m., surely he would have
finished work by now?* Chloe pondered when she realised
that he still hadn't returned her call. Picking up the tray
complete with an empty plate and cutlery Chloe made her
way to the kitchen. Outside it had begun to rain yet again,
not heavy rain but more fine like a mist, the kind of rain
that always seems to soak you to the skin. From her
position at the kitchen sink, Chloe looked out into the
night from the kitchen window, everywhere seemed so
peaceful, wet, but peaceful all the same. At the bottom of
the path near the trees, Chloe could see something
shining, not a bright light but more of a pale yellow.
Wiping her breath off the glass she placed her eyes closer
to get a better look, something was most definitely there
shining between the trees. Opening a drawer, she
rummaged through its contents, "Got you!" she
proclaimed as she held up a torch in her hand, quickly
switching it on and off to test the batteries.

Like the beam of a lighthouse, Chloe shone the torch
from side to side as she stood quietly outside the back
door. The gurgling of the river and the soft padding of
the rain, as it fell onto the ground, were the only sounds
that broke up the stillness of the night. The powerfulness
of the torch's beam made it easy for Chloe to see through
the darkness of the trees as she stood nervously shivering

under the small canopy that hung over the door. The light that she had seen from the window had disappeared, perhaps she had imagined it, maybe it was no more than a reflection on the glass. Chloe took one more scan across the trees with the torch before shrugging her shoulders and returning inside the house, locking the door securely behind her as she went.

"Perhaps she's just gone to bed mate, it is getting on a bit now and you know how Chloe hates late nights!" Alan, Liam's boss said as he laughed, thinking about the dinner parties and how Chloe would be falling asleep by 10 pm.

"That's the fifth time I have tried to call her tonight, but the line just goes dead, her mobile phone isn't ringing either!" Liam said as he sat back down at the table in the hotel bar.

"Perhaps the telephone line is down, you know how rickety and unreliable things like that are in the countryside. I'm sure that she is fine, besides you would have to be a complete maniac to venture down that track at nighttime," Alan said again in the same comical manner.

"Maniac? Thanks, you know nothing like that even crossed my mind but now you come to mention it, perhaps I had better head back over to Millhouse," Liam said nervously as he thought about the situation, and what Chloe might be going through at that very moment.

"Don't be daft! Liam I was joking that's all, and besides you've been drinking there's no way I'm allowing you to drive anywhere tonight," Alan stated as he pointed to the pint glass in front of Liam.

Chloe made one final check that all of the doors and windows of Millhouse were secured before switching out the lights and heading up the stairs to bed. Checking her mobile phone for messages and missed calls one last time she sighed to herself before turning out the small bedside lamp and burying herself deep beneath the duvet.

2:07 am and Annie sat watching as again the key slowly began to sway from side to side building momentum with every swing it took. From her side, Annie could sense the key in the backdoor starting to shake in the lock, gently at first before rattling violently in the keyhole. Along the hallway, Annie could hear the same repetitive actions of the front door key as it too now started to rattle aggressively as if it was being shaken by an earthquake.

Upstairs Chloe lay peacefully asleep, completely unaware of the frantic actions of the keys in the doors below. She was walking along a road, and ahead of her was a woman who appeared to be frightened by something. Chloe called out but the woman seemed to be unable to hear her. She could see the dark silhouette of a man making its way towards the woman, as it reached her Chloe watched on in horror as the man grabbed her before engulfing them both in flames.

The movement of the key on the hook forced it to swing violently before again landing on the cold stone floor where it spun slowly. As it came to a standstill, the keys in the doors stopped shaking, returning to their silent positions inside the locks.

Chloe opened her eyes and sat up quickly as she scanned the darkness of her bedroom. She checked the time, it was 2:15 a.m. Frank would be there early to continue the work on the bathroom, she needed to sleep but the haunting images that had been played out in her dream made it impossible for her to do so. Climbing out of bed she made her way to the studio, if she couldn't sleep then she might as well do something worthwhile Chloe thought to herself as she readied herself to paint.

By the time morning came around Chloe had fallen asleep in her chair in the studio. Outside Frank was happily whistling away to himself as he unloaded the lengths of new copper piping from the van. The sound of Frank and the clanking of the pipes woke Chloe with a jolt, rubbing her eyes and back, she stood and made her way downstairs to let Frank in.

"Heavy night was it?" Frank chuckled as he looked at the sorry state Chloe was in, as she tried to stretch out her back which was aching from a night of sleeping in the chair.

"Something like that," she replied, thinking about the woman in her dream.

"You might want to put that somewhere else," Ted stated as he picked up the key from the kitchen floor and returned it to its hanging place on the hook.

Chloe was about to answer when her mobile phone went into overdrive, announcing message after message. Opening the screen in her hand she saw that they were all from Liam. He hadn't been too busy to call as she had first suspected and had constantly tried to call home the night before. Lifting the receiver of the landline she could hear the dialling tone, the telephone line was most definitely working as she had expected. Typing quickly, she messaged Liam to let him know that she was fine and had no idea why he could not get through. He replied almost instantly, stating that he would call again at lunchtime and suggesting that maybe she should consider having his mother stay for a while, just for the company if nothing more. Chloe huffed as she read the message, there was no way that she was staying at Millhouse alone with her. She would rather suffer loneliness than have his mother constantly rearrange everything while looking down her nose at her. *No, no way!* Chloe thought it wasn't happening and when Liam called at lunchtime she would make it very clear.

Later that morning Frank walked over to Chloe who was again cutting away more weeds from the front garden. "I didn't know you had a cat?" he asked, watching Chloe tugging desperately at a weed.

"I don't!" Chloe replied as her hands slipped on the weed

sending her backwards and landing on her bottom with a thud. "What makes you think I have a cat?" Chloe asked curiously as she held out her hand and waited for Frank to help her.

"It's just the front door, Ted noticed it, small scratch marks at the bottom, here I'll show you," Frank said as he helped Chloe to her feet and led her inside the porch. "See!" he continued to say as he pointed to the freshly scribed marks.

"How strange!" Chloe said as she examined the marks, "I have seen some weird things recently, but I have most definitely not seen nor heard for that matter a cat."

"What weird things would they be Mrs Stevenson?" Frank asked suspiciously as they walked back out into the garden.

"Oh nothing, don't listen to me, Frank. What you hear are no more than the ramblings of a woman who spends too much time on their own. But I will keep an eye out for any feline visitors, you know I always fancied having a cat," Chloe replied smiling as she nudged Frank with her elbow.

"Well, if you're sure Mrs Stevenson," Frank said rubbing the stubble on his chin as though he was deep in thought.

Chloe nodded her surety, "And stop with all this Mrs Stevenson shit and just call me Chloe!"

# Chapter Four

 "You can be so bloody stubborn sometimes Chloe do you know that! In fact, I have lost count of the number of times that you only see things from your point of view!" Liam said sternly as he began to raise his voice. Chloe stood in the lounge, holding the handset of the telephone away from her ear as she mocked him by pulling faces at the receiver.

"I'm sorry, I didn't realise you were keeping a tally chart, perhaps I should count up all the times you have been a PRICK!" Chloe replied as she pulled a 'how fucking dare you face.'

"There is no need to be like that, I just think that having my Mother stay for a while would be a good thing!" Liam stated defensively at her outburst.

"Here we go again! Liam you love your mother I understand that but, how do I put this? She is an interfering busybody that does my fucking head in!" Chloe snapped back, just as Frank walked in through the front door. Hearing Chloe made him laugh out loud as he walked along the hallway. Chloe quickly covered the mouthpiece of the telephone with her hand as she gestured for Frank to be quiet.

"Chloe who was that who's there with you?" Liam enquired as he strained his ear to listen.

"It's my secret lover Liam!" Chloe replied sarcastically as she looked in Frank's direction.

"WHAT!" Liam shouted upon hearing her calm mannered confession.

"You really are stupid, aren't you? It's Frank, you know the man *you* employed to renovate the house. God, I cannot believe that you would think such a thing," Chloe spat as she retaliated. "I'm going now! I have important things to be getting on with, goodbye!"

"But Chloe, hang on!" Liam said despairingly,

"Goodbye!" she replied, quickly placing the handset down and ending the call.

"Oh dear, I take it that there's trouble at the mill?" Frank asked as Chloe entered the kitchen.

"He drives me up the wall sometimes that's all, with his I'm always right attitude. Well, he's not right I don't need his sodding mum here telling me what to do in my own house!" Chloe huffed as she sat down on a stool next to Frank.

"I take it that she's a bit of a battle axe then?" Frank chuckled as he looked across the island.

"Battle-axe? Frank, the woman could be used as a

national deterrent in the face of war!" Chloe fumed, making Frank laugh all the more.

 By late afternoon the temperature had dropped significantly, and Chloe set herself the task of readying the fire in the lounge. Sweeping the remainder of the ash from the fireplace, she placed the small pieces of kindling into the hearth, arranging them to resemble a small bonfire. The careful scrunching of the newspaper made the fire ignite instantly, filling the fireplace with pops and crackles as the dry wood set alight. Chloe sat patiently watching as the flames licked around the small offcuts of timber before slowly placing a well-seasoned log on top of the inferno. "That's it burn!" she said to herself in a sinister voice as she watched the flames licking upwards from the hearth. On the window sill, a small glass vase filled with a selection of dried flowers began to slide slowly to the edge, balancing itself precariously before tipping sideways and falling quickly to the floor. Chloe jumped as the vase shattered into hundreds of tiny pieces across the polished surface of the floorboards. As she sat wide-eyed looking across the room, she heard what sounded like a woman crying. Not a loud wailing but a faint cry as though it came from somewhere in the distance and was carried by the wind. Chloe shuddered as she rubbed the upstanding hairs on her arms, listening as the room returned to the sounds of the burning log again.

The shattered remains of the vase seemed to take her forever to retrieve, and by the time Chloe had swept up the last shard from the floor Frank and Ted were long gone.

The evening seemed to pass slowly, as the recent events surrounding Millhouse played heavily on Chloe's mind. Maybe she should reconsider what Liam had suggested and give in to his demands surrounding the awkward situation of his mother. "Or maybe not!" She said defiantly, quickly snapping herself away from making any rash on the spot decisions.

As usual, by 10 p.m. Chloe found herself yawning uncontrollably as she sat huddled in the armchair by the fire, fighting the compulsion to just allow herself to drift off to sleep. By 10:30 p.m. she could fight it no longer and after locking the doors sleepily made her way upstairs to bed.

Reaching the top of the stairs Chloe stopped suddenly, she could almost feel the blood pumping through her veins as her heart tried to break free from her chest. There it was again, the same distant sound of a woman crying. "Hello?" Chloe called out softly as she stood completely still awaiting a reply. Nothing, as before the sound seemed to just drift away. The air in the bedroom seemed chilled, something that Chloe was not particularly used to at Millhouse, the room always seemed to be warm and welcoming not cold and foreboding. Climbing into bed she pulled the duvet close to her body in a bid to retain its heat. As she lay in bed surrounded by the darkness of the night it happened, for the first time she heard her voice.

"Hear me!" the voice whispered.

"Hello, who's there?" Chloe called out as she looked around the bedroom.

"Hear me!" the voice whispered again.

"I can hear you, can you hear me?" Chloe asked as she sat bolt upright biting her lip, not sure if a reply was what she wanted at that moment to truly hear. The crying began again, but this time it seemed to be closer. Chloe held her breath as she sat listening to the woman's sadness as she wept. The sound of her despair was so clear that Chloe felt that at any moment the figure would be there rocking back and forth at the foot of her bed. Unnerved by the whole situation Chloe switched on the small TV, something that she never did! She preferred to sleep in perfect darkness and complete silence but with the thought of what they both might bring she resided herself to falling asleep to the sound of a late-night chat show.

The rattling of the keys in the locks signalled to Annie that it was 2:07 a.m. unemotional she sat listening as the usual events unfolded in the early hours of the morning. The rattling stopped as the key dropped from the hook and hit the floor. From the trees, the figure in black held the lantern steadily out in front of them as they watched the door of the old outbuilding swing open slowly, its hinges whining in the dead of the night. Chloe turned over in her sleep, grabbing at her pillow to give comfort in her slumber. From the black sleeve of the night visitor, a hand pushed the outbuilding door shut securing it with the bolt, as Frank had done before leaving Millhouse the afternoon before.

Chloe awoke the next morning feeling as though she was coming down with something. Her head ached and her body felt as though she had run the London marathon. Sluggishly she pulled herself up and made her way downstairs, it was 7:30 a.m. and although she was up nice and early Frank would not be there today. Another customer had complained that they wanted him to finish their kitchen extension on time, as he had promised. And Frank being Frank did not want to let anyone down. Chloe had been understanding when he had apologised about not being there to finish the bathroom. Chloe reassured him that it was fine, stating that she had kind of dropped the whole thing on him at the last minute, after all. If she was honest she was secretly relieved at his absence, how her head was banging made Chloe think whether or not she would be able to bear his constant whistling and singing.

"It's very nice of you to say so Annie, but I know I look like shit," Chloe said as she looked over at her sewn-together friend. "Get a grip girl, firstly you're hearing voices in the night and now you're taking compliments from a stuffed toy!" Chloe sighed as she held her aching head in her hands. The key's position on the kitchen floor went completely unnoticed by Chloe as she sipped at the steaming mug of coffee she cradled. The telephone began to ring, from the number she realised that the caller was none other than Liam. "No!" Chloe stated defiantly, she was having enough of a problem dealing with her rationality, never mind having to listen to what he had to say as well. No, Today was most definitely one of those days when she just needed to be left alone, but the separation from society was allowing her mind to work overtime.

By 10: a.m.. Chloe was feeling a lot more like her usual self. Fresh from the shower and dressed she made her way to the studio to busy her mind for the day. Against the wall, the painting of Millhouse stood, the colours on the canvas illuminated by the bright rays of sunlight that shone through the small window behind her. She turned her attention to the canvas that sat in front of her on the easel, although unfinished the features of the face that looked back at her were somewhat striking in their appearance. Chloe sat studying the face that she had started to paint the night when she could not sleep. Had she imagined the sitter? After all the entirety of the work so far had been done without any form of reference as would usually be the case. Chloe spent the day completely absorbed in her work, the subtle shading of the skin tones seemed to bring the painting to life before her very eyes. By 5 p.m. she sat back on her stool as she gazed longingly upon the canvas. "Who are you?" she asked as she looked into the acrylic eyes that stared back at her. The woman in the painting was around the same age as Chloe with hair as black as coal, that curled gently around the lightened tones of her face. Her eyes, brown, seemed to mesmerise Chloe, as though they were drawing her into the painting itself. She felt dizzy, as though she would fall to the floor at any moment. Quickly she turned her eyes away from the portrait, but the attraction seemed to try and draw her attention back. "What is it with you?" she asked the painting as she wiped the remnants of paint from her brush. "Note to self, I must stop talking to things that cannot answer back," she smirked, standing up she walked over to the small window that looked out over the front garden.

"How many worms, I mean could you fit any more in your beak Mr B?" Chloe asked as she stood watching the blackbird that was busy collecting his dinner from the leaf-strewn lawn below. "That reminds me, food!" she said turning around and making her way downstairs.

Entering the kitchen, she momentarily looked at the key hanging on the hook before setting about preparing her evening meal. The telephone began to ring it was Liam, knowing that she couldn't or wanted to for that matter avoid him forever she lifted the receiver and answered the call. "Hey, listen I'm sorry about.." she was about to say when Liam interrupted her.

"No, Chloe I'm sorry I didn't mean to go on, but it's just, well I worry about you being there all alone that's all," Liam said in his best apologetic tone.

"Liam I'm fine, I know you worry, but what with Frank still working here most days, it can get a bit noisy, and I think it would drive your mother up the wall," Chloe said softly, trying her best to sound reassuring and diplomatic, as she crossed her fingers hoping that he would buy it.

"Yes, maybe you are right, she can get a bit agitated by workmen," Liam sighed as he agreed. Chloe looked up and mouthed *thank you*, as she uncrossed her fingers and smiled.

After an hour of talking, not about anything serious just conversations about this and that, they both said their goodbyes and ended the call. It felt good to be back on speaking terms, it made the atmosphere at Millhouse feel more like a home again and she couldn't wait for Liam to return there in a couple of days. Chloe had decided not to mention anything about what had been happening, instead choosing to keep that to herself, at least for now.

In a hotel bar, somewhere up north Liam sat listening to the pleadings of his boss. "Please Liam, I could do with you overseeing the final part of the job this weekend."

"But Alan I need to go home, Chloe needs me!" Liam stated as he shook his head.

"Chloe is fine down there on her own, you have just said so yourself, come on, I will let you go home earlier next week, what do you say?" Alan said as he pretended to grovel, holding his hands together as though praying and looking despairingly across the small round table.

"I'll think about it," Liam sighed as he shook his head slowly, before holding out his empty glass towards Alan.

"That's my boy!" Alan smiled as he stood, "Same again?" he continued, taking the glass from Liam, and making his way towards the small congregation of people at the bar.

Scraping the remains of her dinner into the bin she placed the now empty plate into the sink. After observing Mr B earlier in the garden, she'd decided to cook herself spaghetti Bolognese. However, the ratio of pasta to human had always been a bit of a mystery to her. This always resulted in Chloe cooking way too much and not the loss of her appetite which at first may have been presumed.

Later that evening Chloe sat in the armchair by the fire as she flicked through one of the many books that she had acquired from Simpsons. Chloe, as we know, was not the biggest reader in the world and had only purchased the literature to fill space and look pleasing to the eye. "Huh, I know how she feels," Chloe said to herself as she read about the solitude of the young woman out on the moor.

From upstairs she could hear what at first sounded like a faint knocking. Closing the cover of the book she placed it down onto the arm of the chair and listened more intently. There it was again, although this time it appeared to come from a different location. Chloe stood and walked to the hallway, she waited, and as she listened it started again. Knock, knock she heard from above, a long pause brought an unnerving silence as she edged herself slowly to the foot of the stairs, before knock, knock as it sounded again.

As she made her way up the stairs Chloe heard a thud, she waited for a moment before nervously continuing. The door to the studio was slightly open and through the gap that remained she could see the light shining from inside the room. *Why was the light on? It was bright sunshine whilst I was painting, and I most certainly did not turn it on,* Chloe thought as she neared the doorway.

Taking a deep breath Chloe placed her trembling fingers on the handle and slowly began to push the door open, everything appeared to be just as she had left it. The eyes of the woman in the painting seemed to follow Chloe around the room as she checked to make sure that the window was secure.

"Hear me!" Chloe heard the same voice whisper.

"I know that this is all my imagination playing tricks on me!" Chloe said to herself reassuringly, "I'm not afraid, I've seen the goofy TV shows where they pretend to speak to ghosts. It's always just the wind or an over-suggestive member of the crew putting ideas into their heads!"

Silence, Chloe stood completely still as she waited, "See,

as I thought nothing more than a loose roof tile banging in the wind and the stupid notion that I'm not alone."

As the words confidently left Chloe's mouth, the lights in the studio began to flicker and flash, as one by one the bulbs popped loudly leaving Chloe standing in the darkened room. She turned to leave but her exit was blocked rapidly by the slamming of the studio door. Desperately Chloe fought with the door handle, frantically turning it this way and that as she tried to make her escape.

"Hear me!" the voice whispered again,

"I HEAR YOU, I HEAR YOU!" Chloe screamed, tears streaming down her face as she started to panic. The door handle turned slowly opening the door in front of her. Quickly she rushed out of the room and down the stairs to the kitchen. Spinning the top from the bottle of whiskey Chloe poured a large glass of the fire water before downing its contents in one. What she had just witnessed, was it created in her head? Was she experiencing some form of a breakdown? As she downed the contents of her second glass the reality of what she was thinking hit her. What was she most afraid of? The idea that maybe she wasn't alone at Millhouse, or the thought that she was losing her mind.

# Chapter Five

The following morning found Liam sitting quietly at his desk contemplating what exactly he was going to say to Chloe. The constant flow of alcohol and Alan's more than persuasive manner had found him agreeing to work the weekend, assuring himself that Chloe would eventually understand.

He must have attempted to make that call to Millhouse half a dozen times already this morning, before replacing the handset of the telephone and sitting back in his chair. Liam loved his job and the generous salary that he obtained for being Alan's right-hand man. But since his divorce, Alan's understanding of relationships had somewhat fallen by the wayside. He had adapted quite easily to a life of hotel rooms and takeaway meals where the only person he answered to was himself. He saw Liam's relationship with Chloe as something of a hindrance, a distraction to his career, nothing more than a blockade towards the progress of the business and his success.

"Oh, I see," Chloe replied quietly as she listened to Liam's meaningless words, "Well if it's that important I suppose you have to stay."

"Are you sure that you're okay with it, me staying here to work I mean?" Liam asked awkwardly as he gestured to Alan that he would be with him soon.

"Well, there isn't much that I can say, I was just hoping that you would be home this weekend that's all," Chloe sighed. She desperately needed him to be there, to reassure her that everything was fine regarding Millhouse.

"I'll call you later, Alan is waiting for my progress report, so I had better not keep him waiting," Liam said quickly as he made his excuses.

"Is everything all right? Only you seem a little dazed," Frank asked in a concerned tone as Chloe walked back into the kitchen. She sighed and offered a small smile as she looked at his kind face,

"Oh, it's nothing Frank, just me being needy that's all, Liam has to work the weekend."

"Well in that case you must come to my house for dinner on Saturday. Sandra makes the best meat pie this side of Mamsbury!" Frank stated enthusiastically as he rubbed his hands together.

"It's nice of you to offer, but…" Chloe was about to say when Frank interrupted,

"No buts, I insist! It's about time I repaid you for all the biscuits I've eaten. Besides I'm sure my Sandra would rather talk to you than listen to me banging on about building regulations and football."

"Well, if it isn't too much trouble, then thank you, Frank I would love to come," Chloe said smiling as she accepted his invitation.

The kindness shown towards her by Frank made Chloe feel a lot better about herself and the situation regarding Liam. The next two days seemed to pass by without any strange happenings at Millhouse. The whole atmosphere of the place appeared to have returned to how it was when she had first moved in, with no distant cries or whispered voices to break the stillness of the night.

It was 6 pm and Chloe stood waiting patiently at the top of the track for the arrival of the taxi cab that would take her to Frank and Sandra's house. Chloe could have driven there herself, but this was the first time that she had been invited to go anywhere in what seemed a very long time, and she was most definitely going to make the most of it.

Annie sat motionless in the now deserted house listening to the continuous ticking of the clock. The telephone began to ring, *she's not here,* Annie pretended to say as the answering machine kicked in. It was Liam, the message relaying how he was hoping to speak to her, and that he would try again later if he had the chance to take a break.

"Come in, come in. Sandra, Chloe is here!" Frank called back along the hallway as he ushered her inside. "Let me take your coat and get you a drink," he insisted. Chloe smiled as she handed Frank her jacket, before following him into the dining room.

"I'm very pleased to meet you, Chloe!" Sandra stated in a tone that matched Frank's joyful nature, holding out her hand in front of her rounded form for Chloe to shake.

"And I you," Chloe replied as her small hand became engulfed by Sandra's thickened fingers. "Here, I brought you this," Chloe said as she held out a tissue wrapped bottle of wine for Sandra to take, hoping beyond hope that the circulation would eventually return from the squeezing sensation of Sandra's excitable grip.

The evening was enjoyable, to say the least, and after what seemed like a never ending serving of delicious food and copious amounts of wine the three of them retired to the lounge.

"So, Chloe, how are you finding life over at Millhouse?" Sandra asked as she picked up her glass of brandy, rotating it slowly in her hand.

"I love the place, Frank has done an excellent job and it's starting to feel like home," Chloe replied as she smiled over at where he was sitting.

"Frank tells me that your husband works away a lot. How are you finding the isolation? Sandra asked again as she sipped the warm liquid from her glass.

Chloe felt awkward, how did she answer truthfully

without sounding completely mad? "Do you believe in ghosts?" She asked quickly, completely taking both Frank and Sandra by surprise.

Frank laughed out loud in response, as Sandra glared disapprovingly in his direction having noticed the seriousness in Chloe's voice.

"Tell me dear, why do you ask?" Sandra asked gently, her tone now one of utter seriousness.

"I'm not sure if I am honest, it's just that, well, I have heard things," Chloe replied awkwardly, "A woman crying."

"A woman crying? well I have spent a lot of time over at Millhouse and I can honestly say Chloe dear that I have never heard anything like that," Frank stated, before taking a slow sip from his whisky.

"Well just because you haven't heard anything doesn't mean that it's not true," Sandra tutted. "I mean you're that blinkered it surprises me that you can see to tie your shoelaces."

Chloe smirked at Sandra's outburst as Frank sat quietly shaking his head at her remark.

"A woman crying you say. I'm intrigued Chloe, please do carry on," Sandra said as she sat forward in her armchair.

Chloe retold the events that had taken place while Sandra sat wide-eyed in the chair opposite her listening, she shuddered as the words that Chloe said sank in. Frank began to speak, trying his best to diffuse the irrationality of what Chloe was saying by attempting to give a sense of logical understanding to the whole matter, only to be quietened again by Sandra who tutted and shushed at his suggestions.

It felt strange to talk about it, especially to someone that in all honesty, she had only really just become acquainted with. But that aside Chloe felt as though the burden of carrying the whole thing around with her had now been shared. Sandra appeared to take her seriously, not once did she regard the whole thing to be nonsense made up by someone losing their mind. Chloe felt relieved until the fact that she would soon return to Millhouse alone dawned on her.

"You could always stay here the night we could both take you back in the morning, couldn't we Frank," Sandra suggested as she smiled reassuringly to Chloe and then her husband, who sat nodding in agreement.

Chloe sat thinking about the proposition, maybe it would be the best thing to do. After all the taxi driver would most certainly refuse to drive down the track to Millhouse, which would mean one thing, that she would have to walk it alone, and in the dark.

Upon hearing Chloe's acceptance, Sandra wasted no time at all in showing her to the more than adequate spare room. It had originally been their daughter's before she had made the move to University, met a boy, and subsequently started a life of her own. Chloe thanked Sandra and Frank for their hospitality as she closed the door and settled down for the night. It felt strange to be in such unfamiliar surroundings, but the enjoyment of the evening and maybe one too many nightcaps quickly saw her eyes closing as she nestled herself under the warm duvet.

Millhouse meanwhile stood silent, it would be the first time that it had been left unoccupied overnight since Chloe and Liam had moved in. Outside the willow tree gently bowed its now bare branches to the water as a cold wind blew through the valley, occasionally lifting the fallen leaves from the ground and tossing them into the air like confetti from some long-forgotten wedding. Before leaving, Chloe had the foresight to close the curtains and randomly leave a lamp on here and there to replicate that the place was still inhabited, something that her mother had always insisted on doing when Chloe was a child.

That part of her life was now nothing more than just memories, kept alive by the photographs and keepsakes that she kept safe in a box under her bed. It was five years ago since Chloe had lost her mother, her best friend, to a disease that ravaged her very being. Chloe had watched the slow demise of her mother as her health deteriorated, killing her mobility but never dulling her spirit. Liam had tried to soften the blow surrounding her mother's death by allowing Chloe the freedom to do what she wanted. He knew only too well the aspirations and dreams that Chloe's mother had wished for her daughter. And how she believed that one day she would become a famous artist and take the world by storm with her masterpieces. On the day of their wedding, Liam had made not only a solemn vow to Chloe but also to her mother. Promising that he would do anything to help her achieve those goals.

Annie sat frozen to the spot, as any discerning ragdoll would do. Paralysed in her cloth-bound body she sat propped up on the rocking chair, listening to the night.

2:07 a.m. and Chloe turned over in her sleep, she was back on the same track watching as the frightened woman stood desperately looking all around her. Chloe called out, but as before the woman seemed to be unable to hear her. She began to run towards her, the bareness of her feet making no sound upon the roughness of the rutted earth below her. The woman turned momentarily to face Chloe just as the figure of the man grabbed her from behind. Chloe stopped abruptly and watched as they both became engulfed in flames and disappeared.

2:07 a.m. Annie watched as the time was signalled by the usual swaying of the key hanging on the hook. In Chloe's absence, the keys to the back door no longer resided comfortably in the encasement of the lock. In her wisdom, Chloe had taken the precaution to instead place them in a drawer out of sight, where they sat nestled between rolling pins and cookie cutters. As before the key leapt from the hook landing with a clank as it hit the kitchen floor, spinning slowly to itself.

"Hear me!" Chloe heard as she woke quickly from her dream. For a moment she sat staring around the room, confused by her surroundings. The only familiarity was that of the whispered words that called out from the shadows. From outside the dark figure slowly made its way towards the front of Millhouse, its shadowy silhouette occasionally illuminated by the swaying of the lamp that it carried in an outstretched hand. Gently the latch was lifted allowing the garden gate to open slowly as the figure approached the front door. Crying, Chloe sat listening as the distraught sobbing of the woman could be heard just as clearly as it had been at Millhouse. The figure knelt at the opening of the porch before placing the lantern down on the stone step and pausing momentarily. From its fingertips, something was scattered across the threshold of Millhouse before the figure retrieved the flickering lantern and retraced its steps back into the darkness of the valley.

The crying stopped, and from the door, Chloe could hear a gentle tapping. "Chloe, is everything all right? It's just I could hear you crying," Sandra asked softly from the hallway. Chloe turned on the small bedside light and made her way over to open the door.

"Did you hear it?" Chloe asked as she opened the bedroom door and stood facing a now very concerned looking Sandra.

"Yes, yes I did, is there anything wrong?" Sandra said as she placed her hand gently on Chloe's arm.

"That wasn't me crying, Sandra," Chloe said as she smiled back at her.

"Well, if it wasn't you, who was it?" Sandra asked as he removed her hand and looked around Chloe and into the bedroom.

"I don't know Sandra, but I don't think it's in there," Chloe smiled reassuringly as she turned to look back inside the room. "It's late, go back to bed I'm sure whoever it is won't bother us again tonight."

"Well, if you are sure Chloe, then I will bid you good night," Sandra replied nervously as she took one last look into the bedroom before making her way back to bed. Chloe closed the door and climbed back under the security of the duvet before turning out the light and drifting off to sleep.

The next morning Chloe sat at the breakfast table discussing the event with Frank and Sandra. Frank being the sceptic that he was of course played the whole thing down to being nothing more than a tomcat on the prowl, crying out to defend his territory. Much to the annoyance of Sandra, who sat scowling at him for not taking them both seriously.

"I'm telling you, Frank, I heard it! Clear as anything it was," Sandra stated in defence of what she had witnessed. Chloe watched on from across the table, placing a large slice of buttered toast into her mouth, as Frank chuckled to himself at what he deemed to be complete and utter nonsense.

The journey back to Millhouse was a quiet affair, as both Frank and Sandra seemed to be in some sort of standoff as to which one would speak first. Chloe sat in the same hushed manner in the middle of them both, not sure if she should create a conversation or not. After all, it was her being there that had started all this animosity between them both in the first place. Chloe sighed when Millhouse came into view as the van bumped its way down the winding track. She waited until the van had stopped before removing her seatbelt. "Well, thank you both again for a lovely evening, and I am truly sorry about.." Chloe started to say as she bit her lip at the thought of what she had awkwardly caused.

"No don't be sorry, it was lovely to meet you, Chloe. And as for him, well," Sandra said as she huffed.

"Well, thanks again," Chloe said as she closed the door and made her way to the front gate. As she lifted the latch she heard a vehicle door close behind her.

"Wait, I will come with you, just to be sure," Sandra

called out as she waddled to where Chloe was waiting.

Chloe smiled as she opened the gate, she didn't need a chaperone in her own house, but Sandra seemed concerned and needed her mind to be put to rest. As they reached the porch Chloe rummaged in her handbag for a moment, searching for the front door key before pulling it out of the dark confines of the bag and holding it tightly in her hand. They both turned around quickly as again the clunk of a van door closing drew their attention back along the garden path.

"Here wait for me!" Frank called out as he made his way towards them. Sandra laughed as she watched the thick-set man quickly walk to where they waited.

"I thought you didn't believe in any of this, you said it was all rubbish!" Sandra said, mocking his mannerisms.

"Ah, well, just to be on the safe side I thought it would be better if I came with you, safety in numbers and all that," Frank replied hastily. "Besides I need to check how the bathroom tiles have taken to the walls," he continued.

"More like you're too scared to stay in the van alone!" Sandra said laughing as she pointed at him.

Once inside Chloe made her way to the kitchen, placing her handbag on the island she filled the kettle with water as Sandra stood admiring the room. "I love how it has turned out, you certainly have an eye for what goes with what," Sandra stated as she looked at the shelves littered with various items of both old and new. "I mean there aren't many people that can make a key look interesting," she continued to say as she pointed to the wall where the key was hanging.

Frank by this time had made his way slowly up the staircase and along the hallway to the newly fitted bathroom. He smiled to himself at a job well done as he closed the door and began to make his way downstairs. At first, he tried to ignore it, but he couldn't, turning slowly he made his way back up the staircase and listened nervously to the sounds coming from behind the closed bedroom door. There it was again, a deep groaning, followed by what sounded like unearthly feet dragging themselves across the floor. The doctor had told him a few months ago that he needed to keep an eye on his blood pressure, and at this very moment, he was doing just that!

From the Kitchen Chloe and Sandra heard Frank scream out from above before his footsteps came thundering down the staircase and along the hallway. "Whatever's the matter?" Sandra exclaimed as Frank appeared in the kitchen, his usual tanned and jolly face now replaced by one filled with dread and fear.

"Bloody hell! I've just seen it, the ghost!" he said nervously, as his voice quivered from the shock.

All three of them stood wide-eyed as they listened to the dragging sound now coming from above their heads.

Slowly they made their way to the foot of the stairs ready to face their fears as the dragging got ever closer.

"What did you see?" Chloe whispered as the dragging continued.

"A figure, a white figure moaning and groaning as it came towards me!" Frank whispered back as he tried to control the chattering of his teeth.

"Did it say anything?" Chloe nervously enquired as she looked around the wall towards the staircase.

"I didn't hang around to bloody find out, a ghastly thing it was!" he replied in the same agitated tone.

The dragging sounded like it had stopped, Chloe started to make her way to the stairs, "Where are you going?" Frank asked as he grabbed her arm to stop her.

"To see what it is Frank!" Chloe whispered as she pulled away from him and began to creep up the staircase.

"Well don't just stand there you big ninny!" Sandra said pushing Frank up the stairs to follow Chloe.

"Are you ready?" Chloe whispered as they stood outside the bedroom door, "After three, one two three!" she said quickly pushing the bedroom door open.

# Chapter Six

Sandra screamed as the door flew open to reveal none other than Liam, who hobbled across the bedroom slowly towards them.

"Liam? What the fuck are you doing here?" Chloe asked as she stood in the doorway holding onto her chest. "And why are you limping?"

"Liam?" Sandra and Frank said in unison as they looked at each other with confusion and then into the bedroom to where Frank's would-be spectre was standing.

"I think we could all do with a cup of coffee!" Chloe said smirking as she turned and shook her head at Frank before making her way downstairs, quickly followed by Sandra.

In the kitchen, after he had dressed, Liam explained to them all why he had returned to Millhouse and inadvertently scared the living shit out of Frank. Chloe placed her hand over her mouth in a bid to hide the increasing desire to laugh.

"So, you told Alan that you were going home? I bet he loved that," Chloe asked after she had managed to compose herself.

"Well after he whined on for about an hour about how my not being there would compromise the smooth running of the job he gave in. I think he could see that I wasn't taking any notice," Liam replied, smiling as he thought back to the conversation he had, had on the telephone the evening before.

"So how far away did you get the puncture? I have my van outside so when you're ready we can take a ride over there and change the tyre," Frank said cheerfully, now more relaxed after his experience. Liam smiled and nodded to show his gratitude towards him.

"About 2 miles away, but it was dark, and I only had the small light on my phone!" Liam replied as the others stood listening. "That's why I fell into the ditch because I couldn't see, honestly Chloe it was that deep and muddy I thought I was never going to get out!" Liam continued to say as he rubbed his aching leg. At that moment Chloe couldn't hold back the compulsion to laugh as Liam watched on with a look of dented pride on his face.

Frank took no time at all in changing the wheel and soon Liam was on his way back to Millhouse accompanied by Chloe, who let out a small giggle each time Liam groaned pathetically as he depressed the clutch pedal. "So why did you stay there last night, and why was everyone so jumpy? I mean Frank looked like he'd seen a ghost!" Liam asked as he turned the car off the small country lane and onto the track that led to Millhouse.

"Oh, it was getting late, so they offered to bring me back this morning that's all," Chloe smiled back at him as the house came into view.

"But the whole bursting into the bedroom thing, what was that all about?" he asked as they reached the front gate.

"Oh, we got talking, you know about things that go bump in the night. So, when Frank heard noises coming from the upstairs of an empty house he must have over dramatically put two and two together," Chloe replied placing her handbag down onto the kitchen island.

Chloe for reasons as yet unknown decided not to mention anything that had been happening at Millhouse to Liam. He had stayed in the house alone the previous night and nothing bad had happened to him, although the ability to sleep through anything may have played a big part in him remaining undisturbed. Changing the subject Chloe averted the necessity for any more questions regarding the matter, insisting instead that he accompanied her to the studio to see the paintings that she had been working on.

"Well?" Chloe asked as Liam studied the painting of Millhouse.

"Very good, very good indeed," Liam replied as he placed his arm around her shoulders. "And what do you call this one?" he asked as he turned his attention to the portrait of the woman.

"Imagination?" Chloe replied as she looked at the brush-stroked face staring back at her. Liam let out a small, confused laugh as he listened to Chloe's interpretation of the piece. His understanding of the art world was lacking somewhat and in a bid to not show his ignorance he decided to just accept what Chloe had said.

But he felt drawn to the face, as though the eyes were hypnotising him. Chloe as we know was talented in capturing the true representations of a person, but even by her standards, this was something else. The more he looked at the face, the more he found himself unable to break the attraction of the woman's eyes. "Ahem!" Chloe said loudly breaking Liam's trance-like stare, "Sorry to disturb you, but I am here to you know!"

"Sorry babe, it's just the way you have painted the eyes, they are so life-like, almost mesmerising," Liam replied as he turned away from the painting to look at Chloe.

"Well, I have a dinner to prepare, shall I leave you both to it?" Chloe asked sarcastically as she opened the studio door and headed along the hallway. Liam took one last look at the portrait before following Chloe back down the stairs.

The evening felt just like old times as they sat and chatted and laughed. Yes, she was sad that first thing in the morning he would have to make the journey back to work, but for now Chloe focused on the fact that at least for one night she would have him there at Millhouse.

They fell asleep that night content in each other's arms. Chloe lay soundly, and as she slept she dreamed, the same recurring dream, except something, was different. She could see the distraught woman standing on the track ahead solemnly awaiting her fate. But as the man approached her from behind, she grabbed out pulling another figure into the flames with her, before they all disappeared.

Chloe jumped up as she woke from the nightmare, feeling the bed beside her she noticed that Liam was nowhere to be seen. "Liam! Liam!" she called out as she made her way out of the bedroom and along the hallway, but there was no reply. From the studio, Chloe could hear what sounded like talking. No loud chattering as though there was a full-blown conversation taking place, but more a mumbling, as though someone was talking under their breath. As she entered the door she stopped as her eyes fell upon Liam who was sitting in front of the canvas uttering words to the portrait, before pausing as though listening to her reply. "Liam," Chloe said again softly, as she placed her hand gently on his shoulder in an attempt to distract him.

He jumped as he felt Chloe's touch, confused he looked at her and then at his surroundings.

"Are you ok?" Chloe asked as she looked at the state of

confusion in his eyes. Liam nodded his head slowly as he looked back at her. "Come on let's get you back to bed," Chloe said in the same softened tone, as she helped Liam to stand and led him out of the room. As she reached the door Chloe turned and looked back at the portrait momentarily before guiding Liam back along the hallway to the bedroom.

The next morning Chloe awoke to the feeling of being alone in Millhouse again. Stirring the contents of her coffee mug she read the small note that Liam had left on the island for her before he had headed off to work. In the note, he apologised briefly for any worry that he may have caused but assured her that he felt completely fine and would call her later that evening.

"Well, that was nice, even if it was a little short-lived," she tutted as she looked over at Annie and placed the note back down on the island.

By lunchtime, Frank had disappeared. According to Ted, he had seen an advertisement in the local newspaper stating that the owners of one of the large houses in Wellton were having an auction of its contents, and he had gone there to seek out any bargains there were to be had and generally just be nosey. Safe in the knowledge that she would not be disturbed Chloe set about working on the portrait of the unknown woman. As she sat looking at the face Chloe felt the compulsion to just apply a covering of white paint all over it. The effect that it seemed to have had on Liam unnerved her somewhat, brush in hand she sat contemplating her next move.

It felt at first like a tingling sensation, as though thousands of tiny pins were being pressed into the skin of her fingertips. Her grip loosened on the handle of the brush as the feeling became more and more intense, as it rose through her hands and into her arms. Dropping the brush down onto the studio floor Chloe sat back quickly, rubbing her arm with the palm of her hand as she looked back at the portrait. The eyes of the woman seemed to have changed from those that Chloe had painted, now they seemed dark foreboding and full of intent. Slowly she lifted her hand and moved it towards the surface of the canvas. It appeared to be warm to the touch as her finger stroked the image, she watched on in utter disbelief as the eyes returned once more to their welcoming shades of brown. Whomever it was and for whatever reason, Chloe realised at that point that there was no going back, she had to finish the portrait. What she had witnessed the night before was a calling in some way, Liam had felt it and now so too had she.

It was getting dark outside as Chloe made her way downstairs. From the porch, she could hear a faint cry, not like that of the woman but more delicate as it resounded. Placing her hand on the handle Chloe opened the front door slightly and peered into the porch. Everything seemed to be just as it always was as her eyes were met by the neatly stacked logs and her pair of muddy Wellington boots. Something rushed through the gap in the open door, brushing gently against her legs, she turned quickly on the spot to see a white cat now standing in the hallway, its long and bushy tail standing erect as it blinked in the light.

"Hello," Chloe said as she closed the front door and stood looking at the feline intruder. The cat meowed its reply, turning elegantly on the spot before making its way along the hallway towards the kitchen. Chloe smiled at her unexpected visitor as she followed the cat into the kitchen. "Would you like a drink of milk by any chance?" she asked, opening the refrigerator, and taking out the plastic container, as the cat moved in inpatient spirals around her legs. "I'm sorry but I only have a cooked chicken breast as I appear to be clean out of cat food at the moment."

Chloe watched on as her newfound friend devoured what was supposed to be *her* evening meal before making its way out of the kitchen and into the lounge where it curled up on the armchair purring contently to itself.

It was about 9 p.m. when Chloe finally received the call from Liam, who spent the majority of the time complaining about how much his leg still hurt and how Alan had been ignoring him. At no point did he mention anything about the painting, which surprised Chloe, she had imagined that the previous night's events would be at the very top of their things to discuss. Ending the call with an 'I love you too' Chloe replaced the handset of the telephone and placed another log onto the glowing embers in the fireplace, as the cat stirred momentarily in its slumber.

Liam sat staring at the screen of his phone. Before leaving Millhouse he had entered Chloe's studio and taken a photograph of the portrait, he had no idea why he was driven to do such a thing or keep it from Chloe for that matter. Only the compulsion to see her face and look deep into her eyes had taken over his rationality.

"Well, my little friend I suppose that it's time you were making tracks back home," Chloe said as she gently stroked the back of the purring cat. But the cat showed no interest at all in leaving the comfort of the fire and the welcoming hand of Chloe, as it yawned and curled up tightly in a ball.

Shrugging her shoulders Chloe set about securing the doors and windows of Millhouse for the night. It was fast approaching 10 p.m. and the peaceful sight of the cat sleeping had made her want to seek the refuge of her comfortable bed. "Goodnight," she said, turning off the lounge lights and making her way upstairs. Before she had even reached the top stair the cat came racing up from behind, overtaking her quickly and climbing onto her bed. "Well, I can see that you like the finer things in life puss!" Chloe yawned as she climbed into bed and turned out the light.

2:07 a.m.

"I can't go back, I mustn't go back!" Liam said over and over, and over, rocking back and forth as he dug his fingernails deep into the skin of his arm, breaking the surface tissue and letting blood begin to flow through the hairs.

The key began its movement, Annie sat still, like an incapacitated bystander as the keys in the locks started to shake and rattle violently. If only she had been treated to the sanctuary of the bedroom, then she would not have had to witness such chilling events.

From outside the dark figure slowly made its way to the front of the house. The cat opened its eyes for a moment as the hand quietly lifted the latch and opened the gate before making its lamp-lit way to the porch. Inside the key continued to swing rapidly on the hook before dropping to the floor. The hand opened, sprinkling its contents onto the step as the keys stopped spinning and rattling as though each was controlled involuntarily by the next.

"ARGH!" Liam screamed as his hypnotic state became broken and the reality of the wounds on his arm released their pain. Quickly he ran to the small bathroom and doused his arm with the coldness of the water from the tap. He studied the deep gashes, each one looking like it had been created by something more than just a fingernail. The wounds felt hot, like the burning sensation of sunburn as he carefully dabbed the enflamed skin with a flannel. The air in the hotel room felt stagnant, as though it was choking the very life out of him, he needed to get out. He placed his hand on the cheap brass effect door handle, his palm hissing as he jumped back from the extreme heat emanating from it. He felt dizzy, he felt sick, falling backwards he landed on the bed where he lay unconscious.

The cat jumped up onto the bedroom window sill and watched as the flickering light of the lamp disappeared between the darkness of the trees. All the time Chloe stood on the track watching as the woman cried out. She started to make her way closer, but the shrieking cries forced Chloe back as she covered her ears from the banshee-like sound. The figure appeared in front of her, Chloe screamed out as the woman dragged the unsuspecting soul into the fire before they were both engulfed in the flames.

She woke to the sound of meowing from the windowsill and smiled as the cat distracted her from the vision in her dream, it jumped down and quickly made its way to where she was sitting. "Good to have you around," Chloe said relieved by its company as the cat nuzzled her stroking hand with the softness of the fur on its head.

In a hotel room somewhere in the north of the country, Liam lay still, with only the slow rising of his chest to signal any life within. The dripping of the tap in the bathroom was the only sound to break the silence of the night.

The morning was broken well and truly, by the sound of the heavy rain that was pounding at the window of Chloe's bedroom. "You cannot be serious? You mean you actually want to go out in that?" Chloe asked alarmingly as the cat walked in circles by the front door. "Well don't say I didn't warn you!" she stated adamantly as she spun the key in the lock and opened the door to the now-soaked floor of the porch. Chloe watched as the cat lifted its tail in a satisfied manner and made its way out into the porch, studying the weather more closely before heading off into the garden.

It was 10:30 a.m. and a very impatient Alan stood knocking on Liam's hotel room door. "Liam, open the door, we have a meeting in an hour!"

Liam stirred, he sat up slowly and looked at his arm, the marks had completely vanished. He looked in the direction of the constant knocking and the moaning tone of Alan, as he stood and opened the door. "Sorry mate, I must have overslept," Liam said rubbing his hair as he tried to offer some sort of explanation.

"No, Liam, this isn't good enough! First, you just fuck off home on a whim, and now you cannot even be bothered to get up!" Alan said angrily, pausing slightly as another guest made their way along the corridor, "Get ready, we will have words about this after the meeting!"

"Well, that's the last of it," Chloe sighed as she brushed the remaining water out of the porch. *When Liam comes home at the weekend, we are going to talk about having a door fitted that's for sure,* Chloe thought to herself as she leaned the sodden brush up against the wall of the porch and made her way back inside the house.

# Chapter Seven

Millhouse was now well and truly held within the grasp of Autumn, as the trees that lined the banks of the valley stood crooked and bare from the cold northerly wind that had pulled and tossed at their leafy crowns. Winter would be fast approaching, and if living at Millhouse had taught her anything so far, then it would be that she had to be prepared for its arrival.

The weeks passed slowly. Chloe spent her days working in the studio, occasionally returning downstairs to add another log to the ever-hungry fire in the lounge, which now burned constantly from morning to night. Liam's return to the house had become less and less as the month dragged on, Chloe constantly listening on the telephone to his feeble excuses as to why he wouldn't be back. There always seemed to be something that would appear out of the blue concerning his work. And if she were honest, the last time that he had graced her and Millhouse with his company was not what she would have described or deemed to be a loving experience. He had appeared distant as though his thoughts were elsewhere, conversations were strained and kept to the absolute minimum, and the atmosphere of Millhouse had an awkwardness about it leaving Chloe eagerly awaiting the moment that he would leave. Even the cat, now formally addressed by Chloe as Frosty due to the whiteness of her hair, seemed to disappear whenever Liam was at the house. Usually, she would find herself constantly tripping over the cat as it followed her about like a shadow around the house. Everything about him changed, even his need to be included in everything to do with Millhouse. Chloe had tried to get his attention revived by mentioning the need to fit a door to the porch, something which he had always seen as a necessity, but even this was met by the one-worded answer of 'whatever.'

The portrait was nearing its completion, or so Chloe would tell herself before brush in hand she would find herself setting about making small alterations here and there. Highlights to the darkened hair, or the delicate placing of blues and pinks to the skin. No matter how long she took or how precise her actions were, the face always demanded more.

The news was full of stories depicting how the meteorologists were warning that the country would experience an arctic blast that winter, bringing with it blizzards and strengthening winds.

"As I said, Chloe, all of the bespoke door makers around here are fully booked until next year. The best I can probably do is seal the entrance to the porch from the elements for the time being until we can source something," Frank stated apologetically as he loaded the last bag of rubbish into his van. Chloe sighed as she listened to the words of the man that she had become so reliant on for company recently as they walked back to the house. Ted appeared pushing a heavily laden wheelbarrow full of freshly chopped logs, releasing the handles quickly to the sound of the scraping metal skids on the path outside of the porch. Chloe looked at Ted and then Frank with a puzzled expression on her face, "I noticed that you were getting low, so with Liam not here to chop anymore, I got Ted here to do it for you," Frank smiled.

"This isn't the whole of them Frank, I put the rest in the old outbuilding, should be enough to last you a good few weeks!" Ted said as he continued to stack the logs neatly inside the porch.

"I don't know what to say, except, thank you!" Chloe replied sincerely as she watched the pile of wood grow higher.

"You don't have to thank us, Chloe, you have a lovely new, well old bathroom upstairs that I am sure you are eager to try out. We cannot have you freezing your bi.., er, yourself when you get out now can we!" Frank replied, quickly changing his words to match being in the company of a lady.

"Well, make a note in your diaries for a housewarming party, after all, none of this would have been possible if it wasn't for the both of you!" Chloe insisted as Ted finished stacking the last of the logs and returned outside with an accepting smile on his face.

"Here Frank Listen, while I was chopping those logs I saw something," Ted began to say as they drove along the lanes.

"Not you as well, bloody hell Ted," Frank laughed as he looked across to where Ted was sitting.

"I did I'm telling you! I was stacking the logs in that outbuilding when I saw a woman, clear as anything she was!" Ted replied adamantly, as Frank continued to laugh.

"Well, I believe you, Ted," Frank said sarcastically as he looked back across to the passenger seat.

"You do?" Ted asked, relief resounding in his voice,

"Do I buggery!" Frank replied now roaring with laughter.

"FRANK WATCH OUT!" Ted screamed as he looked out of the windscreen. Frank looked back at the road quickly, but it was too late. They both sat watching in complete horror as the figure of a woman dressed in black suddenly appeared in the middle of the road. Frank desperately fought to regain control of the skidding wheels, but it was all in vain as the woman was hit head-on and the van careered off the road and into a hedge.

"Did you hit her?" Ted asked as his voice trembled, his eyes firmly closed, afraid to open them to the consequences that lay behind them on the road. Frank removed his seatbelt slowly and opened the driver's door.

He took a deep breath as he accepted the facts, it was his fault. If he hadn't been messing around and had concentrated on the road ahead then none of this would have happened.

"There's no one there Ted!" As he looked back along the lane, Frank uttered, "She's gone!"

Ted joined him at the side of the van, they both stood in complete silence as they looked back along the narrow hedge-lined road. A crow cawed loudly from the branch of a tree, as it swooped down low across the surface of the tarmac in front of them and disappeared.

"I suppose this is the part where you tell me that the woman in the outbuilding and the one on the road are the same people Ted?" Frank asked coyly, turning slowly to face him. Ted said nothing, instead he just stood nodding his head slowly, his face pale with fear.

7 p.m. Chloe could not resist running herself a bath, it had been so long since she had, had the pleasure and after the stress that she had been under recently there seemed to be no better time than the present. The bathroom was a room filled with wonder, Frank's attention to detail had once again well and truly surpassed Chloe's imagination as she lay soaking in the mass of steaming bubbles.

"Are you sure that you don't need to go to hospital Frank?" Sandra asked concerned for the welfare of her husband.

"No, I'm sure, I tell you Sandra she was real, we both saw her!" Frank said still shaken by the events as he cradled a glass of whiskey to steady his nerves.

"What did she look like Frank?" Sandra asked as she stroked his back to comfort him. Frank sat in deep thought as he recollected what he had seen,

"She was in her thirties maybe, with dark hair and dressed in a long black dress or maybe a coat of some kind. But her eyes Sandra, her eyes, they seemed to burn into me as she passed through the van!" Frank replayed as he sipped slowly from his glass.

"Wait! Frank, you said she passed through the van, what do you mean? Sandra asked curiously as she stopped her hand's movement on his back.

"Exactly that! She passed through the bonnet and straight between me and Ted. I cannot seem to get the look that was in her brown eyes out of my head, Sandra, do you think that I should contact the police?" Frank asked as he looked alarmingly up at her.

"For what reason? You said yourself that she was nowhere to be seen, Frank. I don't think that the police will take you seriously if you tell them that you ran over somebody who wasn't there!" Sandra replied as she smiled at him reassuringly.

8 p.m. Chloe stepped out of the bath and wrapped herself in a towel that had been warming on the heated ornate

rail, before reaching down and gently tugging on the silver chain to release the plug and the water from the bathtub. Standing in front of the mirror she gently wiped away the condensation on the glass. From behind she could hear *her*, calling out, "Hear me!" she whispered. Chloe turned quickly but there was no one there. "HEAR ME!" the voice called out again, this time louder and with more determination.

"I HEAR YOU, FOR FUCK'S SAKE I'M NOT DEAF!" Chloe snapped back harshly. She turned quickly to the sound of glass shattering, the mirror had split, and its once misted appearance now resembled that of an intricately drawn spider web. "Who are you?" Chloe asked as she stood staring at her broken reflection in the mirror. A gust of wind seemed to come from nowhere, blowing gently across the damp skin on her face. Chloe turned quickly to the window, but as she had suspected it was still fastened tightly shut. "WHAT DO YOU WANT?" Chloe called out as she looked around the room.

Laughter. Chloe rushed to the bathroom door and opened it quickly without hesitation as she tried to pinpoint where the sound was coming from. It was no use, the disquieting sound appeared to be coming from everywhere, as though Chloe was being taunted and teased from the shadows in some sick game of hide and seek. Making her way downstairs she stood listening as the laughter slowly faded away into the night leaving

Millhouse once again quiet and peaceful. Chloe shivered as she stood in the hallway covered only by the towel, she needed to get dressed but the thought of climbing the stairs filled her with dread. As if reading her thoughts of despair Frosty appeared meowing confidently as she made her way to the bottom of the staircase. Chloe sighed a deep sigh filled with gratitude as she followed behind her feline companion. "Well, you're braver than me puss that's for sure," she admitted openly as the cat smugly climbed onto the bed as Chloe entered the room.

"Do you think we should say something, to Chloe I mean?" Sandra asked as she passed another glass of whisky to Frank. "After all Ted did say that he saw something over at Millhouse this afternoon," Frank said nothing, he just sat rubbing the stubble on his chin while seemingly deep in thought. "Frank, did you hear me?" Sandra asked again as she looked at the despondent expression on his face. "Frank!"

He turned slowly to face her, "Sorry love, it's just a lot for me to take in that's all, you know my standing on this type of thing. But you're right, Ted did say that he saw the same woman at Millhouse, so maybe we should say something to Chloe."

"Well, I think it would be best if I popped over there tomorrow, the whole thing would be better coming from me," Sandra replied as she thought about the situation and how unnerved Frank had seemingly become.

"Do I have to come with you?" Frank nervously enquired as he took a long sip from his glass.

"No, I can deal with it, the state of you at the moment is enough to send the poor girl loopy. No, you just drop me off and I will take it from there," Sandra replied reassuringly as she tapped him on the shoulder and made her way back to the comfort of the armchair.

A hotel bar somewhere in the North.

"Oi, just give me another drink and stop being so high and fucking mighty!" Liam slurred as he slammed his empty glass down onto the table and pointed his finger angrily at the bartender.

"Liam, you need to calm down it's late and they are closing, besides, don't you think that you've had enough?" Alan said as he attempted to hush his now drunken friend, before looking around apologetically at the remaining customers that were dotted here and there at the tables surrounding them both.

"And you can shut the fuck up as well! I thought that's what you wanted, a partner in crime to spend the evenings with 'cause let's be honest *mate* no fucker else wants to!" Liam sneered across the table as Alan sat gobsmacked by his alcohol-fuelled remark.

"I would be very careful what you say next Liam, nobody likes a fool, especially an out-of-work fool at that!" Alan replied angrily as he stared back.

"HA!" Liam laughed loudly slamming his hand down onto the table and making the glasses shake violently. Alan stood abruptly, he had seen and heard enough of what Liam had, had to say that evening and he wasn't prepared to listen to anymore as he turned and walked away quickly. "I'll show him who's the fool!" Liam muttered to himself as he stood and staggered away in search of somewhere more accommodating to spend his time. Pushing the large glass door open Liam swayed for a moment as he tried to maintain his balance, from the corner of his eye he noticed the form of a woman looking back at him in the reflection of the glass. She smiled enticingly as a customer heading home for the night pushed past Liam as he held tightly onto the handle of the door to support himself. Regaining his balance Liam followed as the woman curled her finger towards him gesturing for him to join her in the night. The bartender shook his head in discontent at the behaviour shown by the unruly customer as he locked the doors and watched Liam walk away alone.

No matter how hard she tried her eyes would not remain closed, like an eager child on Christmas Eve Chloe now lay wide awake. 2:06 am she read from the brightly lit screen of her phone, "Urgh," she moaned at the thought of being awake at such an unearthly hour as she buried her head in the softness of the pillows.

2:07 a.m. Chloe's heart began to beat faster and faster as she listened to what sounded like someone trying to open the front door. She looked at Frosty who was now intently studying something out of the bedroom window as the rattling of the door continued from below. Slowly and silently, she swung her legs out of the bed. Taking a deep breath Chloe creeped barefoot out of the bedroom and down the stairs, to be met with the horror of the keys swinging aggressively in the lock. From the kitchen, she could hear the same violent shaking, as though both doors were being tried at the same time. *There must be two of them!* She nervously thought to herself. Quickly by the light of the smouldering fireplace, Chloe sneaked into the lounge and picked up the poker before returning now fully armed to the front door. From the bedroom window, Frosty watched as the lamp-guided hand placed something down onto the stone step of the porch before turning and walking away.

The rattling stopped and the keys became still, peering through the peephole in the door Chloe could see no one. Foolishly and without thinking she placed her hand on the key and started to turn it anti-clockwise, the lock clicked, and Chloe slowly opened the door to reveal the coldness of the night air. Gripping the handle of the poker tightly she made her way out to the open doorway of the porch, the feeling of the stone against the bare soles of her feet chilling her to the core as she stood looking out into the darkness.

She stood unable to move as the sound of the woman crying filled her ears, "Where are you?" Chloe called out.

The woeful cries drew nearer and nearer until Chloe felt as though at any minute she would feel the breath on her face as she sobbed. "Why are you crying, are you hurt?" Chloe again asked gently. The cries stopped abruptly, Chloe watched as a grey mist appeared on the path in front of her, she covered her ears to shield herself from the velocity of the scream that followed, the same piercing scream she had heard in the dream, as it rushed within the mist to the opening of the porch before dissipating like the plumes of condensation from Chloe's mouth as she breathed heavily in fear.

Chloe stood in shock with her back pressed hard against the door, as the realisation of what had just happened sunk in. No amount of rational thinking would be able to offer any sort of explanation as to what she had witnessed, the facts were the facts and there was nothing she could do about it.

# Chapter Eight

The next morning found Chloe frantically cleaning the house, it was nearly 9 a.m. and that meant she had been hovering and dusting for nearly 3 hours! It wasn't that Millhouse was messy and unkept, but more of a way to distract her from the thoughts that constantly niggled away at her.

Chloe had sent six text messages to Liam's phone, but so far had received not a single reply. He must have read the urgency for him to get in contact, surely she had made it clear enough in the words she had sent. Switching off the vacuum cleaner at the plug socket, Chloe made her way into the kitchen, she needed a caffeine hit, what she had witnessed in the early hours had made it impossible for her to sleep, and now she was feeling the full effects of the deprivation.

"Now you be sure to call me as soon as you've finished!" Frank insisted as he unlocked the van doors. Sandra tutted as she climbed up into the passenger seat and looked at the untidiness of the cab.

"Really, how do you possibly drive around in this dustbin Frank?" She asked, moving the skin of a long discarded banana from the dashboard in front of her.

"Never mind the cleanliness of my van, did you hear what I said? Call me as soon as…" he started to reiterate once again as Sandra butted in quickly.

"Yes, yes, I heard you, really Frank stop worrying!"

"Stop worrying? Sandra, I'm telling you now that place is haunted!"

"Really, And what brought you to that conclusion then Frank?" Sandra huffed as she fastened her seatbelt.

"There's no need to be flippant! I'm concerned that's all, who knows what could happen!" Frank replied defensively as he started the engine.

"Well, you could always come inside too, you know, if you are that concerned Frank," Sandra scoffed as she turned towards him with a cutting smile. Frank fidgeted in his seat for a moment,

"Yes, well, just as long as you call me that's all I'm saying dear," he said timidly, placing the van into gear and pulling away quickly from the kerb.

Annie sat deliberating what dreams Chloe was having as she sat slumped down at the kitchen island, her half-finished mug of coffee resting next to her as she slept.

She was next to a waterfall, the soothing sound of the cascading river filling her ears as she sat on the bank, her bare feet resting in the water. From behind Chloe could feel a hand gently stroking her hair, she closed her eyes and listened to the voice of her mother as she hummed an all too familiar tune. It now seemed such a long time ago since they had shared this place, Chloe smiled to herself as she thought back to the memories that had been created there. Her mother had always told her that fairies lived amongst the trees that lined the crystal clear water, they sat listening to those that would stop and rest for a while, taking their hopes and dreams and making them come true. "You must not be afraid," Chloe heard her say softly, as she continued to stroke the back of her hair. The humming started again, except this was not the usual tune that her mother would sing to her when she was a child. No, this tune had an eeriness about it, as though each note echoed the sadness of the tale it held within. Chloe turned to look into the blueness of her mother's eyes, she gasped, as her gaze was met by the face of the woman in the portrait smiling back at her. Chloe woke quickly to the sound of rapping on the front door, looking at the clock on the wall she noticed the time, 10 a.m. "I'm coming!" she called out to the impatient sound from along the hallway.

"Sandra? What brings you here?" Chloe asked in a surprised manner as she welcomed her inside.

"Well, Frank was passing this way and I was at a loose end, so I thought I know, I'll go and see Chloe," Sandra lied as she tried her best to sound convincing as she waddled along the hallway. Chloe could sense that there was more to this surprise visit than just being at a loose end, as she watched Sandra nervously look around the kitchen while she positioned her large frame precariously on the edge of a stool. "So how are things?" Sandra inquired suspiciously as again she scanned the room.

"Oh, you know," Chloe replied sighing, thinking about her situation, as she passed a steaming mug of coffee into Sandra's thick welcoming hands. Sandra offered a smile, but it seemed tainted in some way. "Sandra, what's the real reason you're here? Only I have a sneaky suspicion that you want to tell me something." Sandra placed the coffee mug down on the island as she looked awkwardly at the floor. "Well, come on spit it out!" Chloe insisted as she placed her hands impatiently on her hips.

"Well, it's about Frank, but it's a bit delicate Chloe," Sandra started to say in a sensitive tone. Chloe completely misunderstood,

"Oh, are you two having problems, you know in the bedroom department?" Chloe asked tactfully as she lowered her arms to her sides. Sandra sat up on the stool abruptly,

"We most certainly are not! Frank is more than adequate in that area I will have you know!"

"I'm sorry if I offended you, I just got my wires crossed that's all," Chloe said as she offered her apology. "Please, you were saying about Frank."

"Chloe, things have happened, strange things to do with

this house," Sandra began to say as again she became flustered by her surroundings.

"What things? What are you talking about?" Chloe asked now fearing what she was about to hear.

"Ted, he saw something here, yesterday, a woman. Chloe, the same woman then stood on the road, Frank drove straight through her! He's a nervous wreck, he cannot get the vision of the woman's eyes out of his head," Sandra said as she shuddered at the thought of what he had told her the night before.

"Wait, are you saying what I think you're saying?" Chloe asked as she looked up towards the ceiling.

"Yes, Chloe I believe that you have a ghost here at Millhouse!" Sandra said slowly as she picked up her mug of coffee and held it tightly in her shaking hands.

"I know, listen Sandra will you follow me please I need you to see something," Chloe asked calmly as she made her way towards the staircase.

They both stood silently in the studio studying the haunting image positioned in the centre of the room. Chloe felt an overwhelming compulsion to pick up a brush but resisted the temptation as she watched the expression on Sandra's face change as she studied the portrait.

"Who is she?" Sandra asked as she pulled herself away

from the mesmerizing eyes that looked back at her.

"I don't know, I created her with no reference, she just appeared as I painted,"

"Chloe, how Frank described the woman in the road to me," Sandra began to say apprehensively.

"They are the same, yes I know, she comes here, she wants me to listen to her!"

"What you mean you hear her?" Sandra asked as she placed her hand over her mouth in shock.

Chloe nodded, "Yes, remember the crying?"

"What at my house? Oh god, was that her?" Sandra asked now traumatised by the fact that maybe her own home was now embroiled in the whole affair. Chloe said nothing, as she watched the reality of the situation take hold of Sandra, instead she just nodded silently as she feared that maybe she had already said too much.

By noon, Sandra had slowly started to come to terms with the revelation, they needed Frank to verify the woman in the portrait but that would be easier said than done. He had been insistent that he would never cross the threshold of Millhouse again and in Sandra's admission he could be a stubborn old sod at times.

"Do you think that you could convince him?" Chloe asked Sandra who was now sitting deep in thought.

"I'm not too sure if I'm honest," Sandra replied, obviously troubled by what Chloe was asking of her.

"Then what about Ted? He saw her too, maybe we could ask him!" Chloe stated excitedly.

By 1:30 p.m. they were heading to where Ted would be working that day. Sandra had managed to squeeze herself into the small front seat of Chloe's car and sat breathing heavily as she got over the ordeal of having to climb up the steepness of the track. On the back seat, Chloe had carefully placed the portrait of the woman, who caught her eye every time she looked in the rearview mirror of the car.

"What's so funny? I hardly see any humour in this!" Sandra said abruptly as she noticed that Chloe had started to snigger quietly to herself.

"I'm sorry, it's just the irony regarding the whole thing, I mean look at us both, driving to a building site with the painting of a ghost on the back seat. I mean you couldn't make this shit up it's so unbelievable."

"Well, if you put it like that I suppose it is quite comical," Sandra laughed.

The rest of the journey was filled with the same light-hearted approach to the matter at hand until Sandra announced that the building site was next on the right. "Ted!" Sandra called out as she noticed his familiar face as he slowly climbed a ladder laden down with the contents of the bright yellow bucket he was carrying on his shoulder. He paused for a moment to acknowledge her before steadily retracing his steps back down the rungs of the ladder to the ground.

"Hello Sandra, Chloe," he cheerily announced as he made his way over the muddy ground to where they were both waiting. "Frank's not here."

"It's not Frank we want, it's you, Ted," Chloe replied wearing her sweetest smile.

"Oh, I see," Ted replied wearing a look of confusion on his face. He stood listening as Chloe explained why they were there and what they hoped he would do. Apprehensively he agreed, still shocked by the whole ordeal he made his way to where Chloe's car was parked. The look on his face removed any reason to doubt what they both suspected as they watched the fear fill his eyes. "Yes, that's her!" he replied in a dazed manner as he stood staring into the back of the car.

"Are you sure Ted, is this the woman?" Sandra asked calmly.

"Yes, I told you that's her, the same haunting look on her face," Ted confirmed solemnly as he pulled himself away.

He watched from the scaffolding as they drove away before returning his attention to neatly stacking the roof tiles that had been stripped from the roof above him.

"Well, what are we going to do?" Sandra asked as they began the journey back to Millhouse.

"We?" Chloe replied with a sense of uncertainty, this had always seemed to be her problem to deal with, after all, it was Millhouse that appeared to be the epicentre of the whole situation.

"Yes, we! You don't think for one minute that I'm going to sleep soundly until we get to the bottom of this do you?" Sandra stated so matter of factly as she smiled reassuringly.

"Er, Ted!" one of the men at the top of the roof shouted, "Give us a hand!"

Ted looked up at where the voice had called from, "Ok!" he called back as he started to make his way up the roof. A loud crack signalled that the thin roof laths had given way under his feet, his hands scrambled desperately at the remainder of the roof above him, but it was too late, the roof collapsed sending him plummeting through the building and landing hard on the floor below.

From behind her Chloe could hear laughter, "Did you hear that?" she asked nervously. Sandra shook her head,

"Hear what?"

"Laughter, I could hear laughter from behind me," Chloe replied without any doubt in her voice, as she looked in the rearview mirror. The portrait of the woman sat staring back at her, for the brief moment that their eyes met Chloe could have sworn that the face was smiling.

"Stay still mate the ambulance is on its way," Ted could hear someone say, as he lay looking up at the hole in the roof high above him.

"What happened?" he croaked as his eyes tried to focus on the person by his side.

"You fell, we tried to warn you, but it was too late Ted, you dropped to the floor like a ton of lead," the voice replied. He closed his eyes in a bid to block out the pain that was surging through his body, but it was futile. That's when he heard her, calling to him, just as he had heard her call out before he fell. It all came flooding back in a whirlwind of thoughts, the woman at Millhouse, and then in the lane, the portrait and now the same voice softly calling for him to follow her. He couldn't resist, nor did he want to, the gentleness in the way that she spoke commanded his attention. "Ted! Wake up!" The builder at his side called out urgently, as he watched the rising of Ted's chest slow, and his breathing become shallow.

Back at Millhouse Sandra busied herself in the kitchen filling the kettle while Chloe returned the portrait to the safety of the studio. Her mobile started to play 'Club Tropicana' which to Sandra meant one thing, someone was calling her. "Hello, Frank," She started to say, "Frank slow down you're not making any sense, take a deep breath and start again!" She continued as she listened to the flustered voice on the other end of the line. Chloe entered the kitchen to be met by the troubled expression on Sandra's face as she stood holding the mobile phone to her ear.

"Is everything okay?" Chloe whispered as she watched the look on Sandra's face worsen as she ended the call. Sandra placed the phone down on the worktop slowly,

"It's Ted, there's been an accident! Chloe, just after we left he fell, from the roof!" Sandra relayed as she stood trembling by the now boiling kettle.

"What? Is it bad, is he de..?"

"Dead, no Chloe, but he's in a bad way. Frank's on his way over to the hospital now," Sandra replied apprehensively, "Frank asked if it would be okay for me to wait here until he returns?"

"Of course, here let me make you something warm to drink," Chloe said as she made her way over to Sandra and the steaming kettle.

The afternoon passed slowly as they waited for any news from Frank at the hospital. Chloe felt like she should be doing something, just sitting around the house was making her feel somewhat useless. But Sandra was distraught, Frank and Ted had worked together for a while now, and she knew how much Frank thought about him, and how he would blame himself for the accident.

"Chloe, the woman, what do you think she wants?" Sandra asked, watching as she placed another log onto the fire. Chloe shrugged her shoulders as she replaced the fire guard,

"If I'm honest, I don't feel like I know or understand anything anymore."

The telephone on the sideboard began to ring, Chloe jumped up quickly to answer it as Sandra sat nervously watching from the sofa. "Oh, hello Jennifer, no I've not been able to contact him either. In what way do you mean he was acting out of character?" Sandra heard Chloe say as she spoke to the caller. "He said what?" Chloe asked stifling a laugh, "Oh I see, yes of course I will call you as soon as he gets in contact, Goodbye," Chloe said as she quickly replaced the receiver.

Chloe made her way back to the comfort of her armchair as Sandra's eyes followed her, "I take it that wasn't Frank?"

"No," Chloe said smiling, "That was Liam's mother, Jennifer, she hasn't heard from him. But, get this, apparently the last time they spoke he told her she was a stuck-up bitch! She's furious, I said that I would tell him to call her and explain himself, how funny."

Sandra laughed. Frank had often told her all about Liam and his matter-of-fact attitude and how he thought himself to be the lord of the manor. She had often listened to him go on about how if it wasn't for Liam's lovely-natured wife then he would gladly tell him where he could stick his renovation! Frank always was a good judge of a person's character and as she sat looking over at Chloe she knew that again he was right in his thinking.

By 8 p.m., they both stood washing and drying the plates at the kitchen sink. Frank had called earlier to say that Ted was stable for the time being and that he was returning home briefly to get changed before heading back to be by his side. Chloe had insisted that it would be silly for him to drive over to Millhouse to take Sandra home when she could easily stay the night to which Frank begrudgingly agreed.

"You must give me the recipe, the pie filling was delicious!" Sandra said as she stacked the plates back inside the cupboard.

"It was my mother's favourite, I remember my grandmother making it for us when I was a child. So, it's like a family tradition, here I'll jot it down for you," Chloe said as she opened a drawer and pulled out a small notepad and pen.

# Chapter Nine

"That's quite a library you have here," Sandra said, perusing the many titles on display in the lounge.

"Yes, one of my impulse buys as Liam would say," Chloe replied as she mimicked his voice, "Here," she continued handing Sandra a large glass of wine, who smiled gratefully before returning to examine the spines of the books.

"Now, here's something that may be of interest!" Sandra announced excitedly as she lifted down a very old-looking book from the shelf. Chloe walked over and looked at the worn-out cover that Sandra was holding. 'True Ghosts,' they both read in unison. Chloe sat in the armchair while Sandra studied the contents page of the book,

"Any good?" She asked as Sandra sat silently examining the pages.

"Yes, it appears that this book is the journal of a man, What's his name? hang on. Yes, Edward Worthing that's it," Sandra replied as she looked back through the text that she had just read.

"A journal, what like a diary?" Chloe inquired as she sipped slowly from her glass.

"Yes. It appears that he was constantly haunted by the presence of a child, this book documents everything that he witnessed, even down to him actually talking to the ghost!"

"Oh, I see, no offence but I have enough to contend with at the moment, you know with my own persistent spirit," Chloe sighed as she looked in the direction of the staircase. Sandra looked up briefly before continuing to study the book. *Well, this is all very nice, I asked her to stay so that she would have some company tonight, not so she could sit quietly and read!* Chloe complained to herself.

"I believe you know the man very well, Mr.?" the doctor asked as she sat down next to Frank in the waiting room of the hospital.

"My name's Frank, there's no need for all this formality, and yes I have known him for years," Frank replied as he looked at the brown liquid in the take-out cup he was holding.

"Could you tell me please, is he married, or has a girlfriend perhaps?" the doctor inquired as she looked at the paperwork on her lap.

"No, he lives alone, why?"

"It's just that he keeps mumbling a name as he drifts in and out of consciousness," the doctor replied in total bewilderment upon hearing his reply.

"I don't understand Miss, what name?" Frank asked, his voice showing the same lack of understanding as his puzzled expression.

"Well, we are not exactly sure," the doctor replied awkwardly looking back at her notes.

"Can I see him?" Frank asked optimistically,

"It's late, but all being well you should be able to visit him in the morning. Frank go home and get some sleep, if anything changes I promise, you will be the first to know," the doctor said as she touched the back of his hand reassuringly before standing and walking away along the corridor.

It was 11 p.m. and Chloe was struggling to keep her eyes open as she tried to attain the same level of interest in the book as that of Sandra, who had constantly been giving her updates regarding the haunting of the author for the past two hours. In an attempt to save herself from the boredom Chloe stood and made her way to the front door. "Here puss!" she called out into the night from the porch, Frosty had not been back to the house all day and this would be the last chance of entry before Chloe secured Millhouse for the night. "Oh well," she sighed as she closed the door and spun the key in the lock. A few minutes later Chloe returned to the lounge where Sandra still sat engrossed in the book, "Shall I show you where your room is?" Chloe suggested, secretly hoping that Sandra would take the hint and just go to bed.

"Oh, sorry, I was miles away I didn't realise it was so late," Sandra said as she sat up quickly, placing the book down on the sofa beside her.

"It's just I haven't had much sleep, please feel free to take the book with you to bed," Chloe smiled, relieved that Sandra had taken the hint.

"I'm sure that I will be fine in here," Sandra insisted as she looked around the small box room and then at the small single bed. "Now go on and get into bed," she smiled, as she ushered Chloe out of the door.

"Well, you know where I am if you need me," Chloe called out as she made her way along the hallway.

The insistence shown by Sandra was just a mask to cover the insecurity she felt inside about staying at Millhouse. If everything that she had read so far was true to fact then things surrounding the house could be set to get a whole lot worse! Chloe on the other hand had no problem at all in falling asleep, and as soon as her head hit the softness of the pillows her eyes closed, and she drifted off into a world of dreams.

Sandra had reached a crucial point in the book, where Edward had made contact, but it was 1 a.m. and the heaviness of her eyes finally won the battle. The house was silent, apart from the occasional grunting sounds as Sandra turned over in her sleep. Outside the air surrounding Millhouse was eerily still as they slept. An owl hooted from its position high in the branches of a tree as it observed the valley floor below, before spreading its wings and flying to its next point of hunting.

Annie of course did not sleep as she sat in the rocking chair watching over the house. In her short time at Millhouse, she had witnessed the daily comings and goings of Chloe, and the now rare visits of Liam, who if she had an opinion irritated her stitches somewhat. But in the time that she had stayed in her propped-up position, Annie had also witnessed the ever-growing presence surrounding the movement of the keys.

Sandra tossed and turned as she tried to find comfort in the narrow confines of the bed, her rounded figure far outsizing that of the mattress. The duvet slipped and landed in a heap on the floor beside the bed causing her to wake suddenly and fumble desperately in the darkness to retrieve it. Turning on the small bedside lamp she moaned quietly to herself as she noticed the time, it was 2 a.m. Repositioning the duvet on the bed Sandra turned out the lamp and attempted to go back to sleep.

Chloe became restless, she was back on the track, standing watching the woman as she shed tears of utter dismay. She began to make her way towards her, calling out to be heard through the cries as she moved ever nearer. The events replayed, Chloe, shielded her ears as the cries turned once more into screams as the figure of a man was pulled into the flames that surrounded her. She could feel the heat on her face as the woman became engulfed, forcing Chloe to turn away until the brightness of the fire dissolved. Everywhere was still, she turned to where the woman had been standing but she was gone. On the track Chloe noticed something, it was a small piece of parchment, she knelt and held it in her hands. It appeared to have writing on it, but the hurriedness of the hand made it difficult to read. Sandra stood impatiently at the side of the bed tapping Chloe on the arm to rile her.

Chloe felt herself being pulled away from the track, dropping the parchment she woke quickly to be faced with Sandra who looked nervously down at her. "What's wrong?" Chloe asked sleepily as her eyes adjusted.

"It's started, listen!" Sandra trembled as she pointed to the bedroom door. Chloe listened as the sound of the keys rattling in the locks echoed throughout the house.

"What time is it?" Chloe asked as she sat up quickly and jumped out of bed, edging past Sandra as she made her way to the top of the stairs.

"2:07" Sandra replied as she tried to keep up with Chloe's rapid pace.

They both stood listening as they positioned themselves behind the front door, "WHO ARE YOU!" Sandra called out loudly, much to the amazement of Chloe who stood with her eyes wide as she looked back at Sandra the wannabe medium! The keys in the lock rattled violently as she spoke, "I COMMAND YOU TO SHOW

YOURSELF!" Sandra called out again, this time her voice sounding more dramatic.

"What the fuck are you doing exactly?" Chloe whispered as Sandra now stood with her hands in the air.

"Edward in the book, that's what he did, commanded the spirit to come forward," Sandra replied as she stood still, her arms raised high, and her eyes tightly shut.

"Well, I don't know what Edward has taught you, but it seems like it's working!" Chloe whispered nervously as the keys continued to spin in the lock. Sandra opened one eye and looked at Chloe,

"What do you mean, working?" Sandra asked now showing the same amount of nervousness.

"The keys, they have usually stopped by now!" Chloe whispered impatiently as she pointed to the lock on the door.

"So, what do we do?" Sandra asked nervously as the tension built inside her.

"How should I know, you're the one with the magic book why don't you consult Edward or whatever he's fucking called!" Chloe stated in a sardonic tone as they both stood watching the keys still constantly spinning in the door.

From outside the darkened figure stood at the gate watching, as what could only be described as a whirlwind made up of a black mist encircled the house. And then it stopped, the keys fell silent as they returned to their normal static state in the locks. Sandra and Chloe looked at each other as they listened to the house once again fall silent. The figure with the lamp turned and walked away uttering words as it disappeared back into the trees.

"Well, that was interesting!" Sandra stated hesitantly, as she tried her hardest not to look worried.

"I would say that was more than interesting, what the hell did you do!" Chloe asked as she cautiously moved her hand towards the door. As her fingertips reached the handle, a sound reminiscent of thunder appeared out of nowhere. Chloe tried to release her grip on the door, but it was no use. Sandra watched on in horror as Chloe desperately pulled at her wrist to remove her incapacitated fingers, the sound drawing nearer and nearer with every passing second. "DON'T JUST STAND THERE, DO SOMETHING!" Chloe screamed as she pulled hopelessly to free herself. Closing her eyes, Sandra again raised her hands in the air as she called out,

"I COMMAND YOU TO STOP!" she exclaimed loudly.

From outside, the noise rushed forward like a sonic boom, slamming into the door, and throwing Chloe and Sandra backwards along the hallway and leaving them in a heap on the floor. "Something tells me Sandra that they didn't like that remark!" Chloe whispered as she watched the figure of a woman appear at the door, staring at them with eyes as black as peat bogs, before slowly slipping backwards and disappearing silently into the night.

"Did you see, that was," Sandra trembled as she pointed towards the door.

"The woman, yes Sandra I saw her!" Chloe replied apprehensively as she stood up slowly, still looking at the door.

Frank watched as nurses and doctors rushed past him as they made their way to where Ted was lying. He tried to enter the room, but his path was blocked, and he was quickly ushered away. For a brief moment, he caught sight of him sitting bolt upright in the bed his arm stretched out in front of him as he pointed blindly into mid-air. "What's happening?" Frank asked quickly, as he pleaded with the nurse to let him inside.

"Please, do as I say! The doctors are doing everything that they possibly can!" the nurse replied abruptly as she tried to control the now agitated situation. Frank resigned himself to the fact that perhaps now his presence was becoming something of a hindrance. He stopped resisting and held up his hands in a way of showing his white flag of surrender, before quietly making his way back along the corridor and returning to his seat.

"Do you think she's gone?" Sandra asked as she struggled to stand, her knees creaking under the load.

"I think so, but wait, can you smell that?" Chloe asked as she sniffed at the air surrounding her.

"Well, yes but I didn't like to say, I thought that maybe you had, had an accident," Sandra replied as she pointed down below Chloe's waistline.

Chloe tutted loudly at the remark as she shook her head, "Funny! No, it smells like sulphur, where's it coming from?"

Sandra looked around with a puzzled expression on her face as she also began to sniff at the air like a hound dog. "It's all around us, but it seems to be stronger over here!" she said pointing to the open lounge door. Chloe carefully followed the pungent scent over to where Sandra was standing, before turning slowly on the spot and walking to the bottom of the staircase. "Where are you going? The smells here!" Sandra asked in a confused state as Chloe began to climb the stairs. "Wait for me!" She pleaded as Chloe's footsteps creaked on the staircase above her.

"What is it, what are you looking at?" Sandra asked as Chloe knelt in front of a canvas leaning against the wall of the studio. "Chloe! I said what are you looking at?" She asked again in a more urgent tone.

"This painting, the one I did of Millhouse, look," Chloe said anxiously as she pointed, "Originally there was one figure in the trees, now there's two!"

Sandra examined the painting, "Yes, yes I see them, but what do you think it means Chloe, who are they?"

"I don't know, but the smell led me here." Chloe sighed as a single tear appeared in her eye and a feeling of desperation filled her head.

Interference! Why were they meddling with something that they had no knowledge or control over? After all, he had already committed himself to follow, that was what *she* had wanted. They watched the doctor's pathetic attempts from behind a mist-like veil, as medical procedures were carried out to revive the lifeless body of Ted, but their efforts were in vain. At 3:26 a.m. he was confirmed to be deceased, the nurse pulled the sheet up to conceal his body from view as Frank waited anxiously along the corridor, desperate for news.

Frank sat with his head in his hands as he sobbed, while Sandra desperately tried to console him with teary eyes as they sat in the kitchen of Millhouse. For the time being, any fears that Frank had surrounding the house had somewhat been placed to the back of his mind as he wept for Ted. Chloe didn't know what to say or do. The only time that she had properly dealt with grief was when her mother passed away, and now those feelings were back as she watched Sandra and Frank mourn their friend. "I saw him before he died, he was pointing to the corner of the room, and he looked terrified," Frank sobbed as Sandra passed him another tissue.

The morning broke somberly at Millhouse, Chloe stood in the doorway of the porch watching as Sandra and Frank climbed into the van and drove away. She had delicately turned down the requests to go with them, insisting that she would be fine left at the house alone stating that hopefully, Liam would see sense and soon return. She hugged herself tightly in the comfort of her cardigan against the coldness of the valley air as she desperately tried to fight her emotions.

In the kitchen, Annie listened as Chloe broke down, she felt hopeless about the situation. She didn't have anyone to console her as she wept, her mother was dead, and the lack of marital support or love from Liam made her think of him in the same way too!

Crying. Chloe lifted her head and listened as she looked around the kitchen with reddened eyes. It was *her,* "WHY ARE YOU MOCKING ME!" Chloe screamed out as the crying continued. Mocking me, mocking me, Chloe heard echoed throughout the house. "WHAT DO YOU WANT!" She yelled, slamming her fists down hard on the wooden surface of the kitchen island. Again, her words resounded constantly around the house, she covered her ears to block out the sound, but it was no use. The key hanging on the hook swung violently and landed at her feet with a clank, Chloe was about to bend down to pick it up when a dark figure appeared behind her, she could feel the coldness of her breath as she whispered 'You!' gently in her ear., the voices stopped, and the house once again fell silent.

Scratching broke the silence, Chloe walked to the kitchen door and sighed as Frosty meowed eagerly for the door to be opened. Turning the key Chloe unlocked the door, much to the relief of the cat who walked briskly into the kitchen leaving a trail of muddy prints in her wake.

# Chapter Ten

It was supposed to be *their* home together, a place that was filled with happy memories, instead, Millhouse was a place of loneliness.

Picking up a picture frame from the sideboard in the lounge Chloe sighed as she looked at the image, "What happened?" she asked herself. Where had all the promises disappeared to? She needed him to be there, not miles away in some hotel room, only calling when it suited his busy agenda. Ted had died, taken away in his prime and Chloe blamed herself for the tragedy, she needed the supporting arm around her that Liam had so proudly displayed in that photograph when they had first met. But the silence and the coldness that he had shown recently made her question her desire for marital bliss, she needed to know if the feelings that they once shared were still equal between them, or whether the life she now lived was indeed her fate.

No answer, Chloe was beginning to lose hope as she sat huddled in the armchair and ended yet another call. There was always the option to call Alan, but in all honesty, she could not stand the man. Chloe had always thought that he carried a deep resentment for her and used the ability to provide Liam with a career against her. No, he would be the last person that she would ever think about contacting for help, but he was the link, the one person in the world at that moment in time that could shed any light on the problems with Liam.

Scrolling through her book of contacts, the tip of Chloe's fingernail traced the names handwritten onto the pages. People entwined together like the joined-up letters from her pen, doctor, and dentist side by side with the telephone numbers of old friends that promised to stay in touch, but never did. "Aha! There you are, Toad!" Chloe said scornfully as her fingernail halted at his number. It seemed ill-fitting to refer to Alan in this manner, after all, she liked toads, but their slimy appearance was the only creature that matched his persona. Of course, a slug would also match the description, but Chloe had always found them to make her nauseous, even the word forced her to retch.

"Hello, Alan?" Chloe asked through gritted teeth, as she held the telephone receiver just as tightly as she did her disdain for the man on the other end of the line.

"Chloe, what a lovely surprise! Keeping well I hope?" Alan asked sweetly, while Chloe screwed her face up at his sickly attempt at being charming.

"Yes, I'm fine, listen can you tell me where Liam is?" Chloe replied quickly, not wanting to spend any longer talking to him than she deemed necessary. The line went deadly silent for a moment, causing Chloe to imagine all manner of scenarios in her head.

"Are you still there Chloe? only the line went a bit fuzzy for a moment," Alan asked as the noise dispersed.

"Yes, I asked you about Liam," Chloe again asked insistently, as she doodled pictures of obscenities on the page next to his number.

"He's at the dock, can I give him a message, and ask him to call you?" Alan inquired as he looked out across the water to where a ship was being overhauled.

"Yes, can you please tell him to call me, tell him it's important," she asked begrudgingly, as she stabbed the nib of the pen into the page like a dagger.

"Nothing bad I hope?" Alan asked in the same putrid tone, "Leave it with me I will see that he gets the message."

Chloe politely ended the call as she gestured with her hand as to what she thought of him, mouthing *wanker* to herself as she looked angrily at the telephone receiver. It was as though he knew something like he was covering Liam's tracks, his timely pause, maybe he was there when he had taken the call. She could see it now, him telling Liam to remain silent while he kept her sweet.

In her head, she could feel a calling, as though someone was pleading with her to follow. Walking without thought Chloe found herself standing quietly at the back door, the handle grasped firmly in her hand as she looked out at the back garden through the small square pane of glass. "Frosty?" She asked herself, as her eyes followed the white feline's movement along the path towards the woods, how? All morning the cat had been asleep on the sofa. Turning the handle of the door Chloe made her way outside, Frosty turned momentarily before continuing to make its way down the path that led to the bridge. The same feeling of need rushed through her, as she walked barefoot on the coldness of the earth among the trees.

"I promise I will just make sure that she is ok Frank!" Sandra stated as she made her way towards the front door of Millhouse. "Chloe, it's me!" She called out after her constant knocking had aroused no response. Frank watched as she made her way around the side of the house, he sighed deeply as Sandra disappeared from view before opening the door of the van and setting off in pursuit. "Chloe," she called out again as she reached the open back door, where Frosty now sat patiently waiting.

Chloe had reached the bottom of the path and was now standing next to the old stone bridge that spanned the river. Everywhere was silent, in front of her she could see Frosty watching the fallen leaves as they turned and slowly floated their way downstream.

"Chloe, Chloe, where are you?" Sandra called out as she desperately scanned the area.

"You stay here, I'll go and have a look down there!"

Frank called out as he began to follow the path that led down through the valley.

It seemed to be coming from all around her, the same haunting tune that she had heard in the dream. She spun around slowly as she looked up at the bare canopy of the trees that surrounded her. "Where are you?" she called out as the humming of the tune continued.

"SHE'S DOWN HERE!" Frank shouted back anxiously in the direction of the house and Sandra. He watched as Chloe stood at the bridge, her arms held out in front of her as though she was holding someone in a deep embrace. Frank tried to continue, but he couldn't move, his path seemingly blocked by an invisible force.

Chloe could see her watching from the bridge as she held onto her mother tightly, all around the tune reverberating as the haunting melody began once again. "It is time for you to leave now," Chloe heard her mother whisper as she pulled away slowly.

"But I want you to stay!" Chloe pleaded desperately as she watched her mother edge backwards slowly to where the woman stood waiting.

"We will be together again soon," her mother replied in the same whispered tone as the woman stepped forward, surrounding them both in a mist as they gradually disappeared.

She could hear her name being called out, she turned to

see Frank quickly making his way towards her. She looked back at the bridge, but they were gone, on the floor lay a small posy of wildflowers, tied sympathetically with a red ribbon.

"Look, I'm not sure what is going on between you and Chloe, but she sounded desperate when I spoke to her. I would have thought that you being there every weekend would have somewhat cemented things. Listen, whatever it is Liam get it sorted yeah, I need you to be able to focus!" Alan said calmly as he placed his hand on his shoulder.

"I will Alan I promise," Liam smiled reassuringly. He watched as Alan walked away along the side of the dock before *she* appeared on the deck of the ship beside him.

"Remember, what was promised, never return, never return, never return," the woman said as her voice slowly faded away.

Back at Millhouse, she carefully placed the posy of flowers into a small earthenware vase. Frank and Sandra watched quietly as Chloe made her way to the lounge where she placed the vase onto the window ledge of the front window, she smiled to herself before making her way back to the kitchen.

"It's a lovely day, shall we take our drinks out into the garden?" Chloe suggested happily, her tone showing no reference to anything that had happened. Sandra nodded and followed as Chloe led them to the small leaf-covered patio table and chairs, still sodden from the rain. Sandra turned to Frank with a look of concern in her eyes as Chloe sat down, her feet still bare and dirty from the path as her nightdress absorbed the wetness of the leaves.

"Chloe love, don't you think it would be better if we went inside?" Frank asked as he watched her sitting motionless as she stared out into the trees.

"No, I want to stay here! You go, I don't know why you came here anyway!" She snapped as she turned to face them.

"Well, if that's how things are then fine, come on Frank!" Sandra retorted as she turned and began to walk away. Frank looked at the coldness on Chloe's face before turning and following his wife back around the side of the house. "Listen," Sandra insisted as she stopped dead in her tracks. Quietly they crept back to the corner and watched as she sat humming a tune, Sandra shivered as the haunting melody continued to fill her ears. From their hidden position, they watched as Chloe stood up from the table and slowly made her way back inside Millhouse, damp leaves falling to the ground from the back of her nightdress as the door closed sharply behind her.

"After everything, this is how she speaks to us! I tell you now I'm through with little Miss High and Mighty!" Frank fumed as they drove along the narrow track.

"Frank listen, I think Chloe might be suffering from some sort of emotional breakdown, Ted dying may have just tipped her over the edge," Sandra replied as she tried to calm her husband's rage.

"What and you think that I have just brushed the whole thing under the carpet?" Frank sneered as he slammed his hands down hard onto the steering wheel.

"No Frank, no I don't! Please trust me, don't let your anger get in the way of helping her!" Sandra pleaded as Frank stared blankly at the road ahead.

In the studio, Chloe sat on her stool facing the image on the canvas in front of her. The telephone began to ring causing her to briefly look towards the door before returning her gaze to the painting. From his hotel room, Liam sat waiting for her to answer as he looked at his reflection in the mirror fastened to the wall in front of him.

"I have deadly nightshade, so twisted its stems do grow. With berries black like midnight, and a skull as white as snow," Chloe sang to herself as she picked up her paintbrush and began to add layers to the face.

"At last, I thought you were never going to answer," Liam said thankfully.

"Oh hi, sorry I was painting, I thought that you were avoiding me," he heard Chloe say sarcastically.

"No, my phone's been playing up that's all, is everything ok?" Liam asked concerned by the urgency that Alan had said earlier at the dock.

"Everything is fine, when are you coming home?" she asked longingly.

"Soon, I'm nearly done here," Liam replied confidently as he looked down at the job list on the bed next to him.

"Nearly done, yes, yes you are!" she muttered under her breath.

"Sorry, what was that? The lines crackling, I'll call you tomorrow, love.." he was about to say as the line went dead.

Upstairs in the studio, Chloe remained seated in front of the canvas, oblivious to the conversation as she painted, the words of the rhyme going over and over in her head.

Frank was finding it hard to get a grip on the situation, his friend and right-hand man were now gone, and nothing was ever going to bring him back. In his head he wished that he had never set eyes on Liam and Chloe, after all, if what Sandra was suggesting was to be believed then Millhouse was the cause. But it was a house, made of nothing except bricks and mortar, how could a building create something that would be capable of taking someone's life? No, he had worked in the building trade all his life and had restored many an old house, he had often heard talk of the places being haunted but that was just superstition, nothing more than old folk tales retold by over-excitable tongues right? The one thing that did not fit into his sceptical view was the woman, he had seen her, and no one would be able to tell him differently.

Sandra flicked back and forth through the pages of the book she had taken from Millhouse, maybe, just maybe hidden away somewhere inside was the answer to unlocking the mystery of the house and returning everything to normal. She knew that it was a long shot, but how could she turn her back on Chloe? Despite everything that had happened, she had grown fond of her, and unlike Frank, she saw her strange behaviour as nothing more than a temporary glitch in her personality.

The final days of Autumn saw Ted carried to his final resting place, it was a quiet sombre affair witnessed only by the few who stood around the graveside on that cold and damp Tuesday afternoon. The situation surrounding Chloe had meant that Frank insisted that she would not attend the funeral, something that Sandra had no intention of attempting to change. During the time leading up to the day she had witnessed how fragile he had become, and Sandra knew that it would not take much to shatter his self-control completely.

Along the walls of the studio, canvas after canvas stood, each one a masterpiece in colour, as Chloe's obsession with the woman and Millhouse took over. This was how she now spent her days, and nights, only occasionally would she venture outside to walk the paths surrounding Millhouse, always in the same direction, and always barefoot. From the trees her every move was watched by an unseen observer, who listened silently to the humming of the tune as Chloe passed by.

Sandra had convinced Frank that she could easily do the food shopping by herself, she had coped very well all the years he had been at work so there was no need for it to be any different now. She kissed him goodbye and made her way along the road in the direction of the supermarket, where she hailed a taxi cab and gave the directions for him to take her to Millhouse. Sandra didn't know what she would say or if she would even be welcomed when she got there, all that she knew was the impulsion for her to return to Millhouse was greater than the ability to be able to block out the thoughts.

Chloe applied paint to the canvas in a wild and frantic manner, "Meddler!" she uttered deeply as she scratched at the brush strokes with her fingertips.

Sandra climbed out of the taxi at the top of the track much to her disapproval, the driver had refused point-blank to drive down what he considered to be an unsafe road, although unknown to Sandra he was more concerned as to how the car would survive the ruts and potholes with the excessive weight it would be carrying on the back seat. Still, in its usual position, Sandra noticed Chloe's car which showed that it had not been used recently by the heavy covering of leaves on the roof and bonnet. Fastening the buttons on her long overcoat against the bitter wind Sandra began the slow and precarious walk down the track to Millhouse. From either side, she could hear the calling of the woodland as birds announced her impending arrival. The reality of returning to the house gave her butterflies in her stomach as she rounded the bend and Millhouse came into view.

From inside Chloe rocked forwards and backwards on her stool as she stared at the canvas, "Meddler!" she muttered again, this time applying so much force to the brush that the handle snapped loudly in half.

Outside Sandra stopped for a moment to adjust her scarf and steady her nerves before she made the final approach to the front gate. She felt a hand rest upon her shoulder from behind, "Your friend is in danger, you must help her to break free!" a woman whispered insistently in her ear. Sandra could feel the closeness as the hairs on the back of her neck stood upright with fear, she turned but there was no one, only the scent of the damp woodland that filled the air around her.

Sandra shuddered at what she had heard, before returning to face the house. Everywhere seemed eerily quiet as she lifted the latch on the front gate and began to walk towards the porch. From the upstairs window of the studio, Chloe watched as the rounded figure of Sandra made its way along the brick-lined path below her. "Meddler!" she growled.

"Yes, Meddler!" echoed around her as Sandra tapped intermittently on the front door, she re-emerged out of the porch and stood on the path contemplating her next move. At the window, Chloe stood watching unemotionally as Sandra began to walk away. Closing the gate, she took one last look back at the house,

"Chloe?" Sandra asked herself as she looked up at the

window where she was standing. "CHLOE!" she called out waving her hand from side to side above her head. From the window came no response as Chloe stood motionless. From behind her in the studio, the haunting melody started once more as the blackened silhouette of the woman slowly made her way to Chloe's side. Sandra watched on in horror as the spectral mass appeared at the window, the paleness of the woman's skin intensifying the menacing deepness in her eyes.

# Chapter Eleven

"I thought that we had agreed that you would stay away from her!" Frank snapped as he helped a very flustered Sandra into the passenger side of the van.

"I'm sorry, it's just that I needed to see her, you know to make sure that she was okay," Sandra replied breathlessly as she tried to compose herself. Frank shook his head as he placed the van into gear and started to reverse slowly back up the narrow track.

"And? Did you see her, are you satisfied now? He grumbled as the van banged and swayed at meeting yet another deep pothole. Sandra looked down at the floor, she knew that his anger was out of concern for her well-being and the fact that she had somewhat misled him with her plans for the day.

"Yes Frank, yes I saw her and yes I'm satisfied," Sandra lied convincingly. How could she tell him what she had just witnessed at Millhouse? Knowing his protective manner, he would surely have gone off the scale, telling her how he was right and that from now on she was to never venture anywhere alone again.

That evening Liam was once again in the company of Alan in yet another hotel bar, he listened while Alan chatted about work schedules and deadlines, all of it seamlessly going in one ear and straight out of the other as he looked at the screen of his phone. "So did you manage to speak to Chloe?" Alan asked suddenly, breaking Liam's train of thought.

"Oh, yes, she's fine just busy painting," Liam replied as he returned to studying the image on the screen.

*Show him!* The woman's voice whispered in his ear.

"Here look, this is a portrait that she's been working on recently," Liam said following what had been asked of him, as he passed the phone over to where Alan was sitting. He watched as Alan's expression changed and he became mesmerised by the eyes that now looked back at him.

"Who is she?" he asked, still unable to draw his attention away from the screen. Liam shrugged his shoulders as he stood and made his way in the direction of the toilets. Alan waited until Liam was out of sight before quickly sending the image of the woman to his phone, he checked that it had been delivered successfully before placing the handset into his pocket just as Liam returned to the table. "Well, I don't know about you Liam, but I am ready to call it a night," Alan said as he finished the remainder of his drink and placed the glass down on the table.

For once Chloe felt herself, and Millhouse seemed to

have regained its original warmness and serenity, even Annie the ragdoll felt content in her surroundings as she stared at the motionless key on the wall. Looking in the mirror in the hallway Chloe screwed her face up as she noticed the wildness of her usually well-kept hair and the paint-splattered nightdress that she was wearing. "You my girl need a long hot soak!" she stated disapprovingly, pointing her index finger at the reflection in the mirror like a mother scolding a child.

Curses, Sandra read from the page, while Frank tried to ease his mind by watching a football match on the television.

*Curses,*

*There are three types of curses, that I will endeavour to explain here,* Sandra read to herself as she studied the text on page 347 of Edward Worthing's book 'True Ghosts.'

*The first namely that of a quick curse. This type of curse could be performed in more than one way, however, the intention would of course be the same. A quick curse can either be written down for the recipient to read. Verbally, where the sender would of course say the curse out loud, which I shall endeavour to explain further as we look at the matter in more detail as we continue. The evil eye, however, would take a very trained and skilled practitioner in magick to perform successfully, due to several factors, the main one of which is the ability of the sender to maintain the intent of the curse without losing eye contact with the recipient. And finally spitting, which of course is probably the one that is most recognised by people who have refused to buy the wares of travellers.*

Frank tutted when he noticed how engrossed Sandra was in the tatty old book she was reading, the match on the television had been slow and boring and so he loudly sighed before announcing that he was going for a bath. Sandra looked up momentarily and smiled to acknowledge him before returning her eyes to the contents of the book.

At Millhouse, Chloe opened the refrigerator door and lifted out a chilled bottle of wine from which she poured herself a large glass. Annie watched on as Chloe now seemed to have taken on a new feeling of energy as she swayed to the music that was playing on the radio.

Sandra heard the bathroom door close on the landing above her as she continued to the next heading on curses.

*Long-form curses,*

*As the name would suggest these types of curses require time and planning on behalf of the sender to have maximum effect. Both chanting and spell casting are forms of long-form curses. If produced with the correct amount of intent and strength, then as in the case of the* Shipley Witch of 1822 *we can see that they can produce devastatingly powerful results! The self-confessed witch of that time* Mary Baggot *not only cursed the owner of the local manor* Sir Henry Laverty *but also the land on which the manor sat. Subsequently, through time descendants of the Laverty family, took their rightful place as heirs, until the curse would again see their ownership of the manor and their lives both come to a sudden end. But, so powerful was the curse of* Mary Baggot *that neither cattle nor crops would survive her wrath as both would eventually lay dead in the fields.*

Sandra placed the book down onto her lap as she thought about what she had just read and what more to the point she had experienced at Millhouse. She paused briefly as she heard Frank running more water into the bathtub before picking up the book and continuing to read.

At the hotel, Alan took out his wallet and placed it down on the bed, he looked at the image on his mobile phone with distant eyes before typing a message and hitting the send button. Placing the phone down next to his wallet he turned and made his way out of the door and along the hotel corridor as he followed the image of the woman now walking in front of him, who turned occasionally to smile seductively at him as she led him out into the night.

Hi Liam, I am leaving the company in your capable hands, I need to go away for a while, Alan. Liam read from the screen of his phone.

"Go away?" he asked himself out loud as he waited for Alan to answer the call. There was no reply, ending the call he grabbed the keys to his room and made his way in search of Alan for a more detailed answer.

Chloe was feeling much more relaxed as she lay back in the warm water surrounded by bubbles. She closed her eyes and listened to the haunting tune that was playing in her head, all the time her head slipping further and further towards the surface of the water.

"I have deadly nightshade, so twisted its stems do grow. With berries black like midnight, and a skull as white as snow," She began to sing to the melody of the tune, as she slipped under the bubbles on the surface of the water.

From upstairs Sandra heard a loud thud on the bathroom floor, dropping the book down as she stood, Sandra ran as quickly as she could manage up the stairs, all the time calling out to Frank.

"Ye do want to be with me?" the woman asked as she led Alan away from the hotel and along the moonlit streets. He didn't answer with words just nodded his head as he followed closely in her footsteps.

Chloe lay completely still, submerged beneath the surface of the water in the bathtub, as the radio continued to play in the kitchen of Millhouse. On the small table next to the bathtub sat the empty wine glass that she had consumed earlier, her discarded clothes scattered on the bathroom floor.

"FRANK! FRANK! ARE YOU OK?" Sandra called out frantically as she knocked loudly on the bathroom door.

From across the hallway, the bedroom door opened quickly to reveal Frank with a confused expression on his face looking at her while he fiddled with the cord on his pyjama bottoms trying desperately to undo a knot. "What's the bloody matter?" he asked as he looked at the shaking wreck that was his wife.

"I heard a bang, I thought something had happened to you!" Sandra replied as she pointed to the closed bathroom door. He made his way across the hallway pushed the door open and let out a chuckle as he pointed inside the bathroom before shaking his head and making his way back to the bedroom. Sandra looked inside, the bathroom window had been opened by Frank, in his defence, he had always stated that the room became too stuffy with it closed. A gust of wind must have blown in and knocked over the large plant pot stand, sending the house plant crashing to the bathroom floor. She sighed with relief as she dodged the scattered soil on the bathroom carpet and closed the window tightly.

All the time Chloe remained completely motionless, as the woman led Alan closer and closer towards the edge of the water. As though in a dream she watched as the woman removed her clothing slowly, allowing each piece to fall to the softness of the sand as Alan began to do the same. Chloe tried to look away at the sight of Alan naked, but it was as though invisible hands held her head tightly forcing her to watch. The woman walked into the water, holding out her hands for Alan to join her, he stepped forward slowly until they both stood side by side as the waves crashed around them. Helplessly Chloe watched as they walked further and further out to sea until their heads dipped down under the water for one last time and they were gone. On the beach, the ebb and flow of the waves claimed any evidence that they were ever even there. Chloe felt the hands holding her head release as she rose quickly from under the water, breathing in sharply and sitting upright in the bathtub.

"Do you think you could keep the noise down!" Liam heard one of the hotel guests call out from along the corridor. He stopped asking for Alan to answer the door, pulled out his mobile phone and again began to call Alan's number. From the other side of the door, he could hear his phone ringing,

*Something's not right!* Liam thought to himself as he quickly made his way down to the reception desk in the main foyer of the hotel. "I'm sorry sir but I cannot just go about the hotel unlocking the guest's rooms, it goes against the hotel's policy," the night porter stated adamantly from behind the desk.

"But you don't understand I think my boss may be in trouble! He messaged me not so long ago telling me that he had to go away, but his mobile phone is in his room, and he never goes anywhere without it!" Liam insisted as he leaned over the desk in a fit of desperation. The porter sat back in the chair and shook his head,

"Like I said it goes against the hotel policy, if you wouldn't mind keeping the noise down we do have other guests to consider!"

"Well thanks for your help, I will be sure to leave a great review about how considerate you are!" Liam snapped back, slamming his fists down on the desk and causing the porter to jump nervously.

What she had seen, was it true? Chloe deliberated, as she sat huddled in front of the crackling fire. Had she just witnessed the watery demise of Alan, and if it was real, had she somehow caused it?

The telephone began to ring loudly startling Chloe. Making her way over to the sideboard she lifted the receiver and answered the call, "Hello?" she asked apprehensively.

"Chloe? It's me," Liam replied in a trembling voice, as he sat with his head in his hands on the edge of the hotel bed.

Chloe held the receiver away from her ear to shield herself from the crackling of the phone line.

"Chloe, I think something terrible has happened, Alan has disappeared!" Liam announced quickly.

"I'm sure he's fine, maybe he has a new woman that you don't know about, trust me!" Chloe replied reassuringly.

"Maybe you're right, I'll leave it a couple of days and see if he turns up after he's had his fun. How're things with you?" Liam asked in a now calmer manner.

"Everything is fine, I was just going to bed, perhaps you should consider doing the same, you sound tired and need to sleep," he heard Chloe say convincingly as his mobile phone fell to the floor.

"Hello? Hello?" Chloe asked again as the continuous sound of static interference crackled from the handset. "Great, now the telephone is on the blink!" she moaned as she shook the receiver in her hand. Frank had stated earlier in the year that certain branches may cause a problem with the overhead telephone wire as it ran up the valley, but with the huge list of work, the job had simply been overlooked.

For what seemed like an eternity, her time at Millhouse had been like a blur, her recollections of events seemingly wiped from her memory, except for the feeling of being reunited with her mother and of course the tragic events surrounding Ted, and now possibly Alan. Everything else appeared to have just passed her by, even the last time that she had spent an evening with Liam was hard for her to pinpoint, was it over the last weekend? Or was it last month or even a year? But *she* was there to watch over her as a guardian angel shrouded in a black mist, always there to guide Chloe as to what must be done and offering comfort in the haunting melody of the tune.

"Sandra, listen I've been thinking, and I reckon we both need a holiday, some sea air, it would do us both the world of good," Frank suggested as they sat at the table eating breakfast. Sandra shuffled in her seat uneasily, as she thought about the situation regarding Chloe and Millhouse.

"I don't know Frank, it's a bit short notice, besides..." Sandra was about to finish when Frank threw the slice of toast he was holding down on his plate,

"Besides what? If you say no because of that crackpot in the valley, then you're as loopy as she is!" he replied angrily, the legs of his chair screeching as they slid across the wooden floor of the dining room as he pushed himself back away from the table.

"No, I was about to say that I will need some new outfits if we're going on holiday, and to be honest you could do with some new shirts as well!" Sandra replied as she tried to defer his suspicions and calm his quickening mood.

"I knew you would think it was a good idea, we can take a trip into town today, and see if we can get a late deal somewhere hot!" Frank replied eagerly as he retrieved the displaced slice of toast and smiled happily across the table. Inside Sandra's mind, thoughts, terrible thoughts went round and round as she battled with the feeling of leaving Chloe alone with *her*. But Frank would never understand, somehow he was able to block out the vision of the woman on the road. And now he seemed equally able to rid himself of any sadness surrounding Ted with two weeks in Majorca. It was as though he had awoken that morning as a completely different person, the man who always insisted work had to come first, had now taken on a more free and easy attitude to life. She looked at his laid-back attire of striped pyjamas and slippers as he sat munching on a slice of toast, it was as if he had taken early retirement, after all, she would have been waving him goodbye an hour ago if he had still been in the same frame of mind.

Chloe walked into the studio and looked at the array of canvases that lined the walls, the sun blinking intermittent rays of light through the window as it appeared from behind the foretelling clouds of the darkening sky above Millhouse. The portrait still sat on the easel in the middle of the studio, her dark eyes staring coldly across the room. From behind the painted veil of the canvas Chloe could hear *her* sobbing, so pitiful were her cries that Chloe felt compelled to walk over slowly to the canvas and stroke the features of the woman in a way to soothe her. The crying waned as the air in the studio was filled with an icy chill as though she was deep within the depths of winter. "What do you want from me?" Chloe shivered as the temperature in the room continued to drop, "Please just tell me!" She pleaded.

The face of the woman began to move out of the painting, Chloe stepped back as she watched the form taking shape in front of her. "I want you," the face whispered as its eyes glared back at her.

"Want me, for what?" Chloe asked nervously as she edged towards the open door.

The woman screamed, shattering the glass jars filled with paintbrushes and sending them crashing to the ground, Chloe turned to run but the door slammed shut violently to block her path as a dark mist began to surround her. She tried desperately to move but the mist was like ropes that bound her legs and arms tightly to the spot rendering her attempt to escape futile.

# Chapter Twelve

"Please let me go, I'll do anything," Chloe pleaded as she desperately tried to break free from the ever-tightening grip of the mist. The apparition of the woman slowly started to make her way across the room, each footstep landing silently on the floor, leaving a soot-like print in its wake. Chloe fought back the compulsion to scream as tears began to build in her eyes, it was as if time itself had stood still as the woman continued to draw ever closer.

"Shhh, why do you cry?" The woman whispered, now so close that Chloe could feel the spectral iciness of her breath as she spoke.

"Because I'm afraid," Chloe sobbed hopelessly as they stood face to face, the blackness of the mist still spiralling slowly around them. The phantom raised a chilling hand and began to stroke Chloe's hair gently. At that moment she could feel her chest tightening, it was as though her heart would burst from the trauma, as the hand gently wiped away the tears from her cheeks.

"You need not fear me, we are like sisters," The woman whispered through pallid lips, her voice seemingly commanding the wind as she spoke.

"Foolish girl!" the trees in the wood surrounding Millhouse heard uttered, as small hessian bags filled with herbs swung from their branches where they were tied with determined fingers.

"Sisters?" Chloe asked timidly as her eyes followed the woman around the studio, the shards of broken glass from the jars cracking under the soles of her bare feet as she moved across the floor.

"Yes," She replied in the same wind-like whisper, "They mocked me, told me that ye had left me to rot, but I knew ye had not forsaken me."

Chloe felt the restraints of the mist lessen around her, she watched as the woman turned her gaze to the canvas of Millhouse, before feeling to her side with trembling fingers for the door handle. She waited for a moment, constantly watching the movements of the woman before pulling the door open just enough so that she could squeeze through the gap. As she ran Chloe could hear the tormented screams of the spirit behind her. Annie watched on in horror as she fumbled with the key in the kitchen door as the black mist surged along the hallway towards her. The door unlocked and Chloe ran breathlessly out into the garden and headed for the path that led through the woods behind Millhouse. "SISTER!" She heard screaming out from behind, as she veered off the sodden path and into the dense undergrowth. From the edge of the wood, she could see the woman fall suddenly to her knees as she began to cough and gasp for air as though she was choking. Chloe held her hand over her mouth to silence her fearful cries as she crouched down beside the brambles watching as the woman gasped once more and then quickly vanished into thin air. What had caused the malevolent spirit to disappear, Chloe, did not know, the only important thing on her mind, for the time being at least, was that she had gone.

The thought of re-entering Millhouse filled Chloe with dread as she gradually made her way back to the path. She paused momentarily before walking inside the kitchen, everything was normal, with nothing appearing out of place and no signs of the restless spirit anywhere to be seen.

Sandra had managed to persuade Frank that maybe a holiday abroad wasn't necessary after all and that they could easily find somewhere to relax and recuperate a little closer to home. The prices displayed in the travel agent's windows for a week in the sun paved the way somewhat for Frank's sudden change of mind. "Besides, who needs Benidorm when we have Newquay?" he happily announced whilst waving a brochure advertising holiday chalets in Sandra's direction. Satisfied with their decision they headed off along the high street in search of coffee and pastries. All the talk of restaurants nestled along the coast of the Atlantic Ocean in the holiday brochure had made Frank hungry, and Sandra knew that if she was to successfully continue with her shopping trip then his stomach's needs would have to be addressed first and foremost. They found a small café with a table situated next to the window and took their seats. As Frank studied the contents of the neatly folded menu Sandra noticed an elderly woman watching her from across the street.

"Tell the waitress that I will have the lunchtime special, I'm busting!" Frank announced loudly as he stood up quickly and made his way in the direction of the toilets, causing the other diners to look in his direction with astonished faces. Sandra tutted as she watched him hurriedly make his way through the café to join the queue that was now forming at the restroom door. Returning her gaze to the window Sandra noticed that the woman had now gone, she sensed someone beside her and turned expecting it to be the waitress with a daydream face and chewing gum.

"Your friend is in danger! You must make sure that she has this at all times," the elderly woman croaked as she leaned forward and thrust something into Sandra's hand.

"What do you mean, in danger?" Sandra asked as she jumped at the proximity of the woman, who now stood next to her wrapped in a long black shawl.

"Do as I say, before it's too late!" the woman insisted. Sandra nodded slowly, her eyes wide as she listened to the urgency in the woman's pleas. The woman turned her head quickly to the side and noticed Frank making his way back to the table, "Never will she stop, until you all perish!" she uttered. Sandra looked down at her hand before placing what the woman had thrust at her into the pocket of her overcoat.

"Who was that?" Frank asked as he rejoined her at the table.

"Oh, just someone who catches the same bus into town with me on a Tuesday that's all," Sandra replied quickly with the first thing that came into her head. Frank nodded as he accepted the white lie and smiled with relief as the waitress eventually acknowledged their existence as she walked carelessly towards them.

Over lunch, they spoke about their holiday, yes it would be out of season, but the travel agent had assured them that the chalets were very popular the whole year round. For Sandra, the suitability of the holiday accommodation was the least of her worries, she had more important things on her mind. How was she ever going to get to Millhouse? Frank would never agree to her going back, but if what the stranger had said was true then Chloe was in danger. She needed to warn her and deliver the mysterious package that was now in her pocket before it was too late!

Chloe mustered all of her strength as she cautiously climbed the staircase, the thought of re-entering the studio filled her with dread, but she had to know if the spirit had truly gone one way or another. Everywhere was ominously quiet, Chloe took a deep breath and gently pushed the studio door open. Making her way inside she noticed the portrait still resting on the easel, it was now or never. Snatching the canvas with quivering fingers Chloe rushed down the stairs and out into the garden where she threw the painting down harshly before running back into the kitchen to collect the box of matches that were kept in the drawer. Match after match lay discarded on the ground as she desperately tried to get them to light, but each time the flames were extinguished by the wind. It was no use if she was to succeed then something of an accelerant would be needed. "Firelighters!" Chloe exclaimed as she rushed back inside the house to the lounge.

Flames engulfed the canvas, Chloe stood back and watched as the fire took hold, the woman's eyes stared back helplessly as the heat of the fire melted away the features of her face. All the work Chloe had put into the painting was reduced to a pile of smouldering ash within minutes. It was done, over the space of an hour she had completely cleared the studio walls, their acrylic images now rendered to the ground, each suffering the same incinerated fate.

Liam jumped up quickly from the bed, as the afternoon sun lay low in the sky, causing him to shield his eyes from the brightness streaming in through the window of his hotel room. "What happened?" he asked himself as he rubbed the back of his neck. Checking the time, he noticed that he had been asleep since the night before. He stood and walked sluggishly to the bathroom, his head hurt as though he had a hangover from hell. Steam billowed from the bathroom door as he stood beneath the cascading water washing over him from the showerhead. "She tried to be rid of me!" Liam heard whispered from the other side of the shower cubicle door.

"Hello, who said that?" he gurgled as the water flowed over his mouth. Wiping his eyes, Liam watched as the dark figure of the woman appeared within the fog-covered screen of the shower.

"You must do my bidding, you must make her suffer the same punishment!" The woman seethed as her face leered out of the mist.

"You're not real! You're just the result of too much alcohol and too much sleep!" Liam mocked as he turned his face away. The apparition lunged forward, Liam yelped in pain as he felt the sharp point of a needle dig deep into the skin of his back before being drawn down slowly and deliberately as the woman whispered her words of intent. He looked at the floor of the shower and watched as his blood trickled towards the drain.

Sandra needed to speak to Chloe, but the closeness of the guard that Frank was keeping made it impossible to achieve. It was 9 pm and Frank was happily in the bedroom trying on the various items of clothing that he had purchased in readiness for their time away together. Sandra quickly typed a message on her phone as she heard Frank's heavy footsteps clambering down the stairs in his new brown shoes.

**Chloe, I need to speak to you tomorrow! Sandra x.**

Chloe replied quickly, agreeing that she would be available all of the next day. How the message had read puzzled Chloe as she thought about Sandra's urgency. Usually, Sandra would ask how things were, but not this time, no, this time she seemed hurried and to the point.

Although Millhouse was quiet, Chloe had the feeling that at any moment something would happen. After all, if the recent events involving the less than happy visitation were to be considered then anything was possible. Frightened to sleep upstairs Chloe decided to make a temporary bed on the sofa in the lounge, the fire crackled away in the hearth as she drifted off to sleep.

"Checking out sir?" The porter asked as Liam handed in his key and walked towards the exit carrying a large leather suitcase. "Charming!" He stated snootily as Liam swung the door open and walked out into the street.

She was back on the track, Chloe waited as the woman appeared and began to shed tears of discontent, as the same nightmare began to replay. She woke with a jump to the sound of shuffling from above her. Looking at the clock on the wall she checked the time it was 1 a.m., something wasn't right. Her dream would usually happen after the turning of the keys, and that was more than an hour away.

"Chloe, Chloe," She heard,

Sitting up, Chloe listened as the voice called her name, the familiar voice of her mother. She stood up and walked out into the hallway, but it was as though she had gone back in time. Climbing the stairs, she realised that she was back in her childhood home, back to when she revelled in the innocence of a child. From the bedroom door, Chloe watched as her mother sat at the dressing table humming as she brushed her long brown hair. "There you are, come here sweetheart," her mother said as she noticed Chloe's reflection standing behind her in the mirror. She made her way across the bedroom and stood next to where she was seated, "Sit down," her mother said gently as she gestured for Chloe to sit on her lap.

Chloe sighed with contentment while her mother hummed a loving tune as she brushed the small girl's hair. It felt surreal to be back to a time when problems could be solved with a simple kiss on the forehead.

The brush dragged back across her hair tightly, Chloe screamed as she looked at her reflection in the mirror. Her mother's face, once filled with life and the love she held inside her was gone. Only the rotting remains of what she had left behind, now, sat in her place. Chloe fell backwards against the dressing table as she watched the form crumble away like sand.

Chloe jumped as she sat up, desperately trying to breathe as the anxiety of the dream took hold. Tears filled her eyes as she thought about what she had seen, she felt suffocated, she needed air. Spinning the key in the lock

Chloe stood at the front door trying to calm herself as she took in the cold night air. From the darkness, a figure slowly approached the house, and bit by bit the dimly lit light made its way along the track. Chloe began to panic as the figure neared the gate, she reached into the darkness of the porch and picked up the small hatchet used for chopping kindling. Closing the door, Chloe spun the key in the lock and quickly turned out the light in the hallway. She waited in the darkness and listened to the hinges of the front gate creaking as it opened. In quick succession, Chloe heard three loud knocks on the door, trembling she held the handle of the hatchet as she tried to keep control. "Open the door," she heard as again the knocking began.

Chloe stayed completely still in the darkness as the knocking continued, each time growing more and more assertive. From behind Liam could sense *her* as a black mist approached him. He turned and watched as the woman curled her long finger, commanding him to follow. Chloe listened as footsteps echoed in the porch, she exhaled loudly at the sound of the intruder leaving as she lowered the hatchet to her side.

Outside the black shrouded image of the woman led Liam quietly along the path that followed the side of the house and past the old outbuilding. He stood in the small back garden and watched as the woman pointed towards the back door. From inside Annie sat wide-eyed as the key began to turn slowly as if by an invisible hand in the lock of the door. The woman whispered her command, dominating Liam's thoughts as he placed his hand on the decorative handle.

From the end of the unlit hallway, Chloe felt the sudden rush of cold air flow towards her as the door gradually opened. She tried to swallow, but the fear had dried her mouth and cracked her lips as she stood frozen to the spot clutching the hatchet tightly. In the doorway of the kitchen, Chloe watched as the menacing silhouette edged forward, its arms stretched out in front like a monster from some old 1950s horror film. Was this it, the moment that she met her fate? She had no choice, she had to fight.

Her knuckles turned white as she gripped the handle of the hatchet aggressively and charged forward along the hallway, screaming loudly as she ran towards the figure. Liam had no time to react as Chloe entered the kitchen in true warrior guise, slamming into him the hatchet still raised high above her head. In the darkness of the kitchen, Annie watched on as Chloe bravely grappled with the intruder, the hatchet mercilessly flailing above them. "CHLOE! STOP!" Liam shouted as he tried to defend himself from Chloe's barbaric onslaught.

"Liam?" Chloe asked herself out loud as the razor-like blade narrowly missed the top of his head as he ducked. Chloe lost her balance and was sent flying forward with the malice she had put into the swing, sending her straight over the top of Liam, who cowered in the darkness on the floor in front of her in a huddled position. Chloe hit the coldness of the limestone floor hard as her grip loosened on the handle of the hatchet, sending it spiralling dangerously across the kitchen, before coming to rest embedded deeply in the door of a cupboard. Her eyes blinked slowly, as she listened to Liam uttering words above her, she tried to stay awake, but the impact of the fall was making her head spin.

Sandra sat in the quiet of the lounge holding the small package in her hands, she couldn't sleep, the elderly face of the woman still vivid in her mind, *Until we all perish!* She thought to herself.

Chloe woke to the feeling of being dragged, she opened her eyes and tried to scream but something felt tight across her mouth. Her hands had been tightly bound together using the same cutting twine that she could feel biting into the skin around her ankles. She lay helplessly as Liam continued to haul her along on the damp grass, the hatchet hanging low by his side. They reached the wooden doors of the outbuilding, she tried to kick herself free as Liam removed the padlock from the clasp and opened the door. Again, Liam dragged her defenceless body along the ground and into the dark, cobweb-lined interior of the building. She tried to speak, to make him see reason, but her mumbled pleas were met with the same silence as before. Tears filled her eyes as she watched the heavy door swing shut, the padlock securing her imprisonment as Liam walked away.

# Chapter Thirteen

Inside Millhouse, Liam made his way along the hallway and climbed the stairs to Chloe's studio. His eyes filled with anger as he looked around at the empty walls, while the foreboding image of the woman watched his every move from the corner of the room. "She did this!" the figure whispered sinisterly, as Liam paced around in an agitated state. "You know what you must do," the woman hissed as she moved slowly towards him.

"Yes," was his only reply as he walked to the window and looked out into the darkness of the night.

It was morning and Chloe had gradually made her way across the hard stone floor of the outbuilding and propped herself up against the wall facing the door. The tightness of the restraints around her ankles and wrists was unbearable, as she desperately fought to slacken the twine as it cut deeper and deeper into her skin. She paused at the sound of the padlock being removed and watched as the door swung open, blinking incessantly as sunlight flooded the dark interior of her prison. Liam walked sluggishly towards her, "She says you must eat!" he stated abruptly. Chloe sat motionless as Liam stooped over her, she looked at his face, he seemed dissimilar, his expression vague with cold eyes devoid of showing any emotion. She whimpered as the tape stretched across her mouth was quickly ripped away. Tears filled her eyes, as she watched Liam pour water into a glass before placing it on her lips.

"Please Liam, why are you doing this?" Chloe cried hopelessly, as Liam's hand quickly withdrew the glass from her mouth.

"You know why! Because you betrayed her!" he replied angrily, his hands tearing a large piece of bread in half before gesturing harshly for Chloe to eat.

"How, how did I betray her? Liam please you're not thinking straight, untie me and we can get away from here!" Chloe pleaded in a vain attempt for him to see reason.

"Leave? No, you cannot leave, she says that you must suffer, how she suffered!" Liam responded in a mutinous tone as he smirked sadistically. Chloe spat the bread out of her mouth like venom as she screamed desperately in a bid to draw attention to the situation. Liam quickly muffled her pleas with fresh tape, as Chloe frantically shook her head from side to side in a shallow attempt to fend him off. In the struggle that ensued Liam stepped onto the discarded glass, shattering it on the floor into razor like pieces. Chloe looked away as Liam picked up the water jug and made his way to the open door of the outbuilding, he paused momentarily to look back at her before calmly closing the door behind him.

From its position on the sideboard in the lounge, the telephone began to ring. Sandra waited impatiently, as Liam stood in the doorway listening to the constant ringing. "The meddler!" he heard whispered from behind, as a black mist moved all around him, "Speak to her!" the voice whispered again, this time more demanding in its tone as Liam walked forward and lifted the receiver to his ear.

"Hello?" he asked cautiously, while all the time the black mist swirled ominously by his side.

"Oh hello, can I speak to Chloe please?" Sandra hesitantly replied.

"No, I'm afraid Chloe isn't here at the moment, she's on her way to be with her mother," Liam replied as a smile swept across his face.

"Oh, I see, when will she be back? It is quite urgent that I speak to her, Mr? Sorry I didn't catch your name," Sandra asked as she probed the conversation.

"Mr Stevenson, I'm Chloe's husband, I'm not sure when she will return, is there anything that I can assist you with? You said that it was, urgent."

"I have something that I have to give to her in person, on second thoughts, maybe I should call Chloe directly on her mobile," Sandra responded cautiously as she remembered what the elderly woman had said about the package. The black mist spun aggressively at Liam's side as Sandra thanked him for his time and ended the call.

"You have work to do!" the woman's voice whispered from within the mist as Liam replaced the receiver of the telephone and made his way outside.

Chloe could hear movement, she listened in the darkness as someone walked along the path that led to the back garden. She waited, before continuing with her struggle to retrieve a piece of the broken glass between her fingers, while the sound of something being stacked outside echoed in the confines of the outbuilding.

"Sandra, Sandra, where are you?" Frank called out as he searched the downstairs of the house.

"I will be down in a minute!" she replied, quickly hitting the send button, and placing her mobile phone back into the pocket of her cardigan.

"I was in the bathroom, whatever's the matter, Frank?" Sandra asked as she waddled into the kitchen and noticed the concerned expression on his face.

"Nothing, I just didn't know where you were that's all," he replied awkwardly, now realising how silly his urgency must have sounded.

The sharpness of the glass bit into the skin of Chloe's

fingers as she gripped it tightly. Pushing her back against the wall, she leant forward feeling with the tip of the shard for the bindings around her ankles. She winced as her attempts sent the glass sharply into the flesh of her leg, over and over she felt the pain until the broken piece of glass rested directly on top of the twine. She sat in the darkness moving the makeshift knife edge forwards and backwards, as the blood ran down the inside of her leg. The pain was rapidly taking over as any hope of escaping began to diminish, at the point of Chloe's submission the twine snapped, and her legs broke free. From outside the sound of labouring continued, she tried to stand but her legs felt weak. Determined, Chloe battled against the fragile state of her own body as she clambered to her feet and gradually made her way over to the door of the outbuilding. From the gap in the door Chloe could see Liam building something at the rear of the house, she watched breathlessly as he walked away momentarily only to return carrying lengths of timber. Chloe needed to obtain a better viewpoint, but her only chance was a small window covered with a sack in the roof of the building. If she was ever going to find out what exactly Liam was doing, she would have to untie her hands.

The roughness of the stone on the inside of the outbuilding made light work of the twine, as Chloe worked quickly, moving her bound hands up and down the edge of the wall. Pausing only briefly to listen for any sign of advancement of Liam towards the door, for now, at least she was free. From the gap in the door, she could see him as he continued to fetch and carry timber. Chloe searched around in the dimly lit enclosure of her imprisonment for something to enable her to climb up to the window in the roof, if only she could reach the dark beam above her then maybe, just maybe she would be able to reach the opening.

Sandra checked her mobile phone again, still, there was no reply to the message that she had sent earlier. She had questions that she knew Frank would be able to answer, but how would she ever be able to ask them? It was only a week until their supposedly much-needed break and Frank's mood had lifted ever so slightly. How could she possibly head off to the coast knowing that Chloe could be close to some sort of impending danger and live with herself afterwards if anything did happen? No matter how hard she tried to convince herself that she was perhaps acting on the words uttered by a crazy old lady, she could not erase the thought of what she had witnessed at Millhouse.

From her seated position on the rocking chair, Annie watched on in horror at the events that were unfolding before her evenly stitched eyes, as Liam slammed the head of the axe down through yet another log, splitting it sideways with unimaginable force, before continuing the same motion over and over in the same relentless manner.

From inside Chloe listened to the sound of wood being chopped as she continued to feel her way around the objects placed at the back of the outbuilding. To the side of her, Chloe kicked a large wooden packing crate as she made her way around. The size of the crate would easily allow her to reach the beam, but the weight would make it impossible for her to move into position. Tears began to fall from her eyes as feelings of desperation took hold as she desperately tried to pull at the crate. Losing her grip Chloe fell backwards onto the floor, pain shot through her leg as the wounds from the glass opened further. All the time the unceasing sound of wood being chopped continued to echo around her. Chloe looked up, and there above her was another beam similar in size to the one underneath the window. Again, the pain of the wounds coursed through her as she clambered up onto the crate, she stretched as high as she could, but her fingertips only just reached the wooden beam above her. Taking a deep breath Chloe jumped up into the air, her hands grabbing either side of the beam tightly as she began to pull herself up slowly until she rested precariously on the narrow ledge that spanned the building.

Sandra watched from the kitchen window as Frank meticulously trimmed the bushes in the garden, the whirring sound of the electric shears filling the air as he happily toiled away. From the corner of the kitchen, the black spectral mass of the woman watched on menacingly as the electrical cable attached to the shears wrapped itself around the bush as Frank continued to slice away at the shrubbery.

Whispering.

Sandra turned quickly to be met by the ominous gaze of the phantom, who now stood before her. "You're not welcome, I command you to leave!" Sandra stated boldly as she crossed her arms, all the time shaking to the core. The woman's eyes turned jet black as she hissed at Sandra's defiance,

"Meddler!" she replied, pointing her long claw-like finger out of the mist. "If thou wish me to leave then I shall, but ye must give me what is mine!"

"But I don't have anything that belongs to you!" Sandra argued as she pointed back at the spirit.

"Then I shall take one that belongs to thee!" the woman sneered as her face surged forward from out of the mist.

Chloe cautiously placed one foot in front of the other as she made her way along the beam like a tightrope, as dust dislodged by her feet fell to the floor. Gradually she made her way to the window stepping from beam to joist as the wood creaked and moaned beneath her.

Peeling back the hessian material covering the window Chloe gasped. From her position, she could now see fully the fruits of Liam's labour in all its blood-curdling technicolour. Her heart began to race as she looked out of the small window towards the carefully stacked wood of a bonfire that sat waiting in the back garden of Millhouse. Liam had never been one for celebrating such annual events, and now his sudden interest sent fear streaming through Chloe as she thought about his unfavourable intentions towards her.

Sandra stepped backwards covering her ears as the ghostly image of the woman screamed towards the window in a fit of rage. "NOOOO!" She cried as Frank unknowingly cut closer and closer to the cable that the mist-like spiral of the woman was wrapping tighter around the bush.

Chloe froze on the spot as she heard the padlock being removed from the door below her. Holding her breath, she watched as the door swung open and Liam walked into the building carrying a large coil of rope by his side. Her heart began to beat faster and faster as he started to search the interior of the building for her, calling out her name over and over as he scanned the dark corners of the room. Chloe listened as Liam made his way ever closer to where she was balancing, she waited breathlessly until he passed underneath her and again started to search the perimeter of the room.

In an act of survival Chloe quickly lowered herself down and landed heavily on the stone floor of the outbuilding. She yelped at the pain surging through her leg as she hobbled towards the open door. "There you are bitch!" Liam sneered as he made his way out of the darkness, "Where are you going? Your mother's waiting!" he called out laughing.

"LEAVE ME ALONE!"!" Chloe screamed as she tried desperately to make her way to the door. Again, Liam laughed as he drew closer, loosening the coil of rope in his hands as he walked to where Chloe was frantically trying to make her exit.

"Now, now, Chloe darling stop all this silliness and be a good girl," Liam whispered in her ear as he stood directly behind her. She looked at the open door as Liam's hands grasped her shoulders destroying any possible chance of escape.

"You don't have to do this Liam, she's tricking you, please think about this!" Chloe pleaded despairingly as she felt the rope slowly being wrapped around her arms and body.

"Oh Chloe, why do you always have to be so fucking disagreeable?" Liam asked as he pulled tighter on the rope, "I mean out of everything you have ever done that painting was the best and you destroyed it, so yes, Chloe I do have to do it!" Liam sighed as he grabbed Chloe's face in his hand, digging his fingers into her cheeks as he stared into her eyes.

"Please, you won't get away with it, they'll know it's you! Stop this now and let's get as far away as possible from Millhouse!" Chloe sobbed as she tried to get him to see reason, tears falling from her eyes as she was led out of the door and along the path.

Sandra tried to make it to the door, but the mist blocked

her way, from the window she watched as if in slow motion as the blade moved upwards to where the cable lay waiting, the shears now seemingly guided by the movement of the woman's finger.

Chloe's mouth was gagged to silence her screams as Liam pushed her up the makeshift steps and began to tie her tightly to the upright pole in the centre of the stacked wood. From her elevated position, she could see Annie watching, unable to remove her static like stare as she sat in the rocking chair. "Aww, does she want her dolly? Wait there and I'll fetch her for you!" Liam said as he mocked the sounds of Chloe's feeble crying. She watched as he casually walked into the kitchen and returned carrying the small rag doll, which he placed at Chloe's feet. "There at least you can be together, I never really liked the thing anyway!" he grumbled as he clambered down the steps and over to a green can marked petrol.

The woman looked back at Sandra as she readied herself to send the shears through the cable which was now wrapped around Franks calf. Again, Sandra tried to make her way past the mist and warn Frank to stop, but the intense energy concealed within it held her back, forcing her to stay exactly where she was.

Liam seemed unfazed by the situation as he unscrewed the top of the can and made his way over to the readied bonfire. Chloe could smell the distinctive fumes of the petrol as she watched him dousing the wood surrounding her feet. She screamed a muffled scream as Liam flicked the can in front of her, covering her legs in the liquid. He smiled sarcastically as he watched the petrol running over the gashes on her skin as it mixed painfully with the blood that flowed down to where Annie was resting.

Frank looked up to see the face of the woman smiling back at him, as his hands lifted the shears towards the cable. Sandra screamed out as she reached deep into the pocket of her cardigan and pulled out the small tied-up package. The spectre stopped and stared back with enraged eyes at Sandra who stood frantically pulling at the ribbon fastened around the pouch.

Chloe pushed and pulled to try and break free as Liam walked towards her holding a flaming torch, which he held above his head in readiness. She closed her eyes to block out the sight of her impending fate as she prayed to whoever may be listening to make her suffering short-lived.

The ribbon pulled free between Sandra's trembling fingers, she watched as the phantom dropped to her knees, writhing in agony as she knelt on the ground, her hand still gripping the electric cable tightly. "Frank, run!" Sandra yelled as the vision of the woman began to disappear into the mist that was engulfing her. Frank did as he was told, rapidly he uncurled the lead from around his leg and hurried back to the kitchen where Sandra stood holding the small pouch out in front of her.

Not feeling the heat from the fire Chloe slowly opened her eyes, Liam was nowhere to be seen as she scanned her surroundings. The rope that had held her so tightly dropped away to her feet, releasing her from the infernal capture. Picking up Annie, Chloe painfully clambered down the pile of wood and fell to the ground, everything went dark as the pain and shock combined. From the distance, she could hear a voice calling out to her, a calm gentle voice that held no threat nor malice within its words.

# Chapter Fourteen

Grey smoke spiralled gently upon the windless air as a frail hand placed more wood on the fire that sat glowing in the hearth of the small cottage.

In the corner of the room, Chloe lay rambling in a muddled state, beads of sweat running over her pale skin as a fever took hold, "Shh," the woman whispered as she dabbed Chloe's forehead gently with a dampened cloth before placing it back into the small white enamelled bowl which rested on a table next to the bed.

"Mother? Mother, where are you?" Chloe called out feebly as her head rolled slowly to the side to seek out the voice.

"You must rest child," the woman replied softly as she rang out the cloth and placed it back on Chloe's feverish brow.

*It was as though everything that Chloe knew had been taken away from her as she searched around in the darkness. She could hear the softness of a voice, but no matter how hard she tried its location remained undiscovered. Was she dead? Was this the place of life ever after? She couldn't be sure, all Chloe knew at that moment was she felt no pain.*

The woman watched as Chloe became still in the bed,

"Sleep," she murmured gently as she stood and made her way across the small room. She paused briefly to stroke the head of the white cat that lay curled up on a chair by the door, "Watch over her Dandelion," the woman whispered as she made her way outside. The cat meowed as it stood and arched its back before jumping off the chair and making its way over to where Chloe lay peacefully sleeping, Annie placed closely by her side.

Millhouse stood eerily quiet, deserted beneath the tree-lined banks of the valley. It had been three whole days now since Chloe had been rescued, and still, the fever kept its sickening hold over her. From the trees came the rustling of fabric as the long cloak of the woman brushed against the leaves scattered on the ground, as she made her way down to the path that ran alongside the river. She paused momentarily by the small crossing point to the side of Millhouse, before hastily moving forward to where the willow tree stood slowly bowing its leafless head down to the slow-moving surface of the water. From her pocket she took out a small, sharpened blade, holding it firmly between her weathered fingers, as she explained the urgency of her actions to the still-bowing tree. The acceptance of the valley whispered on a gentle breeze that blew through the branches of the willow, pushing them down under the surface of the water, before gently raising them back to their place of rest. The woman nodded gracefully as she moved forward, tightening her grip on the handle of the knife she began to cut with precision small pieces of bark away from the tree, placing each one delicately with respect into a small bag draped over her shoulder. As she made her way back along the path, she could see the wooden pyre still standing in the garden behind the house, where it stood as a reminder of the near demise of Chloe.

From the path on the other side of the river, she could feel eyes watching her. Knowing that the protection within the small pouches that hung from the trees would have now diminished, she quickened her pace as she headed down the path to cross over the low span of the stone bridge.

She stopped as the dark swirling mass blocked her way, "Let me pass!" the old woman uttered as she stared into the foreboding eyes of the face that glared back at her.

"Meddling bitch!" she hissed back from the mist which swirled around her like a nest of angry vipers, "The girl is mine, her time is near!"

The old woman shook her head, "No, Eleanor, it is you that must go! Your time of walking the earth passed many years ago!" she said calmly as she walked towards the spectre, pulling her hand out slowly from the inside of her pocket as she did. Eleanor cowered as she backed away from the frail hand that was held out in front of her, as words were spoken in a bid to repel her. She watched as Eleanor dropped to the floor and vanished leaving only a black dust in her wake, which was carried away by a sudden gust of wind. The old woman pulled at the fabric of the cloak to shield her from the biting coldness as she made her way back to the sanctuary of her home.

Over the following days, she watched as Chloe battled with the fever, listening to her words of delusion as she moistened her lips with the warm liquid that steamed in a blackened pot over the fire.

*She desperately wanted to go home, but in the darkness, there was*

173

*no given direction. From around her Chloe could hear voices calling out, asking for her to join them.*

"I can't see you," Chloe muttered desperately,

"Walk to me child," the old woman whispered as she stroked the back of Chloe's hand.

*Chloe turned quickly in the darkness as she tried to follow the sound of her mother's voice that whispered to her from the abyss.*

"Here, take my hand," she whispered as she held Chloe's hand tighter,

*She felt the security of the hand. From behind Chloe could hear the hissing, seething voice of Eleanor as she made her way out of the darkness. Chloe began to panic, she wanted to escape but the power of Eleanor was becoming overwhelming.*

The old woman watched as Chloe squirmed under the sheets, "Open your eyes child!" she called out as Chloe began to writhe in pain. "NOW CHILD!"

*Chloe held the hand tighter as she felt herself being quickly dragged into a ball of bright light that appeared out of the darkness in front of her.*

The old woman sat back as Chloe opened her eyes and inhaled deeply, "Where am I?" she asked weakly as her eyes scanned the unfamiliar surroundings of the cottage. She tried to sit up, but the fatigued state of her body forced her to stay where she was.

"You must rest child, for now, at least you are safe," the old woman replied as she made her way slowly across the room to the open fire. Chloe watched as the woman stirred the contents of the steaming pot hanging over the flames, before ladling the liquid into a cup and returning to her side.

"Who are you?" Chloe asked in the same feeble tone as the cup was gently offered to her pale lips gesturing for her to drink.

"My name is Aveline," she replied gently.

Chloe coughed as she swallowed the strong-flavoured beverage, that flowed slowly down her throat like syrup. Aveline lifted the cup away and placed it on the table beside her, she paused momentarily, before taking out a small white cotton handkerchief with which she carefully wiped away the remnants of liquid from Chloe's lips. "And I am.." Chloe began to say as Aveline placed a finger to her mouth to hush her,

"I know who you are child, now rest, soon you will need to be stronger than you have ever been."

Aveline watched as the aromatic drink started to take its calming effect on Chloe who lay peacefully beneath the bedclothes, watching the flames of the candles as they flickered from side to side as though locked in some form of hypnotic dance.

In the dark confines of Millhouse, Liam sat huddled in the corner of the studio uttering words of madness to the shadows being cast by the moon as it shone through the window. In his hands he tightly held onto a small wooden picture frame, the glass cracked by the constant pressure of his thumbs, as the smiling face of Chloe looked back at him from beneath the web-like façade. "She is near!" Eleanor hissed as she moved about menacingly in the darkness of the room.

"Show me where and I will finish what I started!" Liam growled as his reddened rage-like eyes followed the swirling mass around the room.

"No! For she will not let you near, it must be another who draws her away," Eleanor whispered sinisterly as she floated within the blackness of the mist.

Sandra tutted as she listened to Frank grunting like a dissatisfied pig as he turned over in his sleep. Night time was the worst, the constant worry about what they would return home to uneased her somewhat, was the restless spirit still at large? Only time would tell, and for her, time was running out fast as the end of their holiday together was quickly drawing to an end. She sat studying the book that she had taken from Millhouse, pondering on thoughts as to what she had read so far. Was it the house? Edward Worthing had stated in depth his understanding regarding the different types of curses, but the last truly unnerved her the most. Picking up the tattered book she re-read the last of the three.

*Object bound Curses,*

*As I have discussed previously, the fundamental requirement of a curse is the intention. But this will of wrongdoing towards another does not have to be performed as words on paper or by chanting.*

*The third type of curse is that of the intention being placed into an object, as with the story of Mary Baggot, the curse in this way has the ability to continue long past its intended use. Items cursed long ago can sometimes find themselves being transferred to the dwellings of others through sales or by way of a gift. The recipient gladly accepts the item unbeknown to its ominous connection to the past, and the effects of the curse of course begin again.*

Sandra shuddered at the thought of household items being cursed, she dropped the book down quickly as she thought about Chloe's eclectic gathering of things inside the house. Frank had often commented as to how the place was decorated with things from the past, and why she couldn't just buy new like everybody else was beyond him. She watched as the mass underneath the duvet grumbled again in his sleep, perhaps he was the one cursed, after all, he had been the one who had transformed the ruinous state of Millhouse into the home that Chloe loved so much. As Sandra watched him sleep her suspicions and nerves for that matter got the better of her thoughts, she decided that it would be in her best interest to keep a closer eye on his behaviour, just in case he started to show any signs that he was possessed.

The following morning Chloe woke to the sound of sweeping. She opened her eyes and watched as Aveline made her way broom in hand around the small room of the cottage. "Ah good morning, how did you sleep?" Aveline asked happily as she stopped cleaning.

"Very well thank you," Chloe replied as she attempted to sit up slowly.

"Here child, allow me to help you," Aveline stated as she leaned the handle of the broom against the wall and made her way over to the waiting body of Chloe in the bed, who eagerly accepted the welcoming frame of Aveline as she aided her into a more upright position.

"How can I ever repay you for your kindness?" Chloe asked as she watched Aveline making her way to the fire where yet more of the steaming liquid bubbled away. Aveline turned slowly as she stirred the contents of the pot,

"The help I offer does not come with any need for repayment child, your actions alone will be what is required when the moment comes, now here drink this before it cools," Aveline smiled as she returned her gaze to the pot as she filled the small cup yet again and held it at Chloe's lips. Begrudgingly due to the strong taste of the brew Chloe accepted the drink and sipped slowly at the contents. "All of it mind," Aveline stated sharply as Chloe paused for a moment to ingest the liquid.

"If you don't mind me asking Aveline, what exactly is this?" Chloe inquired as she cringed at the thought of yet another mouthful.

"An old recipe, one which has been passed down through the ages, everything inside that tea is gathered by hand from nature itself," Aveline stated as she waited for Chloe to finish the contents of the cup. Chloe pinched her nose tightly as she drank the remaining liquid and passed the cup to Aveline's waiting hands. "I never said that it tasted nice child," Aveline laughed as she sat slowly down on the side of the bed.

"It is made from the bark of the willow tree, with just the slightest pinch of cinnamon and chamomile," Aveline continued to say as she gazed deeply into Chloe's eyes.

Chloe sat completely still, it was as though Aveline was

looking deep inside her mind, reading all of her most hidden inner thoughts. A whole lifetime of memories flashed before her eyes in what was seemingly only a fleeting moment as she sat transfixed by Aveline's motionless stare.

"Your insecurity troubles me," Aveline stated abruptly as she broke from her fixated pose.

"I'm not insecure, who said I was insecure?" Chloe asked with a stunned expression on her face, as she watched wide-eyed the outspoken Aveline stand and walk back to where the broom stood resting against the wall

"If *you* are to ever be free of the tormented soul, then you must face the truth about what you hold inside. She will take everything if you continue to lie to yourself, child!" Aveline uttered disapprovingly as she clutched the handle of the broom and continued with the task of sweeping the floor. Chloe felt the atmosphere in the room change as she sat on the bed like a scolded child, embarrassed by the fact that she knew the words of the aged lady were indeed nothing but the truth.

The rest of the morning felt strained as Aveline continued to busy herself cleaning and preparing ingredients that she mixed carefully together, before placing them into small glass jars and bottles that stood in organised row upon row on the shelves that lined the wall next to the fireplace. Chloe was about to ask if she could be of any assistance when the sound of faint scratching coming from the door drew her attention away. Nervously she watched as the door slowly began to open, while Aveline continued to grind the ingredients to fill yet another bottle, somehow completely unaware of the unannounced arrival of the visitor. *Frosty?* Chloe thought to herself as the familiar feline walked gracefully into the small room of the cottage.

"I believe you two already know each other," Aveline stated without even showing the slightest turn of her head as she continued to chop and mash. Chloe watched as the cat jumped up onto the bed and sat purring happily as her hand gently stroked the softness of the fur. "This is Dandelion," Aveline said as she turned around, wiping her hands on a cloth, watching as the two became reacquainted.

"Hello again Frosty, oh sorry Dandelion!" Chloe said awkwardly, correcting herself as the cat meowed loudly in its feline response. Aveline placed the cloth down on the worktop and made her way to where the cat sat patiently waiting, delicately placing her hands on the sides of the cat's face she looked intently into Dandelion's bright orange eyes. Chloe watched as Aveline's brow furrowed deeper,

"It appears that the energy inside Millhouse is becoming restless."

"How do you know?" Chloe asked apprehensively as she watched the wrinkled hands of Aveline release from the cat's face.

"Dandelion here has been watching you and Millhouse for some time, you must stay here child while I see the events for myself," Aveline insisted as she hurriedly wrapped the material of the long dark robe around her body.

"Wait! What do you mean events?" Chloe called out to

Aveline in a confused state. She watched as Aveline paused briefly to cover her head with the hood of the robe as she swung the door open towards her.

"Let no one enter! no one do you hear me, child?" Aveline stated as she swiftly made her way outside, the door slamming loudly as she went. Chloe sat quietly waiting in the safety of Aveline's cottage, as the form of the old woman hastily made her way down through the twisted maze of trees. Nearing the river Aveline waited for a moment to check that the coast was clear before gradually making her way closer to the rear of Millhouse.

From the sanctuary of the trees, Aveline watched as Liam sluggishly carried a handful of clothing over to the open door of the outbuilding, before returning to the house in the same bedraggled manner. Dandelion was right, things were indeed moving at a rate that she had not anticipated. "Aveline," she heard whispered.

"Step back Eleanor!" Aveline called out, drawing the attention of Liam over to where she was hiding within the trees. Dropping the pile of clothes Liam started to make his way down the path leading to the woods. His hands tugged at the handle of the axe and wrenched its sharpened head from out of the tree stump where it rested.

"Who is it?" Chloe called out nervously as three loud knocks resounded on the small cottage door. From the other side, she could hear feet impatiently shuffling on the stone path, "WHO IS IT!" she called out again, this time more demanding in her tone as the knocking continued.

"Chloe, Chloe," she heard a man's voice almost sing in reply, "Open up, I'm cold, so very cold, let me warm myself by the fire," the voice called out in a feeble tone.

"No! Aveline told me not to let anyone in," Chloe replied fearfully as the knocking began once again.

Liam spotted the hooded outline of Aveline and aggressively started to make his way through the thick undergrowth of the wood, violently swinging the axe from side to side as he chopped at the bracken. From her side Aveline noticed the black swirling mist of Eleanor beginning to appear, laughter filled her ears as Liam edged ever closer towards her, grinning a sinister grin.

# Chapter Fifteen

Chloe stayed completely still as she listened to the continuous banging on the door. "Chloe, please I'm so cold," she heard the voice call out again.

"No, I can't!" she replied hesitantly, fear creeping through her body as she listened to the desperation in the pleas as the knocking continued.

"But Chloe please it's me, Ted!"

The knocking stopped. Chloe slowly slid her legs out of the bed and tried to stand, but her recent bedridden state had made her weak. How could it be Ted? Frank had sadly informed her that he had died, but had he? Maybe the brew that Aveline had been insisting that she drank was somewhat hallucinogenic and everything that she thought had happened was all just some fucked up dream. Maybe, just maybe, in reality, she had been tricked by the kindly-faced old woman, after all, she didn't know her. Perhaps she had been abducted, and Ted's insistency was in a bid to rescue her, she had to know as she gradually made her way across the room to the door.

"Ted, is that really you?" Chloe asked as she placed her ear on the wooden surface. From the bed, Dandelion scowled as she watched Chloe's hand grab the door handle tightly.

"Yes, Chloe, please you need to let me in," Ted called out hastily, "I've come to take you home!"

Aveline felt powerless as the dark mist of Eleanor began to twist itself around her body, tighter and tighter it wound until she could no longer move. "I warned thee, but ye wouldn't listen!" Eleanor sneered as Aveline fought desperately inside to summon enough energy to break free. "The maiden is mine to do with as I wish, your foolish meddling must come to an end, and so must ye!" Liam watched as the frail body of the old woman began to lift into the air as Eleanor pointed to the rear of Millhouse.

Tears filled Chloe's eyes as she turned the door handle and thought of home. Her screams echoed through the air at the realisation of the true events, as she stared at the figure now standing before her.

She looked away in disgust as the putrid stench of death filled her senses while Ted indolently dragged his feet across the stone pathway towards her. She could feel the coldness of his touch as he ran his deathly fingers down her arm, "Hello Chloe," he said in a nauseating and ominous tone, as he licked the dryness from his lips. The smell of decaying flesh and damp earth made Chloe swoon as the undead Labourer made his advances towards her, she needed to break free, but her legs refused to assist as they turned to jelly. "It's been a while," he said pressing his face closer to hers. Chloe tried to push him away, but her fingers sank deep into the rotten flesh of his chest. She could feel the skin tearing under her nails as Ted pushed himself even closer to her as he laughed sinisterly.

"What do you want from me?" Chloe cried as Ted nuzzled his face into her neck,

"I could think of a few things, but *she* wants you to return to Millhouse!" he sneered as a worm fell from his mouth and landed on the floor next to Chloe's feet where it squirmed on the stone tiles.

"Well, here we are, home sweet home," Frank grumbled as he parked the van and switched off the engine. "You know, I could get used to living near the sea, maybe we should think about retiring," he suggested as he pulled the last of the suitcases from out of the back of the van.

"Maybe," Sandra sighed as she waddled along the garden path to the front door, while Frank followed behind struggling to carry the multitude of baggage that Sandra had insisted on taking.

"FRANK, QUICK!" Sandra cried out loudly as she disappeared along the hallway. Dropping the suitcases at the door Frank hurried to where Sandra now stood holding her rounded face in her hands as she looked despairingly into the living room. Looking past his wife and into the room Frank saw the reason for her dismay,

"I had better call the Police, don't touch anything do you hear!" He expressed urgently as he made his way to the telephone in the hallway. Sandra nodded nervously as she looked at the mess that was once her tidy home. Mementoes of their life together now lay scattered across the floor by uncaring hands in a bid to find treasure. "The Police are on their way, try not to get too upset," Frank said as he placed a comforting arm around Sandra who now looked around with tear-stained eyes.

Heavy clouds that threatened rain hung low over the valley as Chloe trudged along the muddy pathway that led to Millhouse, her face shrouded with a dazed look of confusion. "She will never succumb to your wicked ways Eleanor, I placed protection everywhere," Aveline stated defiantly as she watched Eleanor moving across the floor of the studio.

"I think otherwise," Eleanor hissed as she turned her gaze to the window and watched as Chloe walked calmly along the path to the house. "Your herbs may keep me from your door Aveline, but what if they are crushed by the foot of another," Eleanor laughed as she watched Chloe nearing the small garden gate. Aveline watched on hopelessly as the black mist surged out of the studio door, slamming it shut aggressively in her wake.

"I'm sorry sir but there does not appear to be any sign of a break-in. Are you sure that nobody else has a key?" Frank shook his head as he listened to the police officer's question.

"No, nobody," Frank replied, "We only went away for a few days, just for some sea air."

"Well, I will leave you both to sort through everything, I have given you the crime number in case you need to make an insurance claim," the police officer replied sternly as he made his way out of the house and headed back to the waiting patrol car.

Sandra could not get the distasteful thought of her home being violated out of her head, and the idea that there were no signs of a forced entry made it worse. What if the crime wasn't committed by the hands of the living? What if the carnage was committed by the hands of the dead? Nobody, especially the police would consider such a thing, after all, nothing had been taken, and hauntings were not what she would consider top of the list when it came to the crimes of the century. The only person who would truly believe and understand her was unreachable since she had gone to stay with her mother. Daily Sandra had tried to get through to Chloe, but each time the call was diverted straight to her messaging service, even the text messages that she had sent were being returned undelivered.

"Are you sure you haven't given a spare key to one of your friends?" Frank asked as he placed the remaining ornaments back inside the display cabinet and started to rewind the flex of the vacuum cleaner. Sandra shook her head adamantly as she displayed her certainty to his question,

"No, not even Chloe!"

Frank looked up puzzled by her answer, "Why would you give her a key? I mean you hardly know the girl and it's not as if the last time you saw her was exactly on the best of terms."

"I didn't mean anything by it, it's just well before we went on holiday in the café there was an old woman who was standing watching me," Sandra began to explain as Frank stood with a bemused look on his face.

"What you think an old lady gained access to our front door key and ransacked the house?" he asked sarcastically while he laughed, "Who was she? Super Gran!"

Sandra's lips tightened as she thought back the

compulsion to retaliate against the mockery being displayed by her husband. "No Frank, I don't think that" she replied calmly, "It's just that she said something to me, something that I fear to be true."

"What, What did she say? I'm sorry for laughing at you, but well you're not making any sense,"

"She told me that she would never stop until we all perish! Frank the woman in the cafe was talking about the ghost of Millhouse. I've been trying to contact Chloe ever since, but she doesn't reply, I found out from Liam that she has gone to stay with her mother," Sandra stated quickly as she tried to get everything off her chest in one mouthful.

Frank scratched the stubble on his chin as he thought for a moment, "No, no you must be confused Sandra, I clearly remember Chloe herself telling me that her mum had passed away a few years ago." Sandra placed her hand over her mouth as she listened to the surety of Frank's words as he recollected on the time that he had sat in the kitchen of Millhouse with Chloe as she spoke about how the day would have been her mother's birthday.

"But why would Liam lie? Frank, I think we should drive over there, just to take a look, you know just to make sure everything is ok,"

"Ok, but we can go tomorrow I've had enough for one day," Frank said as he yawned and stretched, much to the displeasure of Sandra who had been hoping for more of an immediate response to the situation.

The door opened, and Chloe walked confidently over the threshold of Millhouse where she was greeted by the floating mist of Eleanor. "Sister you returned!" Eleanor whispered as she studied the trance-like features of Chloe's face. Chloe remained silent as she bowed her head gracefully in reply. Eleanor smiled full of wickedness, as she commanded Chloe to hold out her hand, watching to see if her fingers trembled with fear. Inside she wanted to scream as Eleanor stabbed the sharp pointed tip of the long needle deep into her palm, twisting and turning as she pushed it deeper and deeper into her skin. She could feel the burn of the metal as it rubbed harshly against the flesh, then bone as Eleanor continued to work the needle through the palm of her hand until the sound of it hitting the floor signalled that the ordeal at least for now, was over.

"Good!" Eleanor hissed menacingly as she led Chloe up the staircase to the studio, all the time the spiralling mist encircling her.

"Child!" Aveline sighed sadly as she watched Chloe enter the room, slowly following the haunting tune emanating from the dark shape of the phantom. Chloe said nothing as she looked unemotionally back at the old woman suspended by mist-like ropes in the corner of the room. Aveline lowered her head as a tear fell silently from her eye,

"I fear she no longer knows thee Aveline," Eleanor cackled as she stroked the back of Chloe's head. "The girl is mine, she will do my bidding until all is complete!" she hissed as the ropes holding the frail figure of Aveline tightened, stretching her arms further to the ceiling.

"And what then? What will you do when she has played her part, Eleanor, throw her away like a bone tossed to a dog? No Eleanor Hurst, all the time that I have the energy of the craft coursing through my veins will I allow you to destroy her!" Aveline replied defiantly as she slowly raised her head and stared directly into the piercing eyes of the spirit. Eleanor lunged forward across the room towards Aveline, sneering, she grabbed the old woman by the throat. Chloe watched on with fixated eyes as Aveline began to choke.

"The energy ye speaks of seems to be fading Aveline!" Eleanor laughed, as she continued to tighten her deadly grip. Chloe stood completely still, as blood dripped down from the hole in her hand, she had to do something, anything to save Aveline, but what?

"Sister," she called out confidently.

Eleanor stopped, releasing Aveline she turned slowly to face Chloe who waited desperately for whatever outcome would follow. She watched fearfully as the face of the spirit appeared to be thinking about the situation, again Chloe confidently spoke out.

"Sister, she is not important now that I have returned, we have more important things to do!"

Again, Eleanor was intrigued by what she heard, "What things do ye speak of sister?"

"The painting sister, surely I must redo what I destroyed before I commit myself to the flames," Chloe replied sympathetically as she looked at Eleanor with remorseful eyes. Aveline watched as the apparition looked at the empty frame of the easel and then back to Chloe.

"Yes, the painting, ye must begin without haste, the time

for me to return is drawing near!" Eleanor whispered eerily as she replied.

From the bed Annie watched the fire in the hearth slowly fade to embers as she sat alone in Aveline's cottage, the cold air of the evening chilling the room from the open door. Dandelion had witnessed the harrowing sight of the newly resurrected Ted and had followed Chloe from a safe distance as she made her way back along the pathways to Millhouse. Hidden deep within the safety of the undergrowth, the feline watcher observed the strange comings and goings of Liam as he continued to shuffle about sluggishly in the fading light. Like a true stalker, Dandelion made her way unseen around the perimeter of the house, looking for any sign of Aveline and Chloe. From the studio window, the cat could feel the faint energy of Aveline, as she watched the shadow of a figure moving along the brightly lit wall of the interior. For now, at least she knew that her old friend was alive. Silently Dandelion made her way to the corner of the cottage garden to where the walls met and settled in for the night in a vain attempt to watch over her.

Chloe watched the studio door close as Eleanor left the room, there were no sounds of turning keys or locks being set, but still, Chloe knew that there was no possibility of leaving. She looked at the palm of her hand as she sat posed on her stool in front of the freshly stretched canvas that rested on the easel in front of her. "Why?" Aveline whispered as she looked across at Chloe from her still elevated position in the corner of the room. Chloe remained silent, her gaze still focused on the blood-stained hole in the centre of her palm. "I know you can hear me, child," Aveline again said in the same whispered tone, as she watched Chloe begin to squeeze the contents of the tubes of paint down onto the surface of her palette. "Child!" Aveline called out in a more demanding voice, forcing Chloe to look up and scowl at the confused face of the old woman.

"Because you lied to me! You tricked me, you wicked bitch!" Chloe sneered as she frantically began to apply brushstroke after brushstroke to the surface of the canvas. Aveline desperately tried to convince her of the truth as Chloe continued to paint, her face hidden from view by the artwork. The old woman was close to losing all hope as she watched Chloe pick up the canvas and turn it carefully to face her,

**If we work together we can escape PLAY ALONG!** Aveline read as she looked at the words painted quickly in yellow ochre. Chloe smiled a small smile of reassurance before returning the canvas to face her, quickly covering the words with more paint as she began the portrait.

From the doorway of the outbuilding Eleanor watched over Liam as he continued to stack any possessions of Chloe in a dark corner. Apart from her still beating heart in the studio no other trace of Chloe ever being at Millhouse remained, as Liam in his trance-like state seemingly began to wipe her from history.

Frank woke to the sound of someone moving about downstairs, he sat up quickly and listened in the darkness. Making his way cautiously down the staircase he waited at the bottom as the sound of movement seemed to be coming from the kitchen, taking a deep breath Frank started to creep along the hallway. As he neared the end, the door of the kitchen opened slowly, gradually he continued to make his way until he stood staring into the darkness of the room. "Frank my old mate," he heard a familiar voice say as he searched in the darkness for the light switch.

"Ted? No, it can't be," Frank uttered, his voice now quivering with uncertainty as his fingers engaged with the switch.

"And then there was light," Ted chuckled as he sat at the kitchen table, forcing Frank to stumble backwards in shock.

"But, but you're dea…"

"Dead? Yes I know, a grizzly affair that was, one minute I'm moving tiles, the next, WHAM!" Ted exclaimed loudly as he slammed his hand down hard on the surface of the table, causing Frank to hold his chest tightly with fear.

"But if you're dead, how are you here?" he asked pulling out a chair opposite his departed friend and sitting down slowly, his mind filled with confusion.

"Because Frank my old chum, I'm here to warn you about Chloe. You see, one day when you left me at the house, you went to be nosey at a clearance sale remember? Ted asked as Frank nodded in response, "Well she tried it on, obviously I turned her down, what with her being married and that. Anyway, I said that I would tell Liam about her infidelity, and that's when she came to the building site, I was on the roof when she distracted me, and I fell."

"What you're telling me that she is the reason you died? Because you turned her down?" Frank asked as he sat back in his chair.

"Yes, and I bet you'll be next, mark my words mate she's trouble!" Ted stated adamantly as he leaned deliberately across the table towards Frank.

# Chapter Sixteen

"Frank, Frank, wake up!" Sandra exclaimed as she shook him by the arm, causing Frank to jump up in the bed, beads of sweat running down his face as he looked anxiously around the brightly lit bedroom.

"What time is it?" he asked, breathing heavily as he looked at his wife with wide panic-stricken eyes.

"Nearly ten past two, you were tossing and turning,"

"He was here Sandra, sitting in our kitchen," Frank replied hesitantly as he thought back to what he had seen.

"Frank you were asleep, who did you see?" Sandra asked apprehensively as she stood at the side of the bed, tying the belt of her dressing gown tightly against her rounded frame.

"Ted, he was here, in the kitchen. He told me that I must be wary of Chloe," he paused momentarily as he looked nervously at his wife, "He told me she killed him at the building site!"

The revelation that Frank had witnessed in his nightmare state played heavy on his mind, so heavy were his thoughts that he could not bring himself to drift back off to sleep. Sandra tried to reassure him that what he had seen was only a dream, probably brought on by the recent stress that they had both found themselves under. But her efforts were in vain as he made his way anxiously downstairs in search of comfort from 'old Jack' the healer himself.

Liam's feet crunched on the grass, covered with a thick frost as he patrolled the area around Millhouse. Winter would soon be upon the valley, yet still, he felt no cold as he acted out the wishes of Eleanor. From the window of the studio, Chloe watched as her once-one true love made his way past the front of the house and along the path that led to the outbuilding. She looked at her watch and checked the time, it was 6:25 a.m. If she was right in her thinking that would give her nine minutes until Liam would again appear at the front of the house, long enough perhaps for them both to escape.

Aveline sat huddled in the corner of the studio trying to keep warm as the coldness of the morning air bit at her bones. "Her power, for now, is failing child but she will soon be back. You must go, and leave this place, I believed that I could control her but the connection she has to this house is far too strong!" Aveline whispered in a tone that mirrored the melancholy in her eyes.

"But I cannot leave you, if I go, then you go!" Chloe stated confidently as the sorrowful expression on Aveline's face changed to a small smile as she chuckled to herself. "What? What's so funny? I didn't think that anything I had said would raise a smile!" Chloe said as she huffed. Aveline climbed slowly to her feet and held out her hands for Chloe to take,

"Look," Aveline said soft-heartedly as she held Chloe's hand in hers. Chloe watched as the wound that Eleanor had subjected upon her had vanished, leaving not even the faintest of traces of injury to her skin. "Nothing more than a shallow attempt to test you."

"It didn't feel like it!" Chloe said as she pulled her hand away quickly and thought about the pain she had been subjected to.

"She wanted to see how powerful her will over yours truly was, after all, it was she who led you away from my home was it not?" Aveline sighed.

"Ted tried to get in, but the moment he stepped through the door things started to change. Aveline, for whatever reason you believe that your 'ability' if that's what you call it is not strong enough, then think again. Whatever you used made him disappear!" Chloe pointed out desperately in admiration.

"But how did you know she would believe that you were under her power? Aveline asked as she watched Chloe begin again to study the movements of Liam from the window. Chloe looked at her watch,

"When all this shit started happening, I used to get thoughts, and the more I had them the more I would paint that stupid fucking picture. I kind of hoped that if I did the same then I would find you," Chloe smiled, "He was ten seconds slower that time!" Chloe thought out loud as she looked back at the window with a puzzled expression.

Aveline shook her head at what this brave soul had done in an attempt to help her, surely the situation was supposed to be the other way around? After all, that was what she had agreed to.

They seemed to wait forever for Liam to appear once

again at the front of Millhouse, as he rounded the corner Chloe grabbed Aveline's hand as they waited silently in the shadows of the porch. Chloe checked her watch as she counted down the next forty-five seconds, knowing that Liam would then be out of sight, "Now!" she whispered as she pulled Aveline quickly along the narrow garden path. Reaching the gate she gripped the latch tightly, the coldness of the metal stinging her fingers as they made their way out onto the track that led to the crossing of the river. The willow tree bowed at their passing as the two desperate figures scurried away into the woods. The iciness of the air surrounding the river sent plumes of steam from their mouths as they hurried down to where the bridge lay waiting to carry their passage to safety. Aveline pleaded for Chloe to stop, the frailness of her body unable to continue at the younger woman's pace. Reluctantly Chloe surrendered to the resistance of Aveline's tugging and stopped. They both stood breathless on the path in the middle of the woods, listening to the sound of nature around them. "Do you think you can go on?" Chloe asked as she took hold of Aveline's hand once more.

"Yes child, for I fear we will soon not be alone!" Aveline replied with an edge of uncertainty in her voice as she scanned the woods on the opposite bank of the river.

"And I'm telling you Frank for the millionth time that Chloe did not cause Ted to fall, no matter what you heard in a dream!" Sandra retorted as Frank turned the van onto the steep rugged track that led to Millhouse. Liam stopped as he heard the sound of vehicle doors being closed. Moving swiftly, he took up a position at the side of the outbuilding, watching as the two figures walked towards the front of the house. "Chloe, Chloe," Sandra called out as she knocked continuously on the front door.

"I don't think anyone's at home love, I knew this was all a waste of time!" Frank moaned as he rubbed the top of his head and replaced his cap.

"Please Frank, can we just take a quick look around?" Sandra asked making her way over to the small window. As she peered inside everything seemed to be just how she remembered the lounge to be, except there was no fire burning in the hearth, much to her surprise.

Crossing the river, the sound of their feet echoed on the stones of the bridge. The safety of Aveline's cottage was near, but from behind they could sense the urgency being created as the black mist of Eleanor made its way towards them.

"All right, just a quick look around and then that's it!" Frank demanded as he became suppressed by his wife's oversized insistency. Sandra smiled a smile that showed her deep satisfaction at winning the situation and watched as Frank began to make his way along the path at the side of the house, as she hurried behind him like a home-bound duckling.

Screams filled their ears as they neared the rows of Hazel trees that surrounded Aveline's cottage like a moat protecting a castle. Chloe could feel the sensation of hands desperately trying to pull her back, as though hell itself was behind her. She watched as Aveline stooped quickly to the ground, grabbing at plants as she began to call out words in a language that Chloe did not understand, before turning abruptly and throwing them into the air. The tormented screaming stopped, "Hurry child!" Aveline said with urgency as she grabbed Chloe by the hand and gestured for her help to reach the small cottage door.

"Hello?" Frank called out as he looked around the side of Millhouse, his every move being scrutinised by Liam as he remained out of sight. "I'm telling you there's no one here, Sandra, except for us silly sods!"

*Go to them!* Liam heard whispered with a vengeance as he nodded to the voice in his head.

"Can I help you both?" he asked suspiciously as he made his presence known, calmly walking from the side of the outbuilding, the axe still held low by his side.

"Chloe, we're looking for Chloe, I'm a good friend of hers and, well I.." Sandra was about to finish when Frank interrupted her, much to her disapproval as she detested interruption in any form.

"We need to see her about the invoice for the work Liam, she told me that you were busy and that she could complete the paperwork," Frank lied as he smiled convincingly at Liam. He waited as Liam seemed to be troubled, as though he had a problem recalling who the man talking to him actually was!

"Chloe's not here sorry, she's away visiting at the moment," Liam replied dispassionately with a sickly smile as he gripped the handle of the axe tightly with his hand, his knuckles whitening with the tension.

"Oh, that's a shame, has she gone anywhere nice?" Frank inquired suspiciously as he watched the frustration building in the muscles of Liam's forearm as he gripped the axe tighter.

"It's a family thing, she has gone to see her mother, poor Chloe's been suffering with her mental health just recently and we thought the change of scenery would do her good," Liam replied in the same unemotional manner as he looked Sandra up and down.

*The bitch has escaped! get rid of the meddlers!* Liam heard Eleanor whisper in his ear,

"Well, I'm sorry that you missed Chloe, I will happily settle the outstanding amount now if you would like to follow me inside," Liam suggested, as he swung the axe up onto his shoulder and beckoned for them both to accompany him. Hesitantly they did as he had instructed and waited in the quietness of the kitchen while Liam went to fetch his chequebook. Sandra watched as he disappeared along the hallway,

"What are you doing?" Frank whispered as he stood observing the rounded figure of his wife as she quickly began to open the drawers of the kitchen cupboards, looking at the contents before hurriedly moving on to the next.

"Something is not right Frank!" she whispered back, just as Liam returned unannounced into the kitchen, the axe swinging slowly by his side. Carefully Sandra moved in front of the still-open drawer of the kitchen cupboard, closing it gently with the bottom of her back as she leaned against the worktop.

Liam said nothing as he placed the shining head of the freshly sharpened axe down onto the surface of the kitchen island, before opening his chequebook and looking directly at Frank impatiently. Sandra could sense *her* presence as she watched Liam fill out the cheque. She looked at the axe resting on the wooden surface as a feeling of dread swept through her, what if the unthinkable had happened to Chloe?

"Nice isn't it!" Liam said abruptly as he noticed Sandra's fixated gaze, catching her completely off guard with his sudden outburst. Sandra uttered not a word, as she stood nervously nodding in reply.

Tearing the cheque from the book, Liam uncaringly handed it over to Frank as he made his way back to the kitchen island. "Well, I'm sure you both have better things to do with your time," he stated as he placed his hand on the shaft of the axe.

"Er, Yes, thank you for your time Liam, be sure to give our regards to your wife when you see her next," Frank replied quickly as he gestured for Sandra to join him as he made his way to the door of the kitchen. "That's some bonfire your building there!" Frank stated as he looked at the sheer size of the stack of wood standing in the back garden.

"Yes, it's a surprise for when Chloe returns, I know how much she likes a good fire!" Liam grinned sinisterly as he ran his finger along the sharpened edge of the blade.

In the small room of the cottage, Chloe sat on the edge of the bed watching as Aveline busied herself with the mixing of various herbs in an earthenware bowl. "What you did was very brave, foolish, but brave nonetheless," Aveline smiled as she turned to where Chloe was resting.

"Are we safe?" Chloe asked nervously as she studied the

actions of Aveline's frail hands.

"For now, child, yes," Aveline replied reassuringly, "Here, you must wear this at all times," she continued to say as she walked across the room and tied a small pouch hung from a black ribbon around Chloe's neck.

"What is this?" Chloe inquired curiously as she held the small hessian bag between her fingers, the strong scent of its contents filling her nostrils. Aveline's lips turned upwards as she smiled a smile aged through time,

"Your only chance of protection child, for now, it is all that you have to defend yourself against her, she will stop at nothing to take control!"

"But Aveline, I've seen what she can do. How is a bag of," she paused briefly to sniff the pouch, "Whatever this is, going to protect me against her?"

"Patience child, all will be revealed as you learn," Aveline replied calmly as she placed a small, blackened kettle to boil over the crackling fire in the hearth.

*Learn? Learn what? There, she was again with her cryptic answers!* Chloe thought to herself as Aveline rested herself down on a chair in front of the fireplace.

Frank sat staring at the cheque in his hands, how could Liam have possibly just forgotten who he was, when everything on the cheque had been completed correctly? It just didn't make sense, why would he create such a lie concerning Chloe's mother? "Frank, I think we had better call the police!" Sandra expressed with an edge of nervousness in her voice, as she thought about what they had witnessed earlier at Millhouse. Placing the cheque down he looked up to see Sandra holding out a mobile phone,

"It's Chloe's!" she said alarmingly as a look of trepidation flooded her face.

"How can you be so sure?" Frank asked, studying the small black handset. Sandra didn't reply, instead, she turned the screen to face him and waited while he observed the evidence for himself.

"You see, the messages that I sent, Frank I have a horrible feeling about this!" Sandra continued, the same look of dread emanating from her eyes.

"I'm not too sure about all of this, I admit he was acting strange but murdering his wife, well that's a bit much Sandra!"

"Frank the ghost, she was there at the house I could sense her! It was as though she was controlling him," Sandra replied anxiously. Placing the phone down on the small side table she quickly headed up the stairs to consult the words of Edward Worthing.

Mist began to creep around the valley floor, covering all traces of life as it slowly blurred everything from sight. Only the naked outlines of the trees that stretched upwards towards the sky were saved from being devoured in its indistinct smog like wake. Everywhere lay silent, even the constant moving of the river seemed hushed by the denseness of the fog, as the death like figure of Eleanor slowly made her way between the trees. "Have I not suffered enough, must I always remain trapped within this tortured body? She mumbled mournfully to herself as she wept.

It didn't seem right to be thinking of food when Chloe could be somewhere suffering, or worse, dead! But Frank insisted that no one would be saved if they starved to death, forcing Sandra to eventually agree as she listened to the rumbling sounds coming from her stomach. Opening the oven door, she carefully placed the chicken onto the rack to cook as she set about preparing the vegetables.

Aveline gasped as she held her chest tightly, her silhouette illuminated by the bright glowing flames that licked and curled in the fireplace. "Aveline, what is it? Are you ill?" Chloe asked, her voice full of concern as she watched the actions of the frail woman in front of her.

"No child, not ill," Aveline replied sadly as she gazed into the fire. "I felt the desperation of another's soul cry out from the darkness as they left this plane." Chloe stood and made her way over to the bowed head of Aveline, placing an arm gently around her shoulders to offer comfort as she silently sobbed in the candle lit room of the cottage.

Frank waited at the table in the dining room as the smell of a roast dinner wafted in from the kitchen. His thoughts concerning the richness of the gravy, as he poured it generously over the contents of his plate, were squashed dramatically by the sounds of Sandra screaming hysterically from the kitchen. Throwing his chair back he stood and rushed to the aide of his now distraught wife, who stood looking down at the roasting dish in front of her. "Sandra, what is it, did you burn yourself?" he asked as he made his way to her side.

"LOOK!" She screamed as she forced Frank's attention

to the dish lying on the kitchen floor.

Frank looked down, he covered his mouth to stop himself from vomiting as his eyes met the gruesome contents of the roasting dish. There on the floor, the chicken that Sandra had so lovingly placed in the oven earlier had changed, now replaced by something so sickening that they both covered their eyes to shield themselves from the horror.

Frank led Sandra away to the sanctuary of the lounge, before returning to the kitchen to remove the mess. From her armchair, she could hear him gagging as he placed the roasted body of the cat into a black sack. Tying the handles of the bag securely he unlocked the back door of the house before lowering the charred feline remains down into the darkness of the dustbin.

# Chapter Seventeen

The door to the outbuilding swung open violently as Liam appeared from inside wiping his blood-stained hands on a rag as the axe rested on the floor by his feet. Turning the key in the padlock he secured the building before making his way back to the rear of Millhouse.

"It is done," he declared without emotion as he slumped down into the armchair and stared at the cold ashes of the unlit fire in the hearth. From the corner of the room, Eleanor stood smiling as she looked at the pathetic image of a man sitting in front of her, who it would seem at that point was prepared to do anything that she asked. Hissing she made her way towards him, the black mist wrapping itself around her body.

"And did thee do as I commanded?" she asked as Liam looked up at her with shallow eyes and nodded deliberately.

"Yes," he replied calmly, "It's in the outbuilding, go and see for yourself if you don't believe me!" he sneered sarcastically.

Eleanor raised her hand forcing the axe to levitate in the air, before sending it sideways towards him, the edge of the blade resting on the bare skin of his neck as he sat perfectly still with fear. "DO NOT MOCK ME!" she screamed, as the coldness of the blade dug deeper into his skin. Liam could feel blood slowly start to trickle down his chest as Eleanor retained the axe's position, she watched through eyes of death the fear building inside of him, as though taunting Liam with the very closure of his life itself.

He exhaled loudly as the axe floated backwards gradually towards the shadowy form of Eleanor, who toyed with it inauspiciously for a moment before releasing her inanimate hold on the handle and sending it down hard on the floor of the lounge. "Tomorrow you must seek out the hoarder, he has things that are mine," Eleanor ordered sinisterly, "But for now ye must sleep!" she said in a mesmerizing tone as Liam closed his eyes.

Sandra could not sleep, much to the relief of Frank who sat bolt upright in bed trying to get things straight in his mind. How could someone have just entered the house without them knowing and switched the chicken for a cat? He knew deep down inside that the whole pattern of events was not caused by something of this realm, and as much as he had tried to convince himself and Sandra otherwise it was apparent that they were dealing with something of a supernatural nature. His usual rationality had been turned completely on its head, leaving him at a complete loss as to what they should do next. He looked to his left and watched as Sandra sat studying the contents of the book, her eyes intently following the text on the pages before continuing to the next.

*Transmutation.*

*The action of changing or the state of being changed into another form.*

*In my research, I have experienced the act of*

*Transmutation before my very eyes, as I witnessed the spiritual form of a female child entering the body of another living soul.*

*Of course, at the time my findings were seen by others as the ramblings of a madman, indeed my sanity was examined by my peers, as they questioned how it could ever be possible. But even to this day, I retain my honesty in what I observed, the account of which I have included below.*

Sandra paused for a moment to take down notes on what she had read, as Frank watched on confused as to why the old book was so important to her.

*March 14th, 1878.*

*My daughter Nell seems more and more troubled by her nighttime visitor, so much so that I now maintain a constant vigil over her as she sleeps.*

*What started as small tapping sounds and strange odours, (their origins which I note are still yet to be discovered) have now developed into objects seemingly moving of their own free will. Only today I have observed the movement of a candlestick complete with candle move a staggering six inches across my dining room table. It would appear that the spirit's restless necessity to communicate has now become somewhat more urgent.*

*March 21st, 1878.*

*For the past week, Nell has become more restless, her*

*mumbling now constant as she sleeps. I have found myself locked in a ceaseless battle to protect her from the entity that haunts the small child's dreams, will I ever help her to be free?*

Aveline watched as Chloe lay peacefully in her slumber, seemingly untroubled by the events surrounding not only Millhouse but her own fractured mind, her only true companion through all of the madness held tightly in her arms. She sighed to herself as she thought about the path that lay ahead, a path that over the years she had walked many times before.

2:07 a.m. Eleanor moved silently through the house humming the same haunting tune. In the kitchen, she stood completely still, her spirit-like form still filled with the anguish she had carried throughout the centuries, as she stared at the key hanging on the wall. Lifting her hand, Eleanor slowly began to move the key from side to side with the pointed nail of her outstretched finger as the words of the tune fell from her cold death-like lips.

"I have a deadly nightshade, so twisted its stems do grow. With berries black like midnight and a skull as white as snow," She sang over and over again as her finger constantly played with the position of the key. Thoughts raced through her head as she swung the key faster, each turn filled more and more with the despair she felt inside. Until seemingly in a moment of rage her hand snatched the key from the hook sending it flying through the air and landing with a clank on the stone floor.

Chloe gasped as she opened her eyes, "I saw her again, just as before crying at the side of a road."

Aveline placed the small wooden tiles down on the table and looked at the troubled candle-lit face of Chloe, as she slowly swung her legs out of the bed. "Except this time, she.."

"She spoke to you as though she was a child?" Aveline asked abruptly as she returned her gaze to the intricately carved symbols laid out on the table in front of her.

"Yes, how did you know? Did I call out in my sleep?" Chloe asked as she rubbed her eyes and made her way sleepily over to Aveline.

"No child, the runes spoke to me, they told me of her desperation to connect with your past," Aveline replied as she pulled out a small stool from under the table and gestured by patting it for Chloe to sit.

Chloe took her position cautiously as she lowered herself down onto the narrow wooden top of the stool, where she sat, her knees folded up uncomfortably like a giant attending a tea party laid out by the little people. Aveline chuckled as she observed Chloe's awkward position at the table, causing her to try even harder not to fidget as the wood creaked beneath her.

"These are beautiful!" Chloe stated as she gazed longingly at the small pictures carved into the surfaces of the wood, "What do they mean?"

Aveline carefully gathered them together in her hands before slowly passing them across the table. Chloe let out a small but nervous laugh as the energy contained within the runes tingled through her hands.

"What you hold there child are messengers," Aveline

pointed out with a deep sense of affection resounding in her voice. Chloe looked at her hands and then at Aveline,

"Messengers?"

"Yes child, ancient wisdom passed down through the ages, they see and hear all that has passed and," Aveline paused as she placed her hands around Chloe's, "What has yet to come." Chloe opened her hands and looked with uncertainty at the runes,

"And what do they say, you know, about what's to come?" she asked nervously. Aveline smiled a smile filled with inner knowledge as she closed Chloe's hands together,

"They say child, that for you to complete your journey and be free of all this misery you must look deep inside your heart. Only when you can look upon yourself without illusions as to who you truly are will you win."

"But you said you knew about her talking to me as a child, how?" Chloe asked as she carefully placed the runes back down onto the surface of the table. Aveline sighed as she held them for a moment before placing them into a small leather drawstring bag.

"That child when you are ready is something that you must answer for yourself. I can only guide you so far along your path, the remainder of the way will be solely of your own doing."

"So, Aveline, when do I start?" Chloe asked as she watched the frail form of the woman make her way over to the fire.

"You already have child, you already have!" she replied as her crooked form bent forward and placed a log on top of the glowing embers, watching intently as the flames surged energetically around it.

The Sun rose lazily in the morning sky, it was three weeks until Christmas and the whole of the valley floor was covered with a thick blanket of frost. A robin flicked meticulously through the piles of discarded leaves, whose hues of brown and orange shone like gold against the whiteness of the ground on which they lay, as it searched for sustenance in the form of an unsuspecting grub.

The metal gate of Millhouse shook as Liam closed it violently behind him, sending the poor defenceless bird fluttering to the safety of the porch roof as it watched the bedraggled figure make its way gradually from the house. From her position at the studio window, Eleanor watched as Liam disappeared from view, her spectral breath fogging the glass. In her hands she pulled and twisted at a length of green cord, constantly shortening it as she created knot after knot, all the time whispering her malicious words filled with intent.

Frank made his way around the bed and looked at the blue shabby cover of the book resting on Sandra's bedside table. Opening it he glanced at the pages filled with words and sketch-like drawings of tortured souls. He continued to turn the pages until he arrived at the point of Sandra's reading so far, marked clearly with a strip of card decorated with colourful birds. He scratched his chin as he slowly sat on the edge of the bed, the book now cradled in his hands as he read the words from the page.

*March 25th, 1878.*

*Nell has now lost any sense of self-control.*

*I write as I sit helplessly watching her as she screams and curses from her bed. The doctor has recommended that for her safety Nell should, at least for the time be placed somewhere secure, a recommendation I might add that I have no wish to allow to happen now, nor in the future.*

"Frank, your coffee is getting cold," Sandra called from the bottom of the staircase, "What's he doing now?" she mumbled to herself as she made her way back into the dining room. Frank replaced the bookmark on the page and closed the cover of the book, he felt compelled to continue but the insistency of Sandra's calling made him think otherwise as he made his way downstairs. "What were you doing up there?" she asked as he made his way into the room and sat at the table. "Frank!" she said with more force in her voice as she noticed his mind seemed elsewhere engaged.

"Sorry love," he replied as Sandra's tone broke him away from his thoughts, "The book, do you think that it's real?"

"Oh, that's what you were doing up there," Sandra sighed, "Yes Frank I do, and I believe that Edward Worthing might just have the answer to solving the problem at Millhouse!" she stated in a very matter-of-factly kind of way as she sipped slowly at her mug of coffee. Frank stood up quickly and made his way back out of the room. Sandra listened as his footsteps thumped down heavily as he climbed the stairs, only for him to return a few moments later carrying the book which he placed down urgently on the table in front of her.

"Then for god's sake Sandra find it and do it quick!" he stated without hesitation as he pointed to the worn out cover.

Old Mr Simpson blew on his hands as he tried to warm them against the cold icy air, business was always quieter at this time of the year, but just like the winters that had passed before he opened the yard anyway, seeing it more as an opportunity to socialise than a way of earning money. His wife Mary had passed away more than twenty years ago, and although the yard offered him financial stability in these his waning years, he now lacked any form of personal company to while away the lonely existence of his remaining life.

From the far end of the yard, Liam watched the aged man make his way to the small office at the front of the buildings. He waited until he saw the grey smoke from the chimney signalling that he was settled in front of the wood burner, before hurrying within the shadows of the barns to the small doorway. Old Mr Simpson sat in an old oak chair placed in front of the glowing fire that was burning inside the stove. Liam could hear the classical music playing on the small transistor radio that was positioned on the window sill as the old man hummed along. He needed to be quick, any form of hesitation could create a problem, and there had to be no sign of an obvious struggle. The rounded brass door handle turned stubbornly in Liam's hand as he opened the door slowly, the music on the radio deadening the sound of the hinges as they groaned under the load. Old Mr Simpson still sat facing the flames of the fire, seemingly unaware of the fate that stood only a few feet away. Reaching into the pocket of his jacket Liam produced a thick length of wire, which he wrapped tightly around his hands as he crept ever closer to where the old man rested. A floorboard creaked loudly below his foot causing Liam to stop dead in his tracks as he watched the old man sit forward in his chair and begin to turn his head slowly.

"Hello, how can I be of assistance on this fine winter's morning?" Old Mr Simpson asked as he shuffled awkwardly in the chair to stand. Liam remained silent as he watched the aged figure slowly climb to his feet. Their eyes met as he steadied himself against the back of the chair, "Take it, take it all!" he stated nervously as he saw Liam standing menacingly in front of him, the wire being pulled aggressively as he grinned. "Please I beg you, I am but a frail old man," Old Mr Simpson pleaded as Liam made his way towards him, raising the wire to the height of the old man's neck. He tried to call for help, but his cries were drowned out by the music as Liam turned the volume of the radio to the maximum.

"Now be a good chap and make this easy on yourself!" Liam said with a smile as he grabbed the old man by his worn-out jacket and began to casually wind the wire around his neck. Old Mr Simpson fought for his life as he frantically lashed out at his assailant. "Steady Grandad you might hurt yourself!" Liam stated calmly as he leisurely overpowered him.

From the studio window, Eleanor laughed as she tied the final knot in the cord, pulling it sharply between her hands and locking the knots together.

Liam watched as the life drained away from Old Mr Simpson's bulging eyes as he gasped for his last remaining seconds of breath. His face reddened from the pressure of the wire as Liam casually stood strangling him, "I do like a good requiem, don't you?" Liam asked as he listened to the mournful music being played on the radio. Loosening his grip the old man fell to the floor in a heap, lifeless he lay beside the old oak chair where he had sat only moments before.

Pulling the door shut tightly behind him Liam made his way to where Old Mr Simpson's car was parked. Climbing into the driver's seat he placed the ignition key which he had found conveniently positioned on the desk in the office into the ignition and drove the car slowly into the main furniture barn.

His actions were cold and calculated as he purposely carried the body of the old man out to the waiting car, where he placed it into the boot, the radio still playing as Liam walked around the barn emptying the contents of the petrol can that in Liam's mind, Mr Simpson had ever so thoughtfully decided to carry in the back of his car.

"Boom!" Liam said as he watched the unfolding events take place as the car exploded inside the barn sending a fireball that ignited the petrol-soaked stock immediately. The shockwave rocked the ground as building after building caught fire. Liam waited, hidden from view as the sound of sirens drew ever closer until he spied his chance and fled the scene, hurrying through fields until he reached where he had hidden Chloe's car down a secluded lane.

# Chapter Eighteen

"Anything interesting?" Chloe enquired as she watched Aveline staring into the flames of the fire.

"Interesting, yes very interesting indeed child. It would appear that Eleanor has lost something most dear to her," Aveline replied, her gaze still fixated on the flickering glow of the flames. Chloe moved forward cautiously as she tried to understand what on earth the old lady was talking about this time. She looked longingly into the flames, but all that she could see was fire, no visions of lost property, just fire.

"What is it? What can you see?" Chloe asked impatiently, causing Aveline to look around sharply as she tutted.

"You are blinded by your rationality, allowing you only to see what your eyes show you. Here, place this onto the flames child," Aveline replied as she handed Chloe a small bag. Carefully she opened it and sprinkled the contents over the flames, jumping back instantly as the fire flared up in the hearth. "Watch!" Aveline whispered as the flames began to part revealing a grey mist in the centre. Chloe watched on in awe as the mist started to reveal an image,

"The necklace?" Chloe asked as the image in the fire showed Eleanor rubbing her neck frantically before dropping to her knees and searching the ground around her in desperation.

"Yes child, the necklace is of great importance to her, she needs it to be complete," Aveline explained as the fire returned to normal. Chloe stood back as she watched the flames entwine.

"I have seen great sadness connected to the pendant since it was taken from her, no good will ever come to one who wears it, only misery," Aveline continued as a sombre look washed over her face.

"Aveline, I know the pendant it was in a load of old stuff that I bought from Simpson's place, I was going to keep it myself but..." Chloe paused as she thought back to that day.

"But what?" the old woman asked,

"But I gave it away, as a Birthday present. Liam's mother had come to stay and what with my dislike for the woman I completely forgot about buying her a gift." Chloe replied awkwardly as she thought about the pendant and what she had done.

"Oh child, the mother, we need to find her and take the pendant back, already many have suffered in her pursuit of the cursed thing. Even as we speak her son is acting out Eleanor's wishes in the wickedest of ways, this is why she manifested at your home child, because you had the pendant, the missing link!"

"Well, malevolent spirit or not I can tell you now she's got her work cut out dealing with Jennifer, her face could crack plaster!" Chloe laughed as she thought about the hard-faced woman and how cutting she could be.

"This is not something that should be laughed about!" Aveline snapped, as her face changed to one displaying her utter seriousness regarding the matter. "If Eleanor takes the pendant before everything is in place then she will grow strong, and if that happens child, then you will never be free, and that is if you live to regret it!" Aveline continued in a hushed sinister tone, causing Chloe to gasp with fear.

Frank closed the van door and stood opposite the town hall with a look of uncertainty on his face. "I'm not too sure about this love. I mean you read about these types of things being full of crooks."

Sandra sighed, linking his arm she directed him to the large queue gathering on the pavement outside the hall. As they waited in line for the doors to open she glanced up and down at the many people all hoping to have a message relayed from beyond the grave. Frank however was more interested in the condition of the masonry, as he thought to himself how much repair work the old hall needed. At 7:30 prompt the doors swung open, and the long line of anxious faces began to file inside, Sandra and Frank included. Taking their seats, they waited for the show to commence, conversations from the audience filling the air as they gossiped amongst themselves, before falling silent as the medium walked out onto the stage from behind the red velvet curtains.

"Here we go," Frank muttered sarcastically under his breath, causing the woman to his left dressed in a bright blue dress to huff at his remark, Sandra nudged him to be quiet as she sat quietly to his right listening as the well-presented man on the stage scanned the audience looking for someone with a connection to the name Rita. Of course, every time his association was correct, the people in the hall all seemingly knew at least one of the names of the deceased that he supposedly connected with as the evening continued. By 8:15 Frank had had enough, whispering to Sandra he stood up and slowly made his way along the row of seats, apologising to the people as they tried to make enough room for him to pass. Reaching the central aisle of the hall, Frank stopped as the medium called out to him,

"You sir, the man walking to the back of the hall."

Frank turned hesitantly on the spot as the medium stood on the stage pointing in his direction, "Me?" Frank asked as he pointed to himself, the hushed audience now staring directly at him.

"Yes sir, you!" the medium replied as he spoke loudly into the microphone he was holding in his fake tanned hand. "Please join me here on the stage."

Frank tried to refuse, pointing to the rear of the hall in a vain attempt to show his urgency for the bathroom, but it was too late, the medium had already created a ripple of applause from the eagerly watching people as they encouraged him to walk forward. Sandra mouthed 'That's my husband' to anyone who looked in her direction as she watched Frank climbing the steps to the stage. The medium took no time at all in dealing with the pleasantries as Frank awkwardly made his way to his side, where he stood shielding his eyes from the brightness of the lights shining down on him. "I have someone here who wishes to speak to you Frank," the medium stated confidently.

"Oh right," Frank replied chuckling as he thought about how stupid he must look in front of all the people who sat clinging on to the mediums every word.

"He says his name is Ted,"

Frank stopped laughing and looked at the medium as he thought back to the visitation in his kitchen.

"From the look on your face Frank I would hazard a guess that you two know each other, am I correct in my thinking?"

Frank nodded his head, "Yes I know him alright, hello Ted,"

The medium closed his eyes, Frank watched as the lights on the stage lowered to a dull hue while the hall fell deadly silent. After what felt like forever he opened his eyes and began to speak, but not as he had previously, now his voice resounded in the familiar tones of Ted. "She's coming for you Frank!" the medium whispered disquietly as he stood in a trance-like state, forcing the audience to gasp loudly.

"Who? Who's coming for me, Ted?" Frank's words trembled as he quizzed the voice from beyond the grave.

"I who walks the paths, I wants thee!" the medium hissed menacingly. Frank jumped back as the microphone in the mediums outstretched hand started to crackle and pop loudly, the speakers of the PA system in the hall distorting with the feedback being created, causing the members of the audience to cover their ears as the squealing from the speakers became more intense.

"FRANK!" Sandra screamed as she watched the microphone explode into an array of flashing electrical sparks. Standing quickly, she tried to make her way to the stage, but her path was blocked by the people around her, who nervously stood covering their gaping mouths with shaking hands as they witnessed the unfolding event. The smoke from the electrical discharge of the microphone encircled the petrified face and body of the medium who was now well and truly back in the land of the living. Throwing the charred remains of the microphone onto the wooden boards of the stage, he screamed like a frightened child, his wide fear-filled eyes staring at the blackened skin of his hand. Frank watched as the mist spun up into the air, breaking contact with the shaking medium's body and flying low over the now hysterical crowd that fought desperately to leave the building.

"SANDRA, OVER HERE!" Frank shouted over the screams and cries of the panicking mass of people as he rushed urgently to reach her. The swirling black mist twisted violently as it made its way over the screaming heads of the audience as they pushed and jostled each other. At the rear of the now fast-clearing hall, the woman in the bright blue dress stood completely alone and defenceless as the mist rushed towards her. Opening her red-painted lips, she tried to muster a scream, but the fear of the situation rendered her silent, as the mist entered her mouth.

"Quick, we need to get out of here!" Frank insisted urgently as he led Sandra to the exit, the woman in the bright blue dress now following in hot pursuit as she licked her lips. "Bloody hell!" he called out in a state of shock as the woman leapt on top of him, covering his face in thick patches of red lipstick as she wildly kissed him.

"SORRY LOVE, NOT ON MY WATCH YOU DON'T!" Sandra roared as she jumped at the woman still clinging to Frank. Tightening her grip around the strap of the handbag she was holding, Sandra swung it forcibly in the woman's direction cleanly hitting her in the side of the face. The ferocity with which she launched her attack sent the woman flying dramatically in the air and landing in a confused state as she lay dazed on her back. Once in the safety of the van they sat silently reflecting on what exactly had just happened. As they slowly drove away, the medium, followed closely by the bedraggled figure of the woman in blue appeared on the steps of the town hall.

"WAIT!" he called out as he noticed the occupants of the leaving vehicle.

"Keep driving!" Sandra cried out as the medium rushed down the steps and out into the road running quickly behind the van like a dog on a rampage. Frank looked in the mirror at the red-faced medium who was rapidly losing momentum, his pace slowing to that of a jog. "Frank, what are you doing? Have you gone mad, Why are you stopping?" Sandra asked frantically as she thought about the possibility of the phantom reappearing at any second.

"I can't just leave him," Frank replied heroically, as he pulled over at the side of the road and waited for the now breathless medium to catch them up.

"That thing, in there," the medium panted as he reached the side of the van and stood pointing at the entrance of the town hall, "What was it?"

"Well, not very nice as I'm sure you realised," Sandra replied apprehensively, as she quickly locked the door of the van as a precaution. The medium looked around nervously before placing his hand into the pocket of his crumpled jacket and pulling out a calling card, which he passed through the small opening of the passenger window to Sandra's waiting hand.

"Please, call me, I need to discuss what just happened, never before have I witnessed something so powerful. Believe me, Frank wasn't it? With the connection your friend has to the other world and my reputation, we could be huge!"

"Huge? You're not suggesting that we profit from this?" Sandra gasped, shocked by the proposition as she looked at the orange-tanned complexion of the medium through the window.

"Think about it! My name is Brian, call me!"

"Drive!" Sandra huffed as she looked over to Frank, "Now!"

They pulled away at speed leaving Brian (the medium) at the side of the road. "The Phoenix!" Sandra laughed as she read from the small card in her hand, causing Frank to shake his head in utter disbelief, "The Phoenix! I mean it's ridiculous, his name is Brian, and he has a fake tan!"

"Sandra love, in there tonight, Ted said she was coming for me. If I'm, to be honest with you, I'm a tad bit scared," Frank stated as he thought about the spirits chilling words.

"Frank nothing bad is going to happen to you as long as I

draw breath, but we do have to revisit Millhouse," Sandra stated harshly as she waited for her husband's reaction.

"But Chloe isn't there, we saw for ourselves that Liam is at the house alone."

"No, we saw nothing except what he wanted us to see. Frank, I know that it's probably not the wisest of suggestions but, we need to find her, whatever the outcome is. Certain things about the place seem odd, her ragdoll was gone, and it always sits in the same place. And.." Sandra hesitated.

"And what?" Frank asked quickly.

"And the bowl, on the island in the kitchen," She replied,

"What? Bloody hell, the Riddler has nothing on you!"

Sandra tutted loudly, "The bowl is where Chloe keeps her car and house keys."

"So, what's so unusual about that?" Frank asked in a confused manner as he scratched his head.

"Well, the keys to the car were gone, yet the car was still there. Why would she take the keys to a car that she never intended to use? And why, if she has gone to stay with her mother, who I might add is dead, did she not drive there herself?

"Christ, that's a serious nose you've got for sticking in other people's business, where did you learn that, at the Wellton school of gossiping?" Frank laughed.

"Then there's the small detail of her mobile phone, which apparently she left behind!" Sandra recounted as the smile dropped away from Frank's mouth.

"Ok, you're right, I suppose it won't hurt to just have another look around the place," he replied agreeably as he turned the van off the main road and headed in the direction of Little Lawton and Millhouse.

Frank dimmed the lights of the van as they neared the top of the track that wound down through the valley to Millhouse. "Look!" Sandra said as she spotted Chloe's car at the side of the road. "It's been moved, someone has turned the car around to face the opposite way!"

In the bedroom of a small and dingy flat, The Phoenix, or Brian as we will address him from now on, was sat on the edge of his bed looking endlessly into the small shaving mirror he held tightly between his fingers. "And will ye come when I call?" he heard the reflection ask in an ominous hissing voice.

"Yes," was his reply as he remained in the same transfixed state. From the shining surface of the glass, a mist began to gather, swirling like a maelstrom of chaos as it rose, surrounding his static body.

"You stay in the van, I won't be long," Frank said in a low tone as he unclipped his seat belt.

"What? No, I'm coming too, Frank!" Sandra insisted loudly as she watched him open the door and climb out. Frank placed his finger to his lips, gesturing for her to be quiet as he slipped away under the cover of darkness towards the front of the house. The whole place was eerily quiet as he gently lifted the old latch on the front gate and sneaked along the garden path. From the side of the window, he could see Liam asleep in an armchair of the dimly lit lounge. Making his way around the side of the house Frank checked the door of the old outbuilding, it was locked securely with the padlock. Feeling in his pocket he searched for his keyring and his spare key to the lock. Chloe and Liam had thought it was best that he had access to the building when they were in the midst of the renovations, and Frank luckily had forgotten to give it back when the work was completed.

The door creaked as it opened sluggishly, once inside Frank switched on the small flashlight on his mobile phone and scanned the interior of the building. In the corner, he could see piles of clothing and boxes, cautiously he made his way over to them. Immediately Frank recognised that everything appeared to be the property of Chloe, the usual dressing gown that she would wear every morning was now discarded across the top of the pile.

From the corner of the building, he could hear a faint scraping sound. Afraid of what might be lurking in the shadows, Frank hesitantly made his way to the door, unwilling to turn his back on whatever was making the noise he slowly retraced his steps in reverse. The sound was getting closer as he pushed his back against the door.

In the lounge, the armchair lay empty as Frank carefully began to close the door of the outbuilding. The scraping sound from inside had stopped leaving him nervously fiddling with the key as he tried to fasten the padlock. From behind a shadowy figure made its way towards him, he could sense that he was now not alone as the outstretched hands reached out to grab him. He screamed as someone took hold of his arm, the fingers clutching the sleeve of his shirt tightly as he turned to face his fate.

# Chapter Nineteen

"Bloody hell Sandra, you nearly gave me a sodding heart attack then!" He exclaimed alarmingly as he recognised the rounded shape that stood before him.

"Well, you were gone a while and I got scared, so I thought I had better come and find you!" Sandra replied defensively as she watched Frank return to the locking of the door. From the rear of the house, they could see light, followed by the sound of footsteps making their way towards them.

"Come on, we had better go I'll tell you what I found out when we have put some distance between us and this place. Frank said as he quickly ushered Sandra in the direction of the waiting van. From the side of the house, Liam watched menacingly from the shadows as the tail lights of the vehicle glowed red in the darkness of the valley as they made their escape.

"I think that we need to call the police love. From what I saw in the outbuilding there's more to this than just Chloe going away for a bit, it's like he's trying to make it look as if she was never even at Millhouse!" Frank said in a serious tone as he watched Sandra pacing up and down the kitchen.

The days passed by, shrouded in the same confusion as the police apparently found nothing amiss when they followed up on the concerns raised by Frank and Sandra.

They were informed that the story regarding Chloe was all above board, after all, Liam himself had telephoned her while the officer was at Millhouse. The police confirmed that they had spoken to Chloe and that she had assured them there was nothing to be concerned about regarding her welfare, but for Frank and Sandra things still didn't make sense.

The power that Eleanor had used to control Liam seemed to be losing its grip as he constantly battled with his thoughts and memories of Chloe. In a desperate attempt to free himself from the madness of his taunted mind, Liam found himself standing in front of the near-completed portrait of Eleanor. He had no choice, he had to break the cycle. Grabbing the edges of the canvas Liam lifted the painting high into the air, before throwing it mercilessly at the wall of the studio. From the corner of the room, the black mass of Eleanor rose up from the floor where the portrait lay. Liam covered his ears from the screams that filled the air as the phantom made her way toward him in a wrath-like rage, the razor-like tips of her fingernails clawing at his face as she grabbed him in her outstretched hands.

He tried to retaliate against Eleanor's attack, but her spectral strength overpowered him as she tore at his clothing, her fingernails ripping into his flesh with the savagery of a beast. Through twists and turns, Liam was thrown against the walls, his bruised and battered body subjected to the constant ferocity of Eleanor as she unleashed her fury upon him. The pain surged through his body as he lay defenceless on the floor, all the time watched by the cold foreboding eyes of Eleanor as she hovered above him. "Ye are like the bitch! Ye wish to be rid of me!" she growled insanely. Liam could feel himself begin to lose control of his senses as the madness of Eleanor filled his head, visions of torture and cruelty flashed before his eyes as the twisting mist flowed all around him, his mind was now not his own and his chance of escape seemingly gone forever.

"What is it, child?" Aveline asked as she studied the look of despair on Chloe's face.

"I'm not sure, it was like someone was calling my name," she replied rubbing her head to free it from the confusion, before returning to filling the bottles with the ingredients Aveline was preparing.

"Hmm," Aveline sighed as she thought for a moment, "It would appear that your connection with those who stand on the other side of the veil is growing stronger."

"What do you mean? The veil," Chloe asked curiously,

"The place where life and death stand side by side child, a gift most precious to have."

"But the voice, it was Liam's. If what you say is true then that means he's dead!" Chloe sobbed as the reality of Aveline's words hit home. The old woman said nothing as she stood in her reticence, listening to the breaking of Chloe's heart as she stood beside her and wept.

"I'm going there and see if what you say is true, and if it is I swear I will tear that malevolent bitch apart!" Chloe snarled, wiping the tears defiantly from her reddened eyes.

"But this is not the way in which these matters work, patience is the key to success child!"

"Patience? I think I've been patient for far too long Aveline. No, if she wants a fight then that's what I'll give her!" Chloe stated adamantly as she slammed the small bottle in her hand down sharply.

"You cannot go there alone child, I will not allow you to put yourself in danger," Aveline demanded as she continued to grind the contents of the mortar thoroughly as she spoke. Chloe rolled her eyes as she listened to the old woman's words, it was as though she was ten again listening to the insistent words of her mother as she denied her the ability to walk alone to the small shop at the end of the street. In her heart she knew that the words Aveline had said were not the same as those that were spoken all those years ago, this was not a case of childhood demands, this was a matter of life and death.

"Then you'll come with me then?" Chloe asked as she smiled sweetly,

"Do I have a choice?" Aveline sighed as she passed another batch of the prepared ingredients to Chloe, who accepted them as she shook her head and continued to smile.

"I didn't think so," Aveline chuckled.

The telephone rang constantly in the small confines of Brian's flat, where he sat completely unresponsive to the incoming call. It was the middle of the day, but the curtains remained closed, blocking out any light from the sun as it hung low in the winter sky. "The other failed, he became weak, you must bring them!" Eleanor hissed as the telephone receiver levitated and landed in Brian's still-charred hand.

"Hello, hello?" Sandra called out as she heard the telephone being answered, "Brian, you told us to call you, at the hall, you remember."

"Yes I remember, you must meet me, today, I must know everything!" Brian quickly replied, his voice relaying the urgency.

"Today you say. I will have to check with Frank to make sure."

"It must be today, give me your address and I will come to you!" Brian insisted in a low deepening voice. Sandra stood in the hallway, the telephone receiver close to her ear as she told Brian exactly where they lived. Frank watched from the kitchen doorway as she ended the call,

"What did he say?" he asked, but there was no reply. Instead, Sandra remained in the hallway, the words of her husband seemingly going unheard. "Sandra what did he say?" he questioned again this time waving his hand in front of her face.

"I'm not sure, I feel like I have just woken up from a dream," Sandra replied hazily as she placed a hand on the wall to steady herself. Frank led the confused woman to the kitchen table where he helped her to sit, placing a cup of sweet tea in front of her Frank watched as she started to return to her usual self. "I don't know what came over me, one minute I was waiting for him to answer, the next, well that bit I'm not too sure about."

It was late afternoon. Chloe breathed in deeply as she stood in the small garden of Aveline's cottage, it was the first time in what felt like forever that she had been outside. Of course, Aveline had her reasons, good reasons, for keeping her out of sight, but the next part of Chloe's readying for what lay ahead involved facing her demons head-on. "Fresh isn't it?" Chloe heard from behind, startled, she turned to see Aveline now wrapped in her long black cloak watching from a short distance away.

"Yes, it's good to feel the coldness of the air on my face," Chloe replied smiling as she walked over to her.

"Here," Aveline said as she held out a cloak of equal blackness to hers, "You might as well look the part."

Chloe took hold of the cloak, as she examined it in her hands she could feel the energy in the material surging up her arms. "How do I look?" she asked, pulling the hood over her head, and turning slowly on the spot.

"More the part than those portrayed in stories," Aveline replied smiling, "Come, let us take in the air as we walk," she continued, holding out her arm for Chloe to take as they made their way side by side away from the cottage and down through the wood that led to the path.

Reaching the familiar old stone bridge Aveline paused for a moment. "Is there something wrong?" Chloe asked as she waited.

"You wish to ask me a question child," Aveline suggested as she rested herself on the long staff in her hand. Chloe looked back through confused eyes at how Aveline could sometimes just read her mind like an open book.

"How long have you been here Aveline? When we took over Millhouse we were told that the valley was completely uninhabited, yet.."

"Yet here I am," Aveline chuckled. "I would have thought by now that you of all people would know child, that I do not discuss my affairs with such things as local councils and their formalities." Chloe accepted Aveline's words with a look of 'fair enough' on her face as the old woman again began to walk. "I came here to wait for you, I was asked many years ago to watch, and if necessary to guide you, this is why I am here, to fulfil a promise," Aveline said as again she linked the security of Chloe's waiting arm.

"A promise, To who Aveline?"

"To your mother. Long before she became ill she would visit me, you were but a child, an innocent little soul. She would tell me stories about how talented you were, and how one day you would be famous. But she also spoke of how troubled you became after your grandfather died. How you would lock yourself away from those that loved you, tormented by the grief of the hole his passing left behind in your life."

Chloe remained silent as she listened to the revelation being retold as they walked along the bank of the river. "Over the years I worked tirelessly to help your mother, time passed, and she became ill, and sadly the visits stopped."

Chloe wiped away a tear from her eye, as the memories of a childhood that she had locked away deep inside of her came flooding back to the surface. She remembered the pain she had felt the day her grandfather lay motionless on the lounge carpet, his last breath taken while cleaning the fireplace. How all she had left was a small leather-bound book and her memories, as she watched the coffin slowly being carried to the graveside from the back seat of a funeral limousine, too afraid to stand with the others as they said their last goodbyes. The book, in which she found no comfort at all, was in her eyes unreadable, the words making no sense as she tried to follow the hastily scribbled ink on the pages. She remembered the arguments that ensued after the passing of her dear grandfather, the misery the house became filled with as night after night she would lay awake listening to the heated discussions between her parents. How one morning she walked downstairs to be met with the reddened eyes of her mother, who explained through the tears that they were now alone.

"How did my mother know you? You said that she would visit," Chloe asked as she wiped away more rogue tears from her cheeks.

"Your mother, my dear sweet friend, was a great believer in shall we say, alternative remedies. She had no time for doctors poking and prodding her, choosing more to fight her troubles with the help of me. Child, your mother knew long before she was admitted to the hospital that her time was drawing near, but she chose to stay at home with you. Of course, I could help no more when the doctors became involved in her care, until now. Now I have returned to finish that which was started many years ago, long before you were even born." Aveline replied, her voice rendered to nothing more than a whisper as she finished, her hand offering comfort as she held Chloe's arm gently.

"So that was the strange-smelling tea that she used to drink, I remember her telling me that it was not for the consumption of children, insisting that juice was so much more suitable for me than the contents of her cup," Chloe smiled as she thought about how secretive her mother was concerning the whole situation surrounding the origin of the tea. Aveline smiled at Chloe's remark regarding the aroma of the elixir as they continued along the path that led to the crossing of the river, where the willow tree still stood bowing its head.

"You spoke of the book child, do you remember what happened to it?"

"No, it just somehow became misplaced when my mother passed away," Chloe replied as she recollected the time she had spent boxing up all of her possessions. "Why? What's so important about the book, you seem very interested in it."

"We go no further than this," Aveline announced as they stood next to the crossing,

"But Liam, I need to know what has happened, how can I do that from here, Aveline I have to go inside!" Chloe insisted as she placed a foot on the stone slab that spanned the narrowed river.

"Wait!" Aveline said sternly as she grabbed the side of Chloe's cloak, holding it tight in her grasp. "There is nothing inside the house that will tell you any more than you already know, she is waiting for you to go to her, do not give her the satisfaction."

"But what if he is hurt? How can I leave him to suffer," Chloe pleaded as she tugged at the cloak to release herself from the restraint she felt from the old woman's hold.

"Child, I fear that what you heard was true," Aveline

retorted sadly as she released her fingers from the material of the cloak and watched Chloe's reaction as she looked back with dejected eyes.

From the window of the studio Eleanor stood watching as the two hooded figures made their way back along the path and out of sight. Only the portrait resting on the easel in the centre of the room broke the emptiness that surrounded her, she yearned to be free of the life she had lived before, but for that, she would need to consume the last breath drawn by Chloe and take over her human form.

Back within the sanctuary of Aveline's cottage, Chloe sat and thought about what she had resurrected, the feelings of despair were back with a vengeance as she wept by candlelight. It was as though she was reliving some kind of nightmare over and over, unable to wake herself from the vivid thoughts that raced through her head. Deep down inside she knew that Liam was gone, but the need to mourn him was missing. Strangely, the feelings she once held for him had vanished, replaced now by utter despise and regret for the times she had allowed herself to miss him while he was away. He would have gladly killed her if she hadn't escaped, and for what? The order of a ghost that's what, she knew that his allowing Eleanor to use him was really just the finale of their relationship, the rot had started to creep in long before she arrived on the scene.

Aveline appeared at her side holding something wrapped in a blue velvet cloth, "Here," she said softly as she handed the package to Chloe, who looked at Aveline and then her hands with confusion in her eyes. Placing it down on the table Chloe carefully unwrapped the velvet covering. She gasped as the cloth opened to reveal the book.

"I don't understand," she uttered, her voice quivering with shock as the tip of her finger gently traced the edge of the book's leather cover.

"Your mother. She passed the book into my care before she was taken to the hospital. It was decided that I would keep the book safe until a day such as this arose. Child, your grandfather purchased the book without knowledge of its true meaning, thinking it something of great monetary value, an heirloom so to speak. But the book was set to be cursed until the day it returned to its rightful owner, something as yet it has thankfully failed at succeeding."

"Failed at? You said it was cursed, wouldn't that mean the curse would be broken if it was returned."

"Yes, that is somewhat true. However, if it was returned then *she* would have the ability to create untold misery and suffering," Aveline replied as she slowly made her way to the boiling kettle hung over the fire.

"Wait, you said *she*, do you mean…"

"Eleanor? Yes, child you are correct, the book is indeed hers. Passed down to her just as it was to you always destined to stay in the family." Aveline continued to say as she poured the boiling water into two readied cups on the table.

"Hang on, do you mean that we are related in some way? You have got to be kidding, right?" Chloe exclaimed as she returned her astonished eyes back to the leather-bound book.

# <u>Chapter Twenty</u>

It would soon be the season to be jolly, yet neither Frank nor Sandra seemed to be in the festive mood. The lounge lay bare of any twinkling lights adorning the absent tree in the corner, as Sandra sat continuously studying the words of Edward Worthing.

*April 1ˢᵗ,1878.*

*Although today would be seen as a time for tomfoolery, I myself do not have any ambitions to play practical jokes or laugh for that matter.*

*Over the past few days, Nell's condition has become increasingly worse, so much so that now I keep a constant vigil at her bedside. Following the recommendation of the doctor I keep the bedroom door locked at all times, for both Nell's safety and the safety of the household.*

*While I attended a meeting in my study to discuss the increasing madness of my daughter, screams could be heard from above us. I rushed to her aid, the frantic pleas of the small child echoing along the corridor as I unlocked the bedroom door.*

Outside, snow had begun to fall. Not in the way of a blizzard, but enough for the ground to be coated with a white dusting of winter. From the window, Frank watched as his neighbours hurriedly unloaded their cars of festive treats and gifts, toys hidden amongst bags of less interesting purchases to evade the eyes of the excitable children as they tried desperately to take a quick peek. Life for them seemed normal as they prepared themselves for the big day, with no malevolent spirits lurking in the shadows, and no missing person to find. "Any luck?" he asked, releasing the net curtain he had been holding at the window and returning his attention to his wife who sat quietly engrossed, as she studied the book.

"The poor child. She became so ill Frank," Sandra replied sadly as she placed the book down on her lap, wiping a tear from her eye as she spoke.

Footstep after footstep remained imprinted in the snow as Brian sluggishly made his way along the pavement, completely devoid of any response to the cheery voices who called out to wish him a Merry Christmas as he passed them in the street. Pausing momentarily, he glanced at the address scribbled quickly by his hurried hand as he looked at the number of the house. With cold-ridden fingers, he placed the small, creased piece of paper back inside his pocket and lifted the latch holding the garden gate shut, before making his way towards the front door along the snow-covered path. From inside Sandra looked up nervously at the sound of knocking coming from the front door. Frank made his way back to the window and carefully drew back the net curtain once more to see who the caller might be, after all that had happened so far, the visitor could be, well anyone, alive or dead.

"It's that crackpot medium, what the bloody hell does he

want?" Frank replied as he stood peering out at the recognisable form waiting on the doorstep. Sandra didn't reply, instead, she sat seemingly fixated on an imaginary spot on the wall. "I'll go and see then shall I?" Frank asked sarcastically as he shook his head and made his way out into the hallway. "Sometimes I think she ignores me on purpose," he muttered under his breath as he grabbed the handle and pulled the front door towards him.

"Ah Frank, we meet again, may I come in?" Brian asked in a desperate manner.

"Well, it's not really a good time," Frank replied as he awkwardly tried to turn him away.

"Let the man in!" Sandra insisted as she appeared in the hallway directly behind Frank, who turned and looked at his wife. Her face still wore the same blank expression, as though her will was not her own.

"But, Sandra," Frank pleaded as he tried desperately to get her to snap out of the dazed state.

"LET HIM IN!" She said again, this time her voice raised and demanding in its nature.

"Now be a good man and do as she says!" Brian insisted in a smarmy tone as he placed a foot forward to step inside the house. Frank acted on impulse as he grabbed the handle of the door and tried to close it. Brian leapt forward, jamming himself between the door and the frame as he tried to overpower Frank and gain access to the house. "Let me in!" Brian growled as he fought to push the door out of Frank's control. The might of the builder over the stage act resulted in Frank winning the battle as Brian was gradually pushed back outside.

"What the hell is wrong with you?" Frank asked as he turned the key in the lock and faced his wife, who swayed for a moment before falling to the floor in a heap. From outside Brian banged on the door,

"Little pig, little pig please let me in!" he sneered angrily as he held the flap of the letterbox up.

"Go now before I call the police you nutter!" Frank called back to the sound of Brian laughing hysterically.

"Look outside Frank, I don't see anyone taking any notice!"

Frank made his way to the lounge window and looked at the street, still neighbours busied themselves as they unloaded their cars, none, as Brian had pointed out so eagerly were taking any notice of the banging and shouting of the menacing medium. "They cannot hear me, Frank, only you!"

"What do you want?" Frank asked nervously as he tried to help Sandra to her feet.

"You!" Brian sneered as he tried the handle of the front door, "Open up Frank, you cannot hide away forever, *she* will have you eventually! NOW OPEN THE FUCKING DOOR!"

Frank held Sandra tightly as he led her into the safety of the dining room, helping her down onto a chair he quickly made his way around the downstairs of the house turning out the lights as he went. If they had any chance of survival against the now Possessed Phoenix then the advantage would have to be solely in their favour.

Outside Brian made his way around the perimeter of the house, checking the security of the windows and doors as he went. "Frank listen, in the book Edward Worthing wrote about spirits having to be invited into a house, as long as we don't open the door we are safe!" Sandra called out into the darkness.

"Little pig, little pig, I will blow your house down if you don't let me in!" Brian laughed.

From the kitchen window, Frank could see the dark silhouette of Brian as he tried to see inside, his face lit up ominously by the flame of the lighter as he flicked it continuously in his hand. "We know your game mate, now piss off and annoy someone else!" Frank growled as his patience began to wear thin. Again, Brian laughed as he made his way to the backdoor, Frank could hear the lid of the dustbin being removed, followed by the sound of scavenging hands as they explored the contents.

"Sandra! What the bloody hell are you doing?" Frank asked desperately as he watched her walk into the kitchen and make her way over to the gas stove. From outside he could hear Brian whistling a haunting tune as he made his way back around the side of the house. The letterbox opened and the sound of newspaper rustling came from along the hallway, as Brian began to push the rolled-up headlines through the slot like a giant wick. "SANDRA PLEASE STOP!" Frank pleaded as he tried to force the hands of his wife away from the gas tap of the oven. It was useless, as the more he tried to prise her away, the stronger her vice-like grip became. Turning to face him Sandra sniggered as she began to rotate the dial, the pungent smell of the hissing gas quickly filling the air around them. From the front door, Brian paused in his actions,

"Read all about it! Couple's bodies found in massive Christmas explosion!" he called out, imitating the sound of a corner-based street seller.

"SHIT!" Frank exclaimed as he panicked as to what he should do. He had no time. Rushing along the hallway he reached the door, fuelled by his desperation he spun the key in the lock. Brian jumped back quickly as the door swung open and Frank appeared ready to fight on the doorstep. In the kitchen, the fumes of the gas slowly began to take effect as Sandra dropped to the floor, the dial still held tightly in her hand.

"You should have let me in Frank, I fear you may have killed her. Of course, there will always be the argument as to whether she did it herself, or you subjected her to the gassing. You hear about this type of thing all the time, couples spending too many years together, until POP just like that, they go crazy and kill the other,"

Still, people made their way along the snow-laden street, oblivious to the unfolding events happening on the doorstep of number 26. Frank saw red, surging forward he grappled Brian to the floor pinning him down on the garden path with his knees as he struggled beneath him. "Better hurry Frank times running out!" Brian sneered as he tried to break loose, the lighter held tightly in his hand. Sandra's eyes closed as the escaping gas made its way along the hallway, filling each and every cavity with its nauseous and deadly perfume. Frank lost all self-control as he continuously pummelled Brian with his fists, blood spilling from his face as he lay on the ground helpless to the attack. He had to finish him, he had no choice. The smell of gas had begun to make its way over the threshold of the house, its scent so strong that it seemed to taint even the crisp winter air.

In one final sadistic act, Brian released the lighter from his grasp and threw it towards the house as he laughed from his blood-sodden lips. Frank screamed out as the lighter skidded along the stone doorstep sending sparks from the flint as it went. The explosion that ensued threw Frank violently backwards into the air and down onto the snow-covered lawn as the escaping gas ignited. He sat sobbing uncontrollably as he watched the house become engulfed by the flames, the heat melting the snow around him. And yet still the people in the street continued to go about their festive duties, as a group of carol singers appeared, happily going from door to door spreading their words of joy. From his collapsed position on the grass, Frank watched as the singing congregation made their way through the gate and up to the front door of the burning house. His pleading still fell upon deaf ears, like the snow that continued to fall silently to the ground. Staggering as he stood, Frank sluggishly made his way to the group of singers gathered around the entrance to the house, he had to make them listen, he had to be heard. Taking hold of their arms he desperately clutched each one in turn trying to get them to take notice of him, his requests went unnoticed as the small congregation broke into their rendition of 'Good King Wenceslas'.

From within the flames, Frank watched in horror as the figure of a person began to make their way along the burning hallway. Screaming from the torture and the pain, the figure neared the open door, as the singers parted. Tears fell from his eyes as he watched the burning body of Sandra reach out her arms towards him. He had nothing left, everything he loved was in front of him suffering. Slowly, Frank walked to his wife's open arms, the carol still resounding in his ears as he made his way between the singers.

As he stepped onto the doorstep the figure of Sandra changed. He watched in horror as the form took the shape of Eleanor, who stood uncontrollably laughing. He could feel the closeness of the chorists as they joined together and encircled him. Spinning on the spot, Frank faced the singers in turn, madness taking over as they moved closer, edging him nearer to the gnarly waiting hands of Eleanor, who stood singing in the doorway. "I have a deadly nightshade," she began as the chorists joined in to accompany her, still moving him ever closer to the clutches of the waiting phantom. "So twisted its stems do grow," Frank covered his ears to block out the mesmerising tune. "With berries black like midnight," they continued, as the razor-like fingernails of Eleanor rested on his shoulder. The faces of the singers became clear, Frank recognising Ted and Liam instantly as they grabbed hold of his arms. Brian stepped forward joined by another who appeared to be soaking wet, "And a skull as white as sno.."

"FRANK! WAKE UP!"

He could feel himself being jostled as hands gripped his shoulders, frantically shaking him. "Where am I?" he asked in a confused state as he opened his eyes to see Sandra kneeling in front of him.

"I woke up and you weren't in bed. I came downstairs and the front door was wide open," She explained nervously, gesturing with her head to the entrance of the house. Frank looked at his surroundings, he was outside,

"But it was snowing and there were carol singers and," Frank tried to say as his thoughts became muddled.

"Come on let's get you inside, you must have been sleepwalking," Sandra stated calmly as she helped him to his feet and led him back through the open door.

"But the house, Sandra, it was on fire! There was an explosion, and you were caught up in it, and it all started with that medium turning up!" Frank urgently relayed as he looked around the still intact kitchen.

"Frank it was just a dream that's all, nothing more. Here drink this, it will help calm you down," she smiled handing him a glass of Brandy.

"But Ted and Liam were there, and *her!*" he replied sipping slowly at the warming contents of the glass. Sandra looked back at him with a concerned look on her face,

"Who Frank, who was she?"

"The woman on the road, the ghost! She was in the flames, I think she was going to kill me! You heard what Ted said at that bloody spiritual night, he said she was coming for me!"

"You're serious, aren't you? Sandra asked as she dropped down on the chair next to him. Frank nodded as he looked over the rim of the glass with panic-stricken eyes.

"We need to find Chloe quickly, Ted we know is sadly no longer with us, but Liam and the medium might be in danger, and the other man, god only knows what fate he suffered!"

"We need to trace Chloe's family it's the only chance we have to find her!" Sandra replied in an anxious voice that trembled with the uneasiness she felt inside.

Rummaging in one of the kitchen drawers Sandra returned to the table holding a notepad and pen, Frank watched as she quickly began to scribble things down onto the paper. "What are you doing?" he asked as she continued to write.

"I'm making a note of everything, just like Edward Worthing did in his book. Now the time, it was 2:07 a.m. when I woke up and found you missing, I remember because I looked at the clock on the bedside table."

Frank listened as she recited the growing list of things that may be of some importance, as he continuously backtracked through the conversations that he had, had with Chloe about her family, in a bid to find some sort of clue as to where in the country she might be. "It's no use love, Chloe told me that she had no family now, she was an only child and never mentioned her dad."

"There must be somebody Frank," Sandra insisted as she sat thinking.

Frank jumped as the silence of the kitchen was broken by Sandra speaking suddenly. "Liam's mother! She'll know Frank!"

"And how do we find her?"

"She telephoned Chloe while I was at Millhouse, I

remember how displeased she was by the call!"

"And how does that help us? Even if she did call the house there would have been more calls after that one, which means it would be impossible to trace the number by the redial button," Frank replied solemnly. Sandra huffed as she feared the realisation that they had perhaps already reached a dead-end.

"The phone, Chloe's mobile, quick where is it?"

"In the lounge, why?" Sandra asked as she watched Frank stand up quickly and leave the room, only to return moments later frantically pressing buttons on the keypad.

"Nothing! Her number, it's not on here!" Frank groaned as he slid the handset across the kitchen table, straight into the hands of Sandra, who whipped up the phone quickly in her hands and resumed the search. "I'm telling you, I've looked, none of the names say Liam's mum!"

"But this is Chloe, she has a real dislike for his mum, and I'm sure from what she told me the feeling is probably equal on both sides," Sandra replied as she studied the list of contacts on the screen.

"So, what has that got to do with it?" Frank tutted as he listened to his wife's ramblings.

"Because my dear, she would use a codename for her, like this one for instance!" She exclaimed, with a look of excitement on her face, causing Frank to lean across the table to take a closer look.

"Well! 'Bitch from hell'," Frank read out loud causing Sandra to chuckle,

"I'd say from how Chloe described her, we my love have found a match. I will give the sweet-sounding woman a call first thing in the morning!" Sandra said smiling as she closed the screen of the phone and placed it on the table smugly.

# Chapter Twenty-One

"I'm sorry Aveline but nothing that I have read so far makes any sense whatsoever," Chloe sighed as she placed the leather-covered book down on the table.

"They will child, they will," Aveline smiled, placing a reassuring hand on Chloe's shoulder.

The wind blew harshly through the trees in the valley, as winter's icy cape now lay heavily across the land. Nothing escaped the grip of the season, as light gave way to the dark side of the year.

Millhouse lay unlit and silent, the home that Chloe had loved so much was now seemingly nothing more than a relic of her past, shrouded in a dark veil of misery. Eleanor was alone, left to her own suffering as she roamed the empty rooms of the house. The discontent that she had shown towards Liam had now rendered him useless to act as her slave in the land of the living, his duties now retained permanently in the place of the dead, just like Ted and Alan. She could feel the closeness of the book, her book, but the protection surrounding Aveline's small cottage had made it impossible for her to infiltrate its perimeter.

"If I may offer a few words of wisdom,"

Chloe looked up from the pages of the book and sighed a hopeless sigh as she waited for the next instalment of riddles to begin.

"Think not what you read as just words, feel them."

"How? How do I feel words, apart from rubbing my hand on the letters!"

"By not being doubtful and sarcastic for a start!" Aveline snapped sharply, causing Chloe to look down to the floor with embarrassment at her rudeness.

"I'm sorry Aveline, I didn't mean to offend you, I can see that you are no stranger to all of this. But me, well if I'm honest I kind of find it all a bit overwhelming," Chloe replied gently, for fear of hurting the old woman's feelings any further.

"You need to open your mind and try again, your connection to the spirit of Eleanor and the book is stronger than you think. Now close your eyes, take a deep breath, and try again," Aveline explained as her voice lowered to no more than a whisper.

Chloe listened to what Aveline had advised and prepared herself to try, inhaling slowly she closed her eyes.

Eleanor felt the connection as Chloe's fingers hovered over the pages of the book as Aveline quietly watched on by her side.

They were in a clearing surrounded by thick undergrowth and trees that stretched endlessly up to the sky. In front of her, Chloe could see the book resting on a small table, its pages open. "Sister," she heard whispered as though carried on the wind, but the air around her was still, allowing the dense smell of the earth to fill her nostrils. From the other side of the clearing, Eleanor stepped forward. "Give me the book, it is mine!"

Still seated at the table in Aveline's cottage Chloe continued to turn the pages, through her fingertips she could feel the intensity of the energy growing stronger and stronger.

"Give me the book!" Eleanor demanded again as she glared impatiently at Chloe from across the clearing.

"No, sister! The book is mine!" Chloe replied as she moved cautiously towards the table.

"Be strong in your actions!" Chloe heard Aveline say from the cover of the trees as she stood opposite Eleanor.

Standing her ground Chloe continued to turn the pages of the book as the energy numbed her hand. "You are dead Eleanor, the book serves you no longer!"

"Dead? No, ye bitch! It is thee that is dead!" Eleanor hissed as she reached out to grab the book.

Aveline watched as Chloe began to shake violently, unable to assist as the battle commenced.

Words started to fall from Chloe's mouth as she stood at the table staring menacingly into the eyes of Eleanor. Over and over, she continued to say the rhyme that flowed through her head,

**'From cradle to grave, In life to death, I hold thee**

**down, 'til drawn thy last breath!'**

From behind Eleanor, figures began to move forward, Chloe watched as men grabbed at the defenceless woman, pulling, and jeering her as she screamed defiantly while they dragged her away into the trees.

Chloe opened her eyes as the clearing fell silent and the tormented soul disappeared. "Is that it? Is she gone?"

"For now, child. You have made the connection and achieved what I feared the most," Aveline replied. "Tea?" she asked, making her way to the boiling kettle hanging over the crackling fire.

"What do you mean when you say feared? Are you actually telling me that I was really in some kind of danger just now?" Chloe gasped as she thought about the possibility.

"There was a slight element of risk, but you connected and that is what is important," Chloe heard Aveline say as she poured the boiling water into the cups.

The days that followed saw Chloe constantly studying the book, all the time under the watchful eye of Aveline. Eleanor had yet to reappear from where the book had temporarily banished her, and even Chloe could now sense that time was of the essence and running out fast.

"It will soon be Yule, child, and I believe that you should return to your home sooner, rather than later," Aveline stated as she took hold of Chloe's hands and held them gently.

"But is it safe? How can you guarantee me that she won't

return?" Chloe asked nervously as she thought back to the torment she had endured at the hands of Eleanor.

"Because *we* will make sure that for the time being at least she cannot get inside, just as she cannot enter my small abode."

Chloe bit her lip as she began to worry, what if her words were wrong? What if she did manage to get through the protection, surely her life would be over! Although Aveline had never proved to be wrong regarding everything else, Chloe still worried, nonetheless, but she knew deep down inside that in reality she had no choice, she had to return to Millhouse.

The following morning Aveline's cottage was a hive of activity, as they prepared all of the things that the old woman had insisted they take to Millhouse. Closing the door securely behind them, Aveline walked around the outside of the cottage, delicately placing the mixture of herbs that had been blended, down onto the ground as she whispered her secret words. Chloe shivered as she waited in the cold morning air for her to return, the hood of her black cloak pulled up to cover her head, while the handle of the heavily laden basket hung low from her arm. She smiled as the reassuring face of Annie peeked out from the side of the cover, where she lay, secretly protecting the book from prying eyes.

"Hello, is that Mrs Stevenson?" Sandra enquired politely as the telephone call was answered. Frank listened as she recited what they had agreed to say, toning down the whole desperation of the situation in a way not to cause distress and alarm to Liam's mother. "Are you quite sure that there are no other family members?"

"No, like I have just informed you, Chloe had no other family members," Jennifer, Liam's mother replied in an assuring tone.

Frank waited impatiently to hear what had been said, as Sandra ended the call and placed the receiver back down on the polished plastic of the telephone. "Well?" he asked. Sandra waddled past him and made her way into the kitchen where she clicked the switch of the kettle to on and continued to prepare the contents of the two waiting coffee mugs. "Sandra, what did she say?"

"Just like we thought no other family, oh and she is catching the first train here in the morning. I told her that you would be more than happy to collect her from the station."

"Did she sound, you know, like how Chloe had described her?" Frank asked in a flustered manner as visions of what a 'bitch from hell' actually amounted to!" Sandra rolled her eyes and tutted at the desperation Frank was showing on his face, as she placed the steaming mug of coffee down in front of him.

From the path Chloe could see Millhouse come into view. Aveline sensed her uncertainty and held Chloe's arm tightly to reassure her that it was safe as they neared the rear of the property. The wooden pyre still stood disturbingly in the back garden, forcing Chloe to turn her head away as they walked to the door. Again, Chloe waited as Aveline made her way around the outside of the house to cast her protection down on the ground, before returning to her side and gesturing for them both to go inside. It all felt different, nothing like she imagined it would be, the whole place felt lost and abandoned as she made her way from room to room.

"We must light a fire, the house feels damp and with my ageing joints that will never do!" Aveline requested as she pointed to the ashes that lay dead in the fireplace. Chloe nodded and set about cleaning the hearth, *the last thing that she needed at this moment in time was for Aveline to come down with a cold,* she thought to herself as she set light to the neatly stacked kindling, immediately filling the room with the sound of crackling wood. "You are perfectly safe child," Aveline said reassuringly as she noticed Chloe's attention being drawn in the direction of the staircase. "The only way that Eleanor can take the book is if you give it to her, at this moment in time she needs you alive, not dead!" Chloe gulped when she heard Aveline's statement, the bluntness of her words chilling her to the core. "Come, we shall see for ourselves," Aveline insisted as she made her way into the hallway and pointed to the foot of the stairs, signalling for Chloe to take the lead.

Upstairs the atmosphere still felt the same, as though the whole place had forgotten how to be a house. Opening the door to her bedroom she sighed as she looked at the bed, her bed, still left as though she had freshly made it that morning. But there was something wrong, terribly wrong, everything was gone. The dressing table where she would sit and apply her makeup was empty, with no hairbrush or lipstick to be seen. Opening the doors of the wardrobe her suspicions were found to be correct, as the rails and shelves lay bare, someone had taken everything! Taking a deep breath to steady herself Chloe slowly opened the door to the studio, in its entirety this room was the one that scared her the most about Millhouse. Again, everything had gone, except the unfinished portrait that sat in the middle of the room. Aveline reached out and grabbed Chloe by the arm in an attempt to stop her as she rushed forward to take the canvas down from its position on the easel. "What are you doing? I need to destroy it!" Chloe demanded as her fingertips fell short of grabbing the picture as Aveline pulled her away.

"No, you do not! If you place your attention towards the image on the canvas then you are willing her to step forward. The painting for now has to stay!" Aveline replied as she lowered Chloe's arms down slowly.

"But how can I stay in a house with *that*?" Chloe huffed as she refused to say *her* name.

"That's the idea, care for it not child it cannot hurt you."

Later that evening Aveline had insisted that Chloe should connect to the elements, and so she found herself taking a long and well-deserved bubble bath, *after all, it was water* she thought. Making her way downstairs Chloe found that everywhere was illuminated by candlelight, that flickered from the windowsills where they had been placed. "We do have electricity you know," Chloe laughed as she entered the kitchen, Aveline turned and scowled from her position by the stove at Chloe's comment,

"From now on, only the flame will light this house, everything has to be as it was. Now chop those leaves, dinner is almost ready!" Chloe lifted a hand to perform a salute but quickly thought better of it as she remembered that Aveline apparently had all-seeing eyes in the back of her head.

Over the small, but palatable meal of wild mushrooms and other plants and herbs that Chloe dared not to ask about, Aveline explained what the coming weeks would entail, and what Chloe must be prepared to do. Pushing her empty plate away Chloe questioned why it would be necessary to call upon Eleanor when everything felt so peaceful. All the time Aveline listened without comment, before standing slowly and making her way over to where the book lay covered in the blue cloth. "When the time is right you will open the book and call upon her to come forward, but, only when everything is in place, do you understand?"

"No, but I'm sure I'll get the hang of it," Chloe said as she smiled a trustful smile.

The fire crackled as the logs blazed in the fireplace, Chloe felt warm inside as she looked at the face of the old woman bathed in the orange glow as she sat watching the flames. This seemingly gentle figure, who contained so much wisdom, and a deep rooted connection to her mother and the past. "Why do you cry?" Aveline asked as she remained focused on the curling flames before her. Chloe wiped away a tear as it rolled down her cheek,

"Because you truly knew my mother, and you upheld the promise that you made to her I guess," Chloe replied as she looked into the fire.

"The pain associated with a loss is a pain that can only be shared with those who understand. I have experienced that loss, many years past now child, but even to this day I still feel the pangs of pain I felt upon the death of my own dear mother." Aveline smiled back through eyes filled with empathy.

The night slipped away as Chloe slept peacefully under

the careful watch of Aveline, who sat in the armchair feeding the fire. She knew that the time was fast approaching as she followed the flame of the candle in the window, flickering as though blown by invisible lips. Chloe became restless as the minutes ticked away, the movement of time resounding from the clock hanging on the wall.

2:07 a.m. Aveline could hear the sound of metal clanging in the kitchen. Silently she made her way out and watched as the key began to swing on the hook.

In her dream, Chloe stood watching as Eleanor wept at the side of the track. She waited but the figure of her captures did not appear, nor did the flames that would usually overwhelm her. Chloe cautiously made her way forward, calmly ready to face the phantom as she walked barefoot along the stony track towards her. Eleanor turned and watched as she drew closer, holding out her arms in desperation as her cries became louder, forcing Chloe to cover her ears.

Aveline watched as the movements started to gain momentum. She turned to face the door as the key began to rattle aggressively in the lock.

"Take me home sister!" Eleanor pleaded as she reached out her hands for Chloe to take.

The noise of the keys was like heavy chains being dragged across stones as they rattled in unison. Aveline placed her hand into the pocket of her cloak and pulled out a small glass bottle. Making her way over to the pendulum-like key on the wall, she removed the stopper and waved the bottle gently in its direction.

Chloe's fingertips brushed against Eleanor's as they stood close together. From behind the spirit, Chloe could see the outline of a doorway appearing, Eleanor turned to look in its direction before beckoning for Chloe to follow her.

The swinging of the key stopped. Aveline lowered her arm and returned the stopper, before placing the bottle back carefully into the pocket of her cloak.

The doorway started to lose its shape, and the image in front of Chloe became distorted as Eleanor disappeared. She woke to find herself lying on the sofa in front of the glowing fire as Aveline re-entered the room.

"Did she show you the way?" Aveline asked softly as she made her way to Chloe's side.

"I think so, she showed me a doorway, but it disappeared."

"Yes, I made it disappear," Aveline whispered as she tapped Chloe's leg in a bid to get her to move over. "You see, it is important for you not to pass through," Aveline continued as she sat down on the sofa beside Chloe.

"Why? Why is it important?" Chloe apprehensively whispered back, as she shuffled across the cushions to give the old woman space.

"Because the door is one way I am afraid, you would be forever trapped on the other side, and that my child, would never do!"

Chloe sat in silence as she contemplated her sleep-state actions, if Aveline was correct then Eleanor was trying to lead her, but if she needed her alive why would she wish to take her through a doorway of death? "Because child, she did not think that I would stop the movement of the key," Aveline smirked as she nudged Chloe with her elbow.

"Don't you think you should knock first or something before entering my head?" Chloe laughed as she nudged the chuckling old lady back.

# Chapter Twenty-Two

12:45 p.m. Frank waited in suspense for the arriving train to stop in the small station of Wellton. Sandra had promised him that sometimes people overreact about a person's traits when they dislike them, and it was quite possible that this was more than likely the case between Chloe and Liam's mother. As she dusted the sideboard, she picked up a photograph of her beloved Frank and thought about how forthright he could sometimes be, and how that could be his downfall regarding the impending meeting with Jennifer. Placing the photograph back down she assured herself that all would be fine, wouldn't it?

The carriage doors swung open, and Frank made his way forward, trying his best to dodge the exiting passengers who seemed to act as though he was invisible. The mass of travellers dispersed leaving the station empty apart from one stern woman, who stood arguing with the guard of the train as to why she had to offload her own suitcase.

"Mrs Stevenson?" Frank asked in a polite and jolly manner as he held out his hand for her to shake. Jennifer turned her attention away from the fuming guard and faced him,

"I take it that I am being addressed by Frank?" she replied with an overexaggerated tone of snobbery. Frank smirked when he heard her voice, he had known Sandra for far too long now to know that she would never put up with someone's airs and graces, no this was going to be interesting.

"Allow me!" he said abruptly as he grabbed the handle of Jennifer's suitcase and began to make his way to the waiting van.

"Oh, I say, wait for me!" Jennifer called out as she watched the thickset man begin to disappear from the station.

"Here we are, your carriage madam!" Frank stated elaborately as he unlocked the passenger door of the builder's van.

"Oh, I say, but this is a van!" Jennifer huffed, quite clearly stating the obvious.

*No shit!* Frank thought to himself as he loaded the suitcase with force into the back of the tool-filled rear of the vehicle, before turning to face her. "I can see all that learning you did at Oxford or Cambridge has paid off!" Frank stated sarcastically. Although his bold take on humour sailed straight over the top of Jennifer's head as she replied,

"No, I studied at Leeds."

Bit by bit Eleanor dragged herself back through the darkness that had been placed around her, as Aveline's temporary banishing began to lose its power. Up ahead she could see glimmers of light sparkling like stars in the veil that hung between the realms of the living and the dead. But there was no way through. Frantically she searched for an opening, but it was to no avail, the gateway was sealed, and Eleanor was trapped back in the place of the muse's remorse.

The kitchen door opened, and Chloe watched as Aveline returned from her walk of protection around Millhouse. "Yes, you would be correct in your assumption child," Aveline muttered as she removed her cloak and hung it on a hook next to the door.

"What about freezing the balls off.." Chloe smiled as she realised that Aveline had again read her thoughts.

"A brass monkey?" Aveline asked as she chuckled.

The journey was 'interesting' to say the least, with Frank constantly trying to engage in humorous conversation and Jennifer trying her hardest to stay dignified as the van banged and bumped along the roads. "Well, here we are!" Frank announced cheerfully as they pulled up outside number 26. Jennifer looked at the house and then at Frank with a confused expression on her face,

"This is not Millhouse!"

"No love, this is my house! My wife Sandra told me to bring you here, I thought that was what you had arranged," Frank stated as he jumped out and began to fetch the suitcase from the back of the van. Awkwardly, Jennifer sat waiting for him to open the door and assist her to the pavement, but as he continued to walk to the garden gate of number 26, she realised that it wasn't going to happen. Sandra appeared at the front door nervously trying to anticipate the mood of Frank, as Jennifer elegantly walked up the garden path towards her.

"Hello, you must be Jennifer," Sandra said politely as she held out her hand, "Chloe has mentioned you on many an occasion."

"Quite," Jennifer replied snootily.

Frank sniggered as he saw Sandra's face change, "I'll put this in the spare room," Frank continued to say as he walked into the house and made his way up the stairs, the suitcase held firmly in his hand.

"Please, do come inside," Sandra said, moving her rounded frame to the side. Jennifer accepted and followed the waddling rear of her host into the lounge.

"Where are Liam and Chloe? I thought that maybe your husband had made a mistake by not taking me straight to their house, are they joining us all soon?" Jennifer asked in a confused tone as she scanned the interior of the well-presented room.

"I think that you should sit down. It must have been a long journey and what I, sorry, we have to tell you may come as a bit of a shock," Sandra replied hesitantly as she tried her best to stall the conversation while she waited for Frank to rejoin them. "Tea, coffee?" She asked quickly making her way to the kitchen.

Chloe sat cross-legged in front of the fire studying the pages of the leather-bound book, searching for the page that would rid the world of Eleanor forever.

"The door that she showed you, can you describe it to me?" Aveline asked gently as she watched Chloe's fingers tracing the words in front of her.

Chloe closed her eyes and thought about the dream, she could see the door surrounded by a haze of swirling mist. "Allow yourself to be open," Aveline whispered as Chloe drifted into a meditative state.

"I can see the door, it's just up ahead on the track, I'm alone Aveline but I feel like someone, or something is watching me,"

"Walk towards the door child, but do not enter," Aveline whispered as she studied the stillness of Chloe's body.

Chloe walked forward, as she neared the door voices started to call out from the other side, strange unfamiliar voices that pleaded to be heard. "I can hear people asking me to save them."

"You are not the one that can help them, child, call out to Eleanor."

Chloe walked closer, "Eleanor, Eleanor are you there?" Chloe asked as she stood looking at the wooden façade of the closed door.

"Yessss," was the reply, "Please sister open the door!" Eleanor pleaded.

"Do not open the door child, but step back. I am here behind you, take my hand," Aveline stated firmly, as Chloe turned and reached out. Opening her eyes Chloe inhaled deeply as she awoke from the vision, her hand still nursing the pages of the book as she looked at the welcoming face of Aveline.

"How did I do that? And more to the point why did I just go and do that?" Chloe inquired impatiently as she uncrossed her legs and closed the cover of the book with a sudden movement of her hand.

"Always, did and whys. At this moment in time, it is more important that you have the ability, than the reason behind it," Aveline said in a forthright manner, causing Chloe to scowl at the non-conclusive answer she had been given.

"Aveline I know that you are trying to help, but I need to know what all this is leading to. I feel the energy of the book, but what I sense is that Eleanor truly needs me. I feel drawn to her in some weird kind of way."

Aveline sighed as she listened to the confusion in Chloe's voice, there was still so much that she needed her to understand, but time was quickly running out. There was nothing for it, the draw of Eleanor was making Chloe eager to help her, forcing the connection between them both to grow stronger. She had to make Chloe understand, and for that, she had to tell her the truth surrounding certain areas of the story so far.

"Child, I must relieve you of your curiosity, for I fear that you will soon be misled if I choose to hold the facts to myself. Your grandfather as you know purchased the book, but his ownership of it cost him dearly. You see child, he became obsessed with solving its mystery, and this obsession guided Eleanor to the location of the book. His desire to understand led him to unknowingly call upon her spirit, thus allowing her to step through the veil. As time went on your Grandfather became taunted by her needs, he tried desperately to resist the spirit's demands but alas, when Eleanor grew tired of waiting she searched for another member of the family to take his place. Child that person was you. Your grandfather quickly became ill and passed over as sadly you are already aware." Aveline paused as she looked endearingly into the tear-filled eyes of Chloe who sat listening to Aveline's painful admittance. "The book became yours, passed down from your Grandfather, but so did the awakening of Eleanor, your grief overpowered her ability to gain access to your thoughts, she needed to be heard and that child is when she made contact with your father."

"You remember only too well the heartache and sadness that was caused by the constant rowing of your parents, as your father's mood seemed to change overnight?"

Chloe nodded as tears streamed down her reddened cheeks.

"His aggressiveness led him to leave the family home, that night would be the last time you would ever see him again, he like the many that followed taken by the wicked hand of Eleanor Hurst."

"Wait! Are you saying that that thing, killed my father, who does that remind you of?" Chloe sobbed.

"That is true in kind, you see your father became so enthralled by the spirit of Eleanor, that, he was willing to do anything for her, resulting in.." Aveline paused,

"What?" Chloe asked slowly as she fought back the tears.

"Him taking his own life, your mother told me how his car had been found in a wood, a hosepipe had been fitted to the exhaust and fed inside, where sadly they found his lifeless body."

"So, what you are saying is that he killed himself for a ghost?"

"Yes, that is what I am saying," Aveline replied with a soft tone filled with honesty. "Your mother carried on as best she could, devoting her life to you. But the book, she saw your hatred towards it. One day when you were at school she took the book from your bedroom and hid it, thinking that maybe you would go back to being the small girl she loved. But under your bed, next to the book were pictures, pictures that you had drawn. Pictures Chloe, that you had unknowingly drawn of Eleanor."

"Wait, I drew her when I was a child, I don't remember," Chloe stated as she tried to think back.

"I saw them, your mother brought them to show me, of course, they were done by the hand of a child, but the likeness was still very apparent. It was only when your mother took possession of the book that she started to become ill. She was locked in a constant battle with Eleanor as she tried to take control of her mind, but your mother was strong and defied Eleanor's attempts. When she knew that her life would soon be over, your mother gave the book to me for safekeeping, fearing that the curse would be passed onto you," Aveline replied as she stroked away the tear-soaked hair that hung down over Chloe's face.

"I'm sorry," Aveline said softly, as Chloe jumped, the caring feeling of the old woman's hands reminded her of her own mother's gentle touch when she had tried to comfort her as a child.

"It's ok, please carry on," Chloe sniffed, as she offered a

small smile.

"The book remained safe, but there were other things that Eleanor cursed that night, so long ago. One of the cursed items now hangs on the wall of your kitchen child, the key is cursed by Eleanor."

"But, I found it, outside in the garden!" Chloe stated suspiciously.

"Yes, it was placed there by the hand of one she commanded, the labourer. He was the doer of her deed, I watched from the trees as he placed the key deep into the corner of your overgrown garden, it was, after all only a matter of time until the garden was tidied, and the key was discovered."

"So, me finding the key started all of this again?" Chloe asked anxiously as she looked in the direction of the kitchen.

"Not just the key, you remember I spoke about the pendant. That which was precious to Eleanor now hangs around the neck of another, and that is why Liam I am afraid became empowered to commit the gruesome acts he was so willing to perform, Eleanor needed him to return the pendant to its rightful owner."

"If Eleanor wants to be reunited with her belongings, then why can't we just give them back to her?" Chloe suggested.

"Because as I have tried to explain if Eleanor takes possession of the book and the pendant on this side of the veil, then she will live once more, she will need a life force, and that life I am afraid will be yours, my child."

"So, how are we supposed to return the book and pendant to a spirit? Chloe asked, flustered by her confusion.

"With magic child, with magic!" Aveline stated confidently. "We must recreate that night when Eleanor was seized, and when all is in place, you child will return the book and the pendant to her, in this way, she will remain behind the veil forever and rest finally in peace."

"When, When will it happen, Aveline?" Chloe asked confidently, now fully committed to playing her role.

"That moment in time is something that you must find, I believe that Eleanor has somehow been trying to show you all along. But there is another part of the jigsaw that we must locate. You see when Eleanor begged for sanctuary that night, it was the door that blocked her way, we must find *that* door."

Chloe slumped down upon hearing Aveline's sudden spanner in the works, how was she ever going to find the exact door from centuries ago? It could be anywhere, and that was if it even still existed. But there was a problem, all the time that Aveline placed protection around the house she was safe, straying away would make her vulnerable, and then there was the matter of contacting the dreaded Jennifer! Chloe's head spun as she tried to come to terms with the revelations Aveline had told her regarding her childhood and the necessity to obtain items from history. Sensing the distress Aveline reached forward and placed her hand on Chloe's shoulder,

"I know the things I have said will have caused you to become confused, but you must understand the importance of the task ahead, failure child, is not an option."

The lounge fell silent as Jennifer absorbed what Sandra and Frank had told her, how could it be true, her son, how could he be capable of such foul acts? Surely they must be wrong, mustn't they? She had to see for herself if she was to believe that it was true. The relationship that she had shared with Chloe over the years had never been filled with respect for one another, but to think that she had been subjected to violence at his hands, made her feel sick to the core. "You mentioned a ghost, I'm sorry, but I am what you would refer to as a sceptic. I do not believe that ghosts are real, they are merely the mind playing tricks on over-excitable people."

"Suit yourself love, but you might find that you change your mind very quickly once you step foot in Millhouse" Frank announced in a straightforward tone, causing Jennifer to question his seriousness.

"That is a chance Frank, that I am willing to take. Just because the police have decided that the whole matter is nothing more than a misunderstanding regarding Chloe's whereabouts, does not mean that I will accept it too!"

"Fair enough, but don't say we didn't warn you!" Sandra huffed, as Jennifer's know-it-all attitude began to irritate her somewhat.

From her position behind the veil, Eleanor could sense the closeness of the pendant as it hung from the neck of Jennifer. It felt so close like she could just reach out and grab it, yet at the same time so far away like it had been cast over an ocean to a distant horizon.

"You will take me to Millhouse!" Jennifer demanded as she stood abruptly.

Frank smirked as he thought back about Chloe's description of Jennifer as she displayed her dominant streak,

"Now!" she reiterated in a more forceful tone, as she stood impatiently waiting by the door. Sandra shook her head in disbelief as she watched the man who usually took no-nonsense, taking barrow loads as he fetched the keys to the van.

"I'm coming too!" Sandra insisted as she waddled through into the hallway and hurriedly fastened the buttons of her overcoat as she stood waiting at the front door, much to the amusement of Jennifer who rolled her eyes at the tightness of the material that was stretched around Sandra's rounded frame.

"Wait!" Sandra said as Frank started the engine.

Opening the passenger door Sandra jumped out of the van and made her way quickly back inside the house, returning moments later clutching the old blue bound book of Edward Worthing.

"What on earth is that?" Jennifer inquired snootily as she turned her nose up in disgust at the condition the book was in.

"Priceless is what this is!" Sandra replied proudly. "Frank to Millhouse!" she continued, applying a generous amount of sarcasm as she mimicked Jennifer's poshness.

# Chapter Twenty-Three

The draw of the pendant was growing stronger as the van neared Millhouse, "Soon we will be reunited," Eleanor uttered as she watched the forming of a vision within the mists of the veil. From her place of entrapment, she could see the front of the house, shrouded by the icy chill of winter, a single flame flickered in the small window, beckoning Eleanor to look closer.

"I must return to my home. The protection that I have placed around Millhouse is weakening, and Eleanor I fear will soon be free,"

"What about me, do I just stay here?" Chloe asked apprehensively, as she watched the frail figure of Aveline slip on her cloak and head for the kitchen door.

"As before, you will be safe all the time you remain inside the house, I will not be long, continue to study the book and I will return shortly," Aveline replied reassuringly as she stepped outside. Chloe watched as the door closed behind her, she was alone again with only the stitched eyes of Annie to watch over her as she resumed her search within the pages of Eleanor's book.

Her lips curled upwards as she watched the hooded figure disappear amongst the trees, "Aveline!" she whispered with a dark and ominous smile spread across her face. If only she could break free, with little in the way of protection Chloe would be easy prey, but still the mist held strong to block her path.

"I'm afraid we will have to walk from here, the track down through the woods looks icy to me, and I would rather not risk sliding down there," Frank stated as he pointed to the bank that dropped away suddenly from the side of the road.

"But I do not believe that I am suitably dressed to take on rambling in the countryside, No! I insist that you continue to drive!" Jennifer implored as she looked down at her fashionable heeled footwear.

"But…" Frank was about to retaliate when Sandra interrupted,

"I must admit Frank that she has a point, I really do not like the idea of going arse over tit, you're a good driver and I'm sure for you it will be easy," Sandra said encouragingly as she smiled at him from across the cab of the van. Slowly they made their way as the ice-filled potholes and ruts of the track cracked beneath the moving wheels of the van. Eleanor watched as the pendant swung from side to side around Jennifer's neck as the van rocked and dipped on the uneven surface.

Aveline was home and quickly set about gathering together enough of the ingredients that she could carry. In her hurried state, she turned sharply, her cloak catching the carefully lined-up bottles and sending them crashing to the floor. Hours of preparation lay scattered across the stone floor of the cottage as Aveline began to rescue what she could from the broken glass.

Nearing the bend Frank gently applied the footbrake, but the slightest amount of pressure locked the wheels instantly, causing the van to skid sideways at a dangerous angle. The veil slipped ever so slightly as the temporary banishing waned, allowing Eleanor to gradually drag herself free from the mist.

Aveline winced as she looked at the broken shard of glass now lodged deep in her finger. She needed to return to Millhouse, but the wound would require her immediate attention. Bracing herself she carefully withdrew the broken, razor-like piece of bottle from her skin as she stood at the small kitchen sink.

Dusting herself down, Eleanor stepped forward, she was free. Ahead of her on the track, she watched as the van slid sideways as Frank battled to regain control. But his attempts were in vain as Eleanor curled her fingernails deep into her palm creating a fist, which she twisted and turned as she took control of the steering wheel. "FRANK!" Sandra yelled out in fear as the van slid dramatically across the track and headed for the tree-lined bank below them. In desperation, Frank gripped the steering wheel, his knuckles white as he fought against the inevitable outcome of the event.

Eleanor smiled as she watched the van slip sideways down the embankment, before lodging itself tightly against the trunks of the trees, that groaned and creaked under the pressure. She was back, and nothing was going to stop her from reclaiming what was rightfully hers.

From the safety of Millhouse Chloe heard the sound of

the collision, slamming the book shut she stood and made her way to the small window of the lounge. "Shit!" she muttered anxiously as she watched the familiar black mist of Eleanor making its way towards the occupants of the vehicle as they scrambled to safety. Not thinking, Chloe rushed to the front door, throwing it open with urgency she set off to warn them of their impending fate. Eleanor hissed as she raced past her, screaming for the travellers to turn and run.

"Chloe?" Sandra asked in a confused state as the figure of the woman ran rapidly in their direction. "Frank, look it's Chloe!"

"PLEASE RUN, SHE'S COMING FOR YOU!" Chloe yelled as she drew nearer.

"Bloody hell, it is Chloe look!" Frank said as he started to run towards her, his feet slipping on the frozen surface as he went.

All the time Eleanor steadily made her way up along the track, her bare feet leaving no trace as she walked silently through the valley.

"Frank?" Chloe exclaimed, "Oh my god am I glad to see you, and Sandra you are a sight for sore eyes! And Jennifer? Hang on, what are you doing here?"

"You said she was coming, who were you talking about?" Jennifer asked snootily as she tried to rearrange her crumpled clothing. Chloe turned and pointed to the black mist-like form of the phantom as she made her way towards them. Jennifer gulped as Sandra grabbed her arm and began to drag her in the spirit's direction. "What are you doing you idiot, Chloe told us to run away, not to it!"

Jennifer said as she trembled with fear.

"In case you had forgotten, we are here because of Chloe! Now shut up moaning and run, or I swear I will feed you to her myself!"

Eleanor's eyes lit up with rage at the sight of the pendant around Jennifer's neck. Surging forward she made her way towards them, the bare skin of her toes dragging along the ground as she made her attack.

"BE GONE!" Sandra roared as she held up her free hand to halt the spectre as it lunged forward.

Jennifer closed her eyes in preparation for her fate as the blackness came down over them in a dense like fog. Frank watched on in fear as Sandra stood her ground, defiantly holding fast against the impending doom that now surrounded them, as Chloe heroically moved forward. From within the swirling mass of despair, Sandra felt a hand take hold of her as she hopelessly fought against the mist to break free.

Relinquishing all fear Frank grabbed Chloe's arm as he watched her disappear within the quickening vortex. The energy of the spiralling mass felt as though it would break his arm in two as he tried desperately to keep hold as the mist quickly engulfed her.

"ENOUGH!" Aveline commanded as she appeared on the track behind them.

"Frank turned to see the frail stranger dressed in black throw something into the mist, dispersing it like ashes to the wind. "Everyone inside, quickly!" Aveline demanded as dark clouds began to fill the sky above them and screams echoed from every corner of the valley.

"What's happening?" Jennifer gasped frantically as Sandra dragged her by the arm towards the house.

"I would say she is slightly annoyed! Or pissed off! in my way of talking!" Sandra retorted desperately as they made their way through the porch.

Outside Eleanor's ferocity raced around Millhouse like a cyclone, banging on the windows and doors as she released her rage. Jennifer covered her ears, as the sound of Eleanor's agonising screams filled the air, she needed to get out and run. Rushing to the door she grabbed the handle, frantically turning it with trembling hands Jennifer pulled the door towards her and attempted her escape, much to the horror of Sandra who desperately pleaded with her to stop. Jennifer took two steps before she was confronted head-on by the menacing face of Eleanor, "GIVE IT TO ME!" She hissed. Jennifer looked away as Eleanor's gnarly hands reached out to snatch the pendant from around her neck.

"GET HER INSIDE!" Aveline shouted loudly to Frank over the din as she watched the disturbed spectre readying herself for the attack. Eleanor grabbed the chain, wrapping it tightly between her pointed nails as Frank took Jennifer by the hand and began to pull her back inside the house. The chain snapped, releasing the pendant, and sending it falling to the ground, Eleanor growled as she watched Chloe quickly jump to where it lay. Grasping it tightly in her hands Chloe scurried backwards through the open door and watched on in horror as Eleanor lashed out at the now retreating Jennifer, who screamed from the pain of Eleanor's nails as they dug deep into her face.

"FRANK!" Sandra yelled out in despair as she watched the skin on Jennifer's face turn red from the blood that spilt out as Eleanor's fingers tore deeper and deeper. He tried to let go, but the tightness of her grip held fast, he started to panic, desperately fighting with the motionless figure of Jennifer who remained still as Eleanor pulled away the skin from her cheek. He felt the splatter of Jennifer's blood as it sprayed from her wounds, he needed to break free, looking around Frank spotted Liam's axe resting against the wall by the open kitchen door.

Eleanor smiled a sinister smile, baring her yellowed teeth as he grabbed the handle. Sandra covered her eyes as Frank swung it high above his head, pausing momentarily before sending the sharpened head of the axe down with force onto Jennifer's forearm, and splitting the flesh and bone in one. The sound of the shattering arm as the razor-like edge cut through filled the kitchen, forcing Sandra to retch as Frank dropped the axe to the floor and quickly began to peel the dead-like fingers of Jennifer's hand from his arm.

Slamming the door shut, Frank breathed heavily as he looked around at the others, who all now stared back at him with the same fearful expression on their faces as to what he had done. "I had no choice, you saw what was happening, I did it in self-defence!" Frank nervously uttered as he tried to come to terms with his actions.

"Oh Frank, you, you.." Sandra began to say, her voice quivering as she spoke.

"Chopped her arm off! I know, my god they'll lock me away for years!" Frank replied as he started to panic, beads of sweat rolling down his face as he looked at his blood-stained hands.

"What have we become?" Chloe asked despairingly as she climbed slowly to her feet, "All of this is my fault, I made this happen!" she sobbed.

"Listen to you all, don't you see this is what she wants! Your friend was not meant to suffer at the hands of Eleanor, but it was her own doing that led her to it. She was the one who tried to flee, at which point your friend potentially put you all in danger of ending your days in the same manner." Aveline announced in a stern tone as she made her way across the kitchen and took the pendant from Chloe's shaking hands. "It was this that Eleanor wanted," Aveline continued to say as she held the pendant out in front of her, "We must be vigilant, now that she knows it is here she will stop at nothing, and I mean nothing to retrieve it. Child, it is now most urgent that you find the page, only then will we be able to stop her!"

"But the page in the book is only part of the problem, we need to find the door, Aveline, we have the book but the door we do not!" Chloe hopelessly replied.

Sandra looked at Chloe, confused as to what they were talking about as Frank peered through the small glass window pane in the kitchen door. "They're gone!" he stated nervously as he scanned the area.

"For now, yes, she has gone. But she will be back, I must go and place enough protection to see us through the night, for it is then when I fear we are most in danger," Aveline explained as she wrapped her cloak tightly around her frail body and ushered Frank to move out of the way.

"You can't just stand back and let her go, did you not see what happened to poor Jennifer?" Sandra pleaded as she watched the old woman disappear out of sight.

"That's Aveline! Try and stop her," Chloe smiled as she thought about the bravery the old woman of the trees had shown her, "Frank, go and clean yourself up, I promise you that nobody will lock you away for murder."

By the time Aveline returned it was evening. Making her way through the kitchen she joined the others in the lounge where they all sat huddled in front of the glowing fire in the hearth. Chloe had explained everything that had happened since she had been taken in by Aveline, and Sandra now sat shell-shocked to find out that in fact, Liam was indeed really dead.

Aveline sat and listened as Chloe continued to tell them both about the old leather-bound book and its connection to not only her life but also to the previous existence of Eleanor Hurst. Everything now seemed to make sense to Sandra, as she retold the experiences of Edward Worthing and the saddening possession of his daughter Nell, to Chloe.

Frank sat in quiet contemplation as he thought about the demise of his friend Ted and his connection to the placing of the key. Over and over, he searched his memory to remember where Ted had been working previously in a bid to find out where he could have obtained the key. It was an ancient house, he could still hear Ted going on and on about how much of the original features had remained in situ after all the years, but the name evaded him. Aveline watched as Frank remained in a transfixed state as he stared into the fire, "Frank, please, there is no need to wallow in self-pity, what has happened, happened," Chloe said, trying to offer reassurance as she noticed his quiet remorseful expression.

"That's it, Wallowmead. That's where Ted was working!" Frank announced abruptly, causing Sandra to jump up in shock.

"Ah yes, the place of Eleanor's sister," Aveline said as she listened, "I believed that the house had been taken apart piece by piece, destroyed by all the misery that dwelled there."

"It was, I remember going to look around the place to see if there was anything worth buying," Frank said as he remembered the sale. Sandra shuddered at the thought that he had seen sense against purchasing something cursed from the house of doom. "But there wasn't anything that took my eye, to be honest, stuffed animals were never my thing. No, the whole place was loaded into shipping containers and sold onto old Mr Simpson. Come to think of it Chloe, no forget it, it must just be a coincidence."

"What Frank, what is just a coincidence?" Chloe asked suspiciously.

"Well, it's just that when you had that bathroom delivered, you had a door dropped off too. It was Ted who mentioned it first, and then I knew that I had seen it before. Chloe in the outbuilding, you have the front door that belonged to the house in Wallowmead, don't you remember when you said that it would be perfect for the porch and not to worry about Liam because it was originally his idea," Frank replied as the picture became clear in his head. Chloe looked at Aveline, who smiled a knowing smile in return.

"You must enter the outbuilding and retrieve the door, Frank," Aveline stated as she pointed her frail hand in his direction.

"Not bloody likely, have you seen what's out there!" Frank replied nervously as he folded his arms and shook his head to show his defiance at the request.

"Frank, you must do as she said! You don't have a choice, either you go, or I do!" Chloe replied in the same demanding tone.

Frank sighed as he looked at the three women, who all carried the same united expression on their faces. He had no choice, he had to do the deed. Since he had known Chloe he had always felt a little responsible for her well-being, and after his own daughter had left for University and started a life of her own he was left with a hole, a hole that Chloe filled perfectly. "Fine, but I'm going in the daylight, and Aveline, after what I saw you do today I would appreciate it if you came with me."

"Of course," Aveline smiled, "You're a good man Frank, a good man indeed!"

2:06 a.m.

Aveline sat patiently waiting in the kitchen as Frank and

Sandra took turns to grumble and snore loudly in their sleep, as they leaned against one another on the sofa in the lounge. In the armchair, Chloe turned over as the same dream began once more.

2:07 a.m.

The key began to swing gently as Aveline moved closer, "Soon," she whispered, "Soon sister, you will be free."

Chloe watched as Eleanor stood waiting at the door, beckoning with her hand for Chloe to join her. As she stood watching, surrounded by the haunting tune, Chloe noticed a woman walking out of the mist to join Eleanor. They embraced each other as though they had not felt each other's arms for an eternity before slowly releasing and turning to face Chloe, who woke suddenly from the dream and stared around the candlelit room.

# Chapter Twenty-Four

It was morning, and the atmosphere inside Millhouse felt tense and filled with trepidation, as Chloe sat alone studying the pages of the book. It seemed that no matter how hard she concentrated, or connected with the writing on the pages, nothing came forward. Sandra watched from the doorway of the lounge, observing the fraught expression on Chloe's face as she desperately tried to seek out the answer. She wanted to help, but her assistance would be futile, Chloe had already told them both that it was her sole duty to find the answer hidden within the written text in the book. Aveline tapped her on the arm and gestured for Sandra to join her in the kitchen, where she pointed out what she must do. It seemed a minuscule task to complete within the greater circle of the problem, but Sandra accepted the request if only to feel as though she had at least played her part, even if that part was a small one.

The kitchen island had been laid out with the provisions that Aveline had provided, but nobody had the appetite to eat it. It seemed wasteful to Frank, whose usual morning eating routine would have devoured it within minutes. But the dread of leaving the house and entering the outbuilding made him feel sick to the stomach, he watched as Aveline finished her conversation with Sandra, he knew that the time had come.

"It is time Frank," Aveline whispered as she placed the cloak around her shoulders. Frank uttered not a word as he grabbed his coat and nodded in the direction of the old lady.

From upstairs Sandra heard the kitchen door close. She watched as Frank and Aveline swiftly made their way towards the padlocked door of the outbuilding from the small window of the spare bedroom, where she placed a large white candle as Aveline had instructed. "Be safe," she said quietly, her breath misting the glass as she watched them sneak out of view, before making her way to the next room, and the next window.

"Remember Frank, we are here for the door, nothing more, nothing less. Whatever happens, try, and block it out, Eleanor no doubt will attempt to confuse, but this must not dissuade you from your duty, do you understand?" Aveline asked as Frank removed the small key from his pocket and placed it into the padlock fastening the door.

"I get the picture, please can we just get this whole thing over and bloody done with," he asked as the padlock opened with a click.

Inside, the musty smell mingled with something far more disturbing and putrid as they carefully made their way to where Frank had leaned the door against the wall when it had originally been delivered. "Here it is!" he announced as he pointed to the white sheet covering the door. "Can you smell that?"

Aveline nodded as she pointed to the sheet, "Remove the covering."

Frank took a deep breath as his hands grasped the edges of the material, pulling it to the floor in one swift action. "ARGH!" He screamed alarmingly as he jumped back in fright. Stretched out on the door was the mangled body of Dandelion, its paws nailed to the surface in a sickening act of crucifixion. Undeterred by the sight, Aveline tried to encourage Frank to continue with his task, as he stood unresponsive, traumatised by the mutilated corpse

"Frank," he heard whispered, "Frank, you hurt me!" The same voice muttered again, this time more forceful in its tone.

"No, it can't be, Jennifer?" He asked, looking back at the face of the bloodstained cat.

"Yes Frank, it's me, how could you do such a thing?" Jennifer's voice wailed from the feline's mouth, as maggots fell from its lips to the floor. Frank watched on in horror as the cat began to tug and wrench at the nails fastening it to the wooden surface of the door, the rotten flesh of its paws ripping as they worked their way free.

"ENOUGH!" Aveline shouted, throwing the contents of a small bottle in the cat's direction, as it hung by one leg in front of him. "Frank the door, we must get the door!" Aveline demanded as she grabbed the now lifeless body of the cat and unemotionally discarded it across the room. Not wanting to hang around for any more of Eleanor's party tricks, Frank grabbed the weighty timber and began to lug it towards the open door of the outbuilding, quickly followed by the now vigilant Aveline.

The wind seemed to have picked up from nowhere and was constantly gathering momentum as Frank leaned the door up against the front of the porch. "My tools, I won't be able to do anything without them!" He said to Aveline, pointing in the direction of the van that still rested on its side between the trees.

"Very well," Aveline agreed as they made their way out along the track, from the window of the studio, Sandra watched as they walked away. Passing the portrait Sandra paused to look, she remembered when she had first seen Chloe's artwork, and how long ago now that all seemed to be. Making her way out onto the hallway she collected the remaining candles from the small occasional table and made her way down the stairs.

Tools at the ready, Frank set about measuring the door so that he could make the alterations needed to fit it into place. From inside Chloe could hear the sound of sawing, looking up she noticed Sandra enter the room, where she placed the candle into the holder on the windowsill. "Any luck?" Sandra inquired with a sense of hope in her voice, Chloe shook her head slowly, before returning her gaze to the pages in front of her.

"Do you think that this will work? Chloe doesn't seem to be able to find anything and I'm scared she's going to give up," Sandra frantically asked Aveline as they stood in the kitchen.

"By doubting her you are willing her to fail, this is not something that you will find in the kind of book you read Sandra," Aveline replied in a serious tone as she pointed to the blue cover of the book on the kitchen worktop, "This is real magic!" Sandra watched as the eyes of the old woman sparkled as she said those words, perhaps there was hope after all.

Outside Frank battled against the changing weather as he looked at the dark clouds that signalled a storm was gathering. The door was made of oak, ancient oak, which made shaping it impossible to do quickly as Frank tugged at the saw which buckled and snagged as it cut. Stopping to wipe the sweat away from his brow, Frank looked around at the trees as he sensed eyes watching him, clutching the small pouch that Aveline had placed around his neck for protection, he steadied his nerves and continued with the job in hand.

Chloe sat on the floor of the lounge, her eyes closed as she gently passed her hand over the pages. She was on the track, but the image of Eleanor was nowhere to be seen. Alone she stood, looking at the door in front of her, the same door that she had seen before. From her side, she could sense someone drawing near, Chloe turned to face the mist but there was no one there. She opened her eyes to see Aveline sitting in front of her smiling a sad smile.

"It was you, in my vision, you were the one that comforted Eleanor,"

"Yes child, you are correct. I was the one that you saw," Aveline replied softly.

"But why? Why would you offer her comfort?" Chloe asked in a confused tone as she tried to make sense of what she was hearing.

"Because I am the sister to which Eleanor refers, I could

have saved her, but instead I saved myself," Aveline replied sadly as her eyes fell to the floor. "It was only when the book was taken in by your family that it awoke the curse, I had a chance to redeem what I had done to my poor Eleanor, but when she started to seek her revenge I knew that I had to stop her."

"So, all of this is down to you and your sister having some sort of family domestic? Aveline, my Grandfather is dead, my mother is dead, my Father is dead and so is Liam, my whole life has been destroyed because of it!" Chloe growled as she slammed the book shut and attempted to stand, only to be pulled back down by the hands of Aveline.

"But do you not see child, now you can resolve everything, all that you need is what lies inside that book."

"I'm sorry, but I think that you had better leave before my usual calm manner explodes and I kick your decrepit arse out of my house!" Chloe snarled as she snatched herself away from the frail woman's hands.

"CHLOE!" Sandra shouted as she stood in the doorway, "That is no way to speak to someone, Aveline is here to help!"

"Oh yeah, help is that what you call it? Leading us like lambs to the slaughter more like!" Chloe snapped back.

"Listen to me young lady, I might not know as much as the 'great witch' here, but what I do know is that there is one hell of a scary bitch waiting to do goodness knows what to us. My husband, your friend, is outside alone as we speak doing the best he can, don't you think that we should all do the same?" Sandra stated as she stood with her hands resting on her rounded hips, in a stance of defiance, as she waited for an answer.

"Fine! But when all of this is over that's it, Aveline can go back to her cottage in the woods, and I can get the hell out of here!" Chloe huffed as she realised that Sandra was right in what she had said. Sandra offered a small smile to Aveline who looked back with sorrow in her eyes as Chloe's words echoed in her head. "Now if you don't mind I have things that I need to do," Chloe said coldly as she returned her attention to the book.

The day seemed to disappear quickly and before Frank knew it dusk was fast approaching. Without stopping he continued to sculpt the door to fit the opening of the porch, the ground beneath him covered with the curls of planed wood that stayed for a moment before blowing away on the cold strengthening wind. "Come and take a break," Sandra pleaded as she watched him struggle to lift the door into position,

"Not until I have finished," Frank replied without even looking in her direction as he lifted the door up onto the hinges.

Inside Chloe could feel the energy racing up her arm as the book connected with her, page after page she turned as the energy grew stronger. Outside Frank lowered the door down onto the scrolled hinges, the heaviness of the wood dropping with a thud as it rested into position.

"I'VE FOUND IT!" Chloe exclaimed as the book gave up its secret and the page revealed itself.

"What did you see?" Aveline asked as she looked down at

the ancient scripture,

"I saw the way, I know what I must do," Chloe smiled as she picked up the book and climbed to her feet.

Frank quickly collected his tools and made his way back inside the house to where the women were gathered together in the kitchen. "So, what happens next?" he asked as he gulped at the hot tea that Sandra had made for everyone.

"I guess we just wait," Chloe replied as she looked at Aveline with a confident expression on her face.

"The time will show us when," Aveline said as she looked at the key hanging from the hook on the wall.

Outside a storm raged into the night as the four occupants of Millhouse sat together, none uttering a word as rain lashed at the candlelit window of the lounge. Silently they waited for the moment Eleanor would return, each not knowing what the darkness would send forth, everyone except Chloe who seemed to be relaxed in her thoughts as she cradled the book in her arms. Lightning flashed across the sky as the sound of thunder boomed in its wake, shaking the very foundations of Millhouse as the storm gathered above the valley.

2:00 a.m.

Chloe stood silently and made her way into the kitchen where she stood facing the hallway, followed by Aveline, who placed her hand into the pocket of her robe and handed Chloe the pendant. There she stood, waiting for the moment Eleanor would return as the clock ticked away loudly in the background. In the lounge, Frank grabbed Sandra's hand tightly, lifting it to his mouth he kissed it tenderly, "I just want to say," he began as tears filled his eyes.

"Shh! I know Frank, I know," Sandra whispered as she stroked away the tears from his face.

2:05 a.m.

Chloe held the book tightly as she prepared herself. Collecting the key from the wall she made her way into the lounge where she waited by the window. Staring out into the night, her face illuminated by the solitary flicker of the candle. Frank and Sandra stood and watched as Chloe replayed the role.

Within the wood, Eleanor ran to escape the gathering hoard as they neared ever closer to her. Breathlessly she hurried through the undergrowth as the brambles tore at her skin. Reaching the edge of the trees she looked back momentarily at the flaming torches of the men, before hitching up her tattered clothing and running towards the sanctuary of her sister's house.

From the window, Chloe could see the figure of a woman running helplessly towards her, pleading to be saved. Pressing her face against the glass Chloe could see Eleanor, not as a phantom but as a young woman screaming out in desperation. Sandra held on tightly to Frank's arm as the sound of the tormented soul pierced everything that surrounded it.

2:07 a.m.

Eleanor saw the face at the window peering out as she screamed for help, making her way to the door she tried to turn the latch, but the door was locked from the inside.

Aveline looked at the door as the handle began to rattle violently.

Eleanor banged her fists helplessly on the solid wood of the door as the burning torches carried by the jeering crowd surrounded her, "We have thee, Eleanor Hurst! Thy mercy is now in the hands of God!" she heard as fingers began to grab and pull at her.

Chloe turned and faced Frank and smiled a sweet smile, one that he had not seen grace her lips in a very long while, as he thought how they would share their mornings, just talking in the kitchen. Sandra watched as Chloe walked out of the hallway and made her way into the porch, placing the key in the lock of the old door she turned it slowly.

From outside Eleanor felt the door open behind her.

Aveline watched as the doorway became bathed in a white glow, as Chloe stepped forward, holding out the book and pendant for Eleanor to take. "Sister," she smiled as she looked at Chloe, "I knew ye would not forsake me."

"Never," Whispered Chloe as she watched Eleanor turn and walk away.

Chloe looked into the light, she could hear the same soothing melody that her mother used to sing. She stepped forward towards the open doorway, as Aveline called out for her to stop.

She had a decision, everything she ever loved was there

waiting for her in that light, she looked back inside the house. The screams and pleading actions of Frank and Sandra as they begged her to stay seemed to fade away as she smiled and walked through the doorway. Frank tried to support Sandra as she fell to the floor and wept as Chloe disappeared into the light.

Chloe lay back as her mother's fingers gently stroked her hair as she sang, they were together again, and nothing would ever keep them apart.

10 years later.

"Excuse me, but could you tell me the price of the ragdoll in the window please?" The suit-clad businessman asked as he entered the shop and approached the counter.

"Ah yes, she is a beauty are you a collector? The salesman asked as he pulled the doll from the display.

"No, it's for my daughter, she will be eight soon and I know she will love it."

In a pink-painted bedroom somewhere in England.

"What's this you're hiding?" the little girl asked as she pulled a small but neatly folded piece of paper from under the ragdoll's dress. "It's a letter!" she gasped as her small fingers opened it.

This is Annie,

She is the best friend anyone could ever have.

Always there to make you smile when you are sad,

or watch over you when you are scared.

But the time I have shared with her must soon come to an end.

Please keep Annie safe, and remember me to her,

All my love,

Chloe x

# ABOUT THE AUTHOR

Darron lives in Devon with his fellow writer wife and children. When he is not teaching or writing, Darron spends his time composing music, walking the moors and coastal paths, always in search of inspiration!

Follow Darron on Amazon, where you will find his other titles, Queen of the Moor and Over the Wall, or head to the website below to find all the latest titles, special offers, and new releases.

www.undertheoaks.co.uk

Printed in Great Britain
by Amazon